JOAN RILEY

# Romance

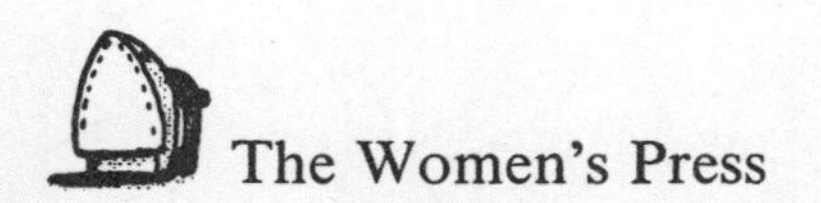

First published in Great Britain by
The Women's Press Ltd 1988
A member of the Namara Group
34 Great Sutton Street, London EC1V ODX



British Library Cataloguing in Publication Data available

Typeset by AKM Associates (UK) Ltd,
Ajmal House, Hayes Road, Southall, Middlesex
Printed and bound in Great Britain by
Hazell Watson and Viney Ltd,
Aylesbury, Bucks.

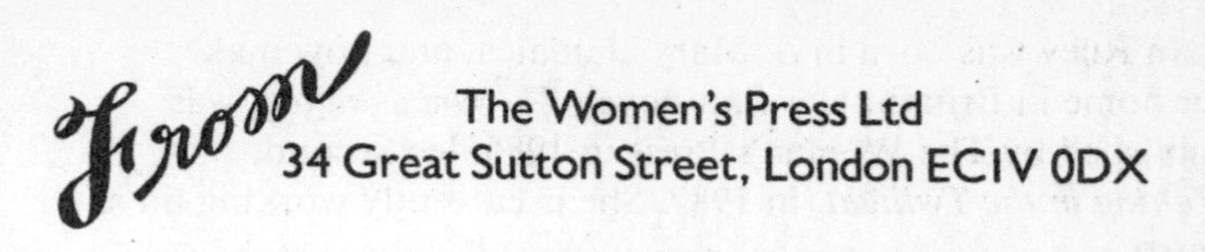
From
The Women's Press Ltd
34 Great Sutton Street, London EC1V 0DX

Steaming ahead

Joan Riley was born in St Mary, Jamaica, and now makes her home in Britain. Her first novel, *The Unbelonging*, was published by The Women's Press in 1985, her second, *Waiting in the Twilight*, in 1987. She is currently working on a fourth.

For Lethna and Bayhano

# Acknowledgments

The following people have been invaluable in the shaping of this book.

Margaret Busby, without whom I might not have resolved major difficulties in characterisation. She was willing to discuss and suggest with never-failing patience, and demonstrated the value of reading back to narrow the gap between what I had written and what I intended to say.

Beverley Hue, who read paragraphs and half-pages which could have made little sense out of context, yet whose response was invaluable to me; who also provided a sounding board for ideas and gave blunt (if not always welcome) assessment at every stage of the book's development. Somehow our friendship survived it.

Rachael Calder, who offered encouragement and coped with my moods.

Jacqui Roach, for her sharp and not always tactful criticisms during the initial stages of the book. Jacqui along with Katy Nicholson provided a sounding board for my first ideas and picked up on the more improbable ones, while Katy acted as guinea pig reader for much of the original draft.

Jen Green, for her helpful suggestions.

All the women whose speech patterns I attempted to absorb, and finally my daughter and nieces, observation of whom helped to breathe life into the children in the book.

# Acknowledgements

The following people have been invaluable in the shaping of this book:

# One

She saw them before they saw her, the two men leaning against a dusty red Cortina and looking out of place in the regimented grey street. Her heart lurched and her stomach sickened. There was a stitch in her left side and she leaned heavily into it, pressing her palm hard against the spot, her breathing ragged as she came to a dead stop.

Surely they hadn't been inside already! Why hadn't they been prepared to wait? They had agreed to hold everything until tomorrow . . .

Verona inched forward on reluctant feet, her face glistening with moisture. She had rushed home after the ordeal at work, and even now her lungs felt raw from the unaccustomed exercise. The lumpy folds of flesh on her body were damp and clammy with trapped sweat, and under her grey duffel coat the drab, unfashionable brown dress clung uncomfortably to her skin. She hardly felt the icy fingers of the January evening cold as she gazed numbly at the men. Her deep brown eyes looked hunted and at bay. She felt as guilty as a child caught in an act of forbidden mischief. *If only it were as harmless as that!* she thought.

The wild idea of retreating around the corner came to her but she forced herself to approach the men. Her whole being concentrated on them. They were deep in conversation and she toyed with a half-formed notion of slipping past and into the safety of her sister's house. She had nearly reached them when the taller one, younger than his rounder, balding companion, looked up, straightening as she came alongside.

'Miss Harris.'

Verona stiffened, eyes darting nervously around the deserted street as she instinctively side-stepped away from the man. Her plump brown hands clutched her shopping-bag tightly, nails digging into the coarse fabric. For a moment, past and future merged, as old fears surfaced, echoing in her mind, threatening to swamp her.

'I wonder if we could have a word.' The man's voice came through the pounding in her ears.

She hesitated, trying to pull herself together.

'It won't take a moment,' he insisted, moving forward as he misinterpreted her swift recoil.

She sidled past him and edged towards the pale yellow gate and the neat box-like front garden of the house.

The man's mouth thinned and he directed his eyes to the house in a speaking glance. 'I think we'd better keep your sister out of this.'

Verona looked at him in surprise, feeling a little more secure as her fingers closed round the solid reassurance of wood, slid along and clumsily unlatched the catch.

'I thought I was to see you tomorrow,' she said tentatively.

The smaller man twitched with impatience, drawing her attention, and her heart sank at the open dislike in his small blue eyes. 'The situation has changed since then,' he said.

Verona's gaze moved longingly to the warm glow of the stained and varnished door. Her stomach fluttered on a sudden thought: *Supposing Desiree doesn't believe me!* She told herself that was stupid; her sister had always stood by her. Look how Des had taken her back when she had run away to the hostel after that awful row about her books.

Yet the creeping doubt remained. She had never been accused of anything like this before, certainly not when it was everybody's word against hers.

'We'd rather have our little chat in the car,' the short man said abruptly as she pushed the gate.

She froze, fear radiating out of control again.

'No need to involve anyone else in our little business, is there?' he said, stoking her panic. Had she been less preoccupied, she might have seen the unease he was trying to disguise. His face was large and round, with freckles that went well beyond the boundaries where hair once stood. She looked anxiously at the other man, hardly noticing the redness that started at the roots of his hair and disappeared into the open collar of his shirt.

The out-of-control feeling had stifled her voice in her throat. Verona felt rooted in a bad dream that wouldn't let her run. How could she speak to them on her own? With an effort, she found courage in a defiant anger. She was safe in the protection of her large body – and her experience of that other night, more terrifying than this could ever be. Recurring images of it replaced her fears of imminent dismissal.

*He* had told her no one would believe her word against his; after all, he would say she had given herself willingly . . . She had been so frightened, afraid of the blood and the pain, terrified that Desiree would find out and that their father would have to know. Her hands went automatically to her belly, pressing it in remembered pain. It had hurt for so long afterwards, she had wondered if he had bored a hole in her. At night she would lie stiff and watchful, straining to make out every shadow, listening to the heavy footsteps and the shuffling gait of late-night revellers.

She had felt so apart from everything, dirty and alone. It was as if she had been cast outside the warmth of her family, too afraid of what they would say, what they would think, to ever dare tell them what Ronnie had done. Ronnie had been her sister Desiree's first real boyfriend and he had got on so well with her father. If only –

'Miss Harris?' As the tall man touched her arm she jerked away, suffocating with the contact and the painful memory. 'We need to discuss the situation,' he said.

It all came back to her in a rush, banishing the past. The accusation, the humiliation of being searched. *How dare they assume I'm guilty!* she thought, indignation clearing her head.

'I thought you were supposed to be my union rep,' she accused.

The men were unmoved, the taller one still bland and

pleasant-faced beside his dour companion.

'I'm everyone's rep,' he corrected mildly. 'Both Mr Benson and I are here to help you out of this mess.'

'We have to consider everyone's rights in a case like this,' Mr Benson emphasised. 'The woman you stole the money from has as much right to justice as you.'

'I didn't steal any money,' Verona insisted. 'Miss Marsh from Security searched me, and you can go through my bag again if you like.'

He looked at her as though she were simple. 'Listen, love, we've been through all that. Like we said, Stoneford's isn't going to insist you give back the money, so if I were you I'd stop pushing it.'

'We're only here to sort this mess out,' the tall man said, giving the other a reproving look. 'Now if you'd just slip into the car for a minute I'm sure we can have the matter over and done with in no time.'

Verona's eyes darted involuntarily to the blank, shuttered and curtained windows along the street. So much for neighbourhood watch. *I could be raped right here on the street and no one would notice*, she thought unhappily. A vision of her bulk sprawled across the pavement came to her mind, bringing an incongruous flash of humour to her predicament, and her face creased into a fleeting smile which transformed her features, hinting at a woman who never took herself too seriously. It steadied her, eased the tension pounding at her temples and biting at the base of her skull.

She faced the men more calmly, resigned to giving in to their unyielding pressure. There seemed no way she could get rid of them without at least discussing the accusation.

'You'd better come in for a while,' she said evenly, bracing herself against the hostility equally visible on both faces now. She longed for a sweet, something to chew on to ease her nervousness.

'We already had a word with your sister,' the tall man said. Her unexpected attitude had obviously squeezed all trace of friendliness out of him as he added: 'Of course, she doesn't yet know what we've come about, but strikes me she'll be none too pleased to hear the evidence, especially if it gets in the papers.'

'Hello, love!'

Verona's heart sank as she heard and saw Mrs Evans coming down the street, pulling a heavy shopping-trolley behind her. *Nosy Dora, that's all I need.* She groaned inwardly.

Mrs Evans lived in the house opposite and doubled as the neighbourhood gossip. She was a small, stocky woman who always appeared when trouble happened, her bleached hair looking lank and dead in a style from some bygone age. Her eyes always reminded Verona of an inquisitive mouse, constantly shifting around to absorb information.

'Friend of yours?' the tall man asked, looking knowingly at the advancing figure.

Verona's mouth tightened; she knew she was cornered.

Still some way away, Mrs Evans called out: 'Who's your friends?'

Doing her best to ignore her question, Verona tried again with the men: 'I think you'd better come in.' She was annoyed to hear the edge of desperation in her voice.

The short man grinned nastily. 'Nice area this,' he said pointedly. 'Wonder what the neighbours would say about you thieving?'

Verona glanced nervously towards Mrs Evans, whose approaching figure looked like some descending winter crow. Verona had to shift the men before any damage was done. Her anger swelled. They knew they had her in a bind. No way could she risk her sister's peace of mind. Not when Desiree was so ill. Life in this part of Croydon was hard enough at the best of times, with the isolation and the silent hostility of the neighbours. Verona thought ruefully of the many times Desiree had bailed her out of difficult situations, and she knew the least she must do now was avoid involving her sister in this unpleasantness.

'What do you want me to do?' she asked flat-voiced.

The man's face relaxed immediately and he even managed a smile. 'If you could just step into the car for a moment,' he repeated, 'there are one or two little things we need to clear up.'

He held the passenger door open in readiness.

'What's happening, love?' Mrs Evans asked, peering into the car suspiciously. She stared brazenly at the union men. 'Haven't seen you two around before – friends of the family, are you?'

Verona felt her nails digging into her palm, sweat trickling down her spine. If they told Nosy Dora why they were here, it would be up and down the street by the following evening. She had often enough seen how the woman worked, moving from door to door, ringing the bell and making aimless conversation before dropping her load of gossip. The only door she avoided these days was Desiree's and that simply because she had been met with flat dismissal on the several occasions she had tried.

Desiree peered anxiously out of the window, opening it a crack and straining without success to hear the conversation going on outside the gate. When she saw Verona enter the car, and the panic on her face as she looked from the men to Mrs Evans, she knew something must be badly wrong.

*V must afraid of something*, she thought unhappily. *Why else she so scared of Nosy Dora overhearing?*

She looked at the grey-coated woman in disgust, hating the way she hovered near the car obviously consumed by curiosity. That woman was a pest. Desiree had christened her Nosy Dora less than a week after they moved in, much to Verona and John's amusement. The woman had been round several times in the first few days, poking about in an attempt to prise out secrets they might have hidden. At first Desiree had put up with her in a spirit of neighbourliness, inviting her in for coffee and sitting patiently while she gossiped non-stop about the other people on the street. Within the first hour, she had found out that her neighbour to the right, with the large, unfriendly Alsatian, was living in sin with a man half her age, after her husband ran off up North with her best friend. Her neighbour to the left was a social climber who looked down her nose at everyone on the street. True to Mrs Evans's prediction, she had soon moved out, being replaced by an equally reserved professional couple.

It was when Mrs Evans started on the few black families that Desiree lost patience, even though she did find them unfriendly and unwelcoming. She had no intention of discussing any black person with Nosy Dora, refusing to be mollified by the woman's assurance that she was different. It might have been fine if she had confined herself to telling tales of white people, but talking about black people was quite another thing.

A movement outside caught her attention, and she looked up to see Mrs Evans moving reluctantly away, disappearing out of sight on her way to another neighbour. Why couldn't she mind her own business? Desiree felt mortified at the idea of her sister being the subject of gossip.

'Oh, V, why you don't get out, tell them you will finish talking in the house?' she muttered, gripping the white aluminium window frame.

The memory of the men's grim, official-looking faces worried Desiree. Only the thought of Verona's reaction to her interference stopped her from going out there now to demand to know what was going on. She sighed, impatient with her sister's need always to prove herself. 'Is the same stupidness make her run away just before Papa die.' Look how much trouble that had caused, Verona nearly ending up in a children's home because of it.

What had Verona done this time? Desiree let the curtain drop back slowly, then pulled it closed across the chilly darkness.

Her wretchedly thin body was stooped and shambling, giving her the appearance of an old woman, all vitality swallowed by long months of suffering. The dull ache in her belly sharpened and she drew a ragged breath, half-staggering to lower herself into the yielding softness of a high-backed, brown velour easy chair, gripping the arms with bone-thin hands. Sweat broke out on her forehead, and her features distorted with an effort to control the stabbing pain inside her.

*Perhaps I shouldn't have driven them away*, she thought, as the pain subsided. Perhaps she had been a little hard.

When the men had presented themselves at the door earlier, asking for Verona, she had invited them in; feeling instinctively that something was wrong, she had not wanted to antagonise them before she found out more.

'Why you wanting to see Verona?' she had probed cautiously, as they made themselves comfortable on the roomy settee, relaxing with the tea she had supplied at their request.

'It's not the sort of thing we can discuss without Miss Harris's permission,' the taller one, who seemed to act as spokesman, apologised. His face was almost the same colour as the shock of ginger hair on his head.

'I'm her sister – you telling me I can't know what business you have with her?'

The man shook his head. 'I'm sorry, missus, it's something we have to speak to Miss Harris about in private, like.'

The short man, barrel-bellied and freckled, nodded agreement, his eyes never leaving the plate of biscuits from which he stuffed himself continuously, with only small pauses for a gulp of tea.

Desiree's temper, already frayed by constant pain, had snapped at the evidence of unconcern in their attitude. 'Look, you,' she said sourly, 'this is my house. I didn't ask you to come knocking on my door, but you came and you sitting there drinking my tea, telling me you have something on my sister and I can't know about it.'

Both men exchanged uneasy glances. The shorter one reached for another biscuit, his reddening face betraying his annoyance. Neither spoke and the air was thick with guarded hostility.

'I want to know what it about,' Desiree went on. 'It's obvious you all just trying to cause my sister trouble and I not resting till I find out what you all up to.'

They seemed surprised by the reaction of this mild-looking black woman glaring down at them.

'We're not at liberty to discuss Miss Harris's problem with you,' the short man spoke for the first time, his voice patronising. 'Mr Battle was trying to explain: against the rules, you know.'

Desiree hissed air through her teeth, arms on hips, unconsciously like her mother when she had felt any of her children threatened.

'Don't you talk to me like that!' she snapped, pain forgotten in her indignation. 'Who you all think you are anyway? All you is the same –'

'I hope you don't imagine we're here to get at Miss Harris,' the tall man butted in feebly. 'Honest, love, we just want to do what we can for her.'

'Like what so?'

He ignored her sarcasm. 'Believe me, love,' he continued, 'whatever we do will be best all round.'

Believe them! Of course she didn't believe them. She had come across men like this before, full of wind and bluster, ready to bully anyone who would let them. She wasn't fooled by the false niceness of the ginger-haired spokesman. These types were all the same. Well, she'd lived among working-class Whites long enough to know they'd as soon step on a black person as help them.

'Look, love, we're sorry –'

'I don't want your apology,' she cut in, 'I want to know what you trying to do to my sister.'

The man sounded exasperated: 'Look, we don't mean to upset you –'

'I think we'd better wait outside,' the short man had interrupted, draining his cup and putting it beside the now empty plate on the low table in front of them. 'It's obvious you don't want us in your house.'

'Too right! You can come back when Verona gets home, and don't expect to stuff your face here again.'

Remembering, Desiree stretched her legs carefully, cautious of the pain building up again. She shouldn't have driven them out. If Verona was on one of her independence things, she would end up in a load of trouble, of that much Desiree was sure. *Maybe I protecting her too much. Sometimes I forget she a big woman now.* But Verona was all she had left of family. With the death of their father all contact with Guyana had gone, and Desiree knew she would never have the nerve to go there in search of family.

Of course, there was John, but it was years since she had really been able to count on him. It was not that he didn't try, but he had so much else on his mind, what with his grandmother in Jamaica not well and another promotion chance coming up. That was the problem with her marriage. These days John was so preoccupied, he could spare little worry for her. *Still, if only he could realise I suffering as well*, she caught herself thinking with some pique, before pushing the thought away guiltily. *I have a duty to support John*, she admonished herself. *If he don't get loyalty from me, where he supposed to get it?*

She had explained that to Verona just last week.

'Crap!' her sister had responded with the vehemence any mention of John provoked in her of late. 'The only duty you have is to yourself and the children. Des, John is a big man – he's not your child – and he have plenty enough time for his flipping Granny Ruby and Grandpa Clifford.'

Even her friend Mara dismissed the excuse that John's thoughtlessness had developed only since Rathbourne's closed down. 'Other people lose their job and survive without stepping on someone else,' Mara pointed out, 'and if he so full of problem, how come he don't forget his grandparents?'

Desiree shrugged, making allowances for the fact that her friend had been forced to leave her husband.

Mara had been dogged. 'Des, you mark me: the way that man is carrying on . . . stay with him and you're going to regret it.'

The clock in the hall chimed a quarter to the hour and Desiree shook her head to clear it; this was not the time to think of John. She leaned forward to switch on the standard lamp, liking the soft, restful glow it cast on the room. A bright blue shape behind one of the settee covers caught her eyes, and her mouth tightened when she realised what it was. *Another of V's damn books. I sure I took them all upstairs*. She sighed wistfully. If only V had married that Leonard, maybe she wouldn't need to use romance as a substitute for real life. Easing to her feet, Desiree went to retrieve the book, looking at the cover with distaste. *If I don't keep picking them up we all going drown in them*. As it was, Verona's room was bursting with them. At the very least they were a fire hazard.

The clock struck eight as she reached the bottom of the stairs. Desiree hoped Verona didn't stay outside too long; the last thing she needed was Mara coming back with the girls in the middle of whatever discussion was taking place out there.

Inside her sister's room Desiree looked about despairingly, before adding the novel to a pile by the door. Verona had become no tidier with the years. Out of habit, Desiree moved about picking up discarded clothes, folding them neatly or putting them on hangers.

She was sorting through the wardrobe when she came across the loose shirtwaister dress, incongruously small among the more ample garments. She took it out slowly, examining it with surprise. It looked so tiny and insignificant, a splash of colour among the drabness of the other clothing. Why had Verona kept it? It had been Desiree's fourteenth-birthday present to her and the younger girl had loved it. Come to think of it, not too long after that V had started putting on weight and had become moody and secretive. Neither Desiree nor their father had been able to get through to her and it had hardly come as a surprise when she ran away.

Hugging the dress unconsciously to her, Desiree tried to make sense of the changes in Verona. At first she had put it down to growing pains, not knowing what else to think. *If only Mama had been alive*, she mused sadly, *she would have known what to do*. Their mother had always been so sure of everything, so calm; she would never have allowed V to get into such a state. These thoughts brought on the usual guilt in Desiree. She had failed to look after her sister properly. Why else should she have turned out this way? Desiree's eyes swept involuntarily around the endless piles of romance novels that seemed to cover every available inch of floor space. *Still, at least V is dependable*, she consoled herself, thinking of her sister's ability to take charge of the children, even if she refused to do for John. This illness would have been harder to bear without her, and lately Verona had practically taken over the running of the house.

Desiree frowned; that was what she least understood. How could V be so confident and reliable with the children, and around the house, yet be in such a mess herself? The question defeated her as it always did, and with a sigh she put the dress back, fingers lingering on the soft material. It was hard to believe so much had changed.

The sound of the front door closing snapped the mood.

'V, what those men want?' she called anxiously, moving to the stairs.

Verona's heart sank. What had they told Desiree? She chewed at her bottom lip with angry indecision. They had no right coming and worrying Des. It was bad enough them getting her to sign the lies they had concocted. But this! It must have been obvious to them that Des was ill. God, she seemed to be wasting away right in front of everyone's eyes. Verona only hoped they had the decency to keep her sister out of it.

She heard Desiree approaching the lounge with the slow, hesitant steps that measured out the pain she was feeling.

*If only she would to go the doctor's.* Verona sighed. If only Desiree would stop seeing her as a baby sister. On their mother's death, Des had taken charge, though barely ten at the time. *And when I ran away, after Ronnie . . .* She swallowed, skirting the thought. Later, when their father died and the local authority wanted to take her into care, Des had fought that too. They had both been so scared, huddling together in the single bed which, apart from a lop-sided ancient wardrobe, was the only furnishing in the dingy little room. It was the best Des could do on her wages at the time and Verona still thought with bitterness of how the bank had foreclosed on the house almost as soon as they heard that Mr Harris was dead.

'What those men want?' Desire asked again now, pushing open the lounge door and resting heavily against the frame.

Verona thought fast as she saw the worry on her sister's pain-drawn face. 'It was about me credit account,' she lied, eyes not quite meeting the anxious query in the other's. 'They've brought in a credit limit and mine's already overdrawn.'

'But you never had no trouble with your account before.'

Verona seized on the first thing that came into her head: 'It's the lawnmower I ordered for John from the sales.'

'So why they come all the way down here and wait so long?'

'I don't know.' Verona knew she sounded lame. 'Head office

probably told them it was urgent or something . . . apparently the firm have money problems,' she threw in as an afterthought.

'You don't expect me to believe that, V?' Desiree looked openly sceptical. 'Look, if you in trouble you know you can tell me.'

Verona resisted the temptation. No, she had to deal with this on her own. With Des so ill, she could not dump this on her. After all, wasn't that the main reason she had just signed their lying piece of paper?

'Honestly, Des, you are a worrier!' She forced a laugh. 'Getting all hot and bothered over a lawnmower and I can't even get you to see a doctor.'

Desiree refused to be distracted. 'V, before Mum died I told her I'd look after you . . .'

'Well, I never asked you to!' She regretted the words as soon as they were out, hating the hurt in her sister's eyes. 'I'm sorry, Des.' She gave her sister's stiff, unresponsive form a hug. 'But you know how I hate being babied . . . I'm twenty-seven, for God's sake. You can't keep trying to look after me for ever.'

'V, we're all the family we have left; we have to stick together.'

The ring of the doorbell cut the conversation and Desiree glanced at the star-shaped wall-clock behind Verona's head.

'That must be Mara and the kids,' she said, straightening tiredly.

Some of the tension eased out of Verona as she watched her go. She could hear Mara's voice, bracing and cheerful as ever, and the excitement in the children as they erupted into the house.

'Hello, Auntie V,' Carol breezed in, 'you'll never guess what we did!'

Verona smiled; you couldn't help but like Carol, rude and unruly though she was. She knew she ought not to indulge her as often as she did – at eight she was more than old enough to be a little more considerate – but there was no malice in the child and she could always find excuses for her.

'What did you do?' she asked, as Carol stood bursting with impatience.

'We went ice-skating and Lyn fell over and started to cry.' Laughter bubbled in the child's voice. 'And Mara said she was being silly.'

'That's not true!' Lyn's voice signalled that she was spoiling for a fight, her puffy eyes showing her upset. Quieter than her younger sister, she always seemed to have the responsibility for them both, uncomfortably reminding Verona of Des and herself. 'She pushed me over, Auntie V!'

'No, I never!'

'Yes, you did!' Lyn's voice squeaked in indignation. 'You were showing off, just 'cause you went once before with that soppy friend of yours.'

Carol's eyes flashed. 'Denise is not soppy, not like that giraffe-neck Mick what fancies you.'

'All right, you two, stop it,' Verona said sternly. 'Your mother is ill and the last thing she wants is to hear you two going on at each other.'

Both children looked contrite. 'Is Mum really sick, Auntie V?' Lyn asked with concern.

Verona felt remorseful, wishing she had chosen her words more carefully. 'I'm sure she'll be better soon,' she said comfortingly.

Although only just turned ten, Lyn understood so much more than Carol, and Verona wished she could teach her more around the house.

'I think we'd better get ready for bed,' Lyn said to Carol.

'Awww!'

'Carol, Mum's sick – c'mon!'

Carol sobered at once. 'Sorry, Auntie V,' she whispered, going meekly after her sister.

Verona could hear Desiree and Mara over the retreating sound of the children's steps and wondered if she should join them.

'Hey, V, you not talking or something?' Right on cue, Mara's cheerful tone lifted to include her.

Verona grinned. Mara was Des's only true friend, and she really liked her, especially since she had left Winston and gained so much confidence. 'I thought you weren't staying,' she said, coming into the passage.

'I'm not, I'm just trying to persuade your idiot sister that the house won't fall down, the children won't starve and the world will keep going while she go to the doctor . . . in fact I've a mind to drag her there myself.'

Desiree gave a reluctant smile, shaking her head. 'I told you I'd get round to it. Anyway, I'm not that bad.'

'Tell it to the birds,' Mara dismissed. 'Listen, I gone, you hear. The way Charleen and Jay were at each other, they probably done batter one another and half the house as well.'

'Yeah, I'll see you then,' Desiree said listlessly.

'Don't forget I'm coming weekend,' Mara reminded. 'V, I'll talk to you, hear.'

'Take care, Mara.' Verona closed the door behind her, leaning against it as she watched Desiree's stooped progress towards the kitchen. Who would believe her sister was only thirty-two? She looked like an old woman, bent and twisted from years of pain.

Verona followed slowly, fighting down an impulse to plead with her yet again to see a doctor. Her sister was too stubborn to take any notice and Mara had said enough for the time being.

'There's dinner in the oven, V,' Desiree said over her shoulder.

'I'll just go check the kids first,' Verona responded.

Light from a fluorescent strip flooded the long, narrow kitchen and she watched Desiree move automatically to the sturdy pine dresser in one corner, her skeletal fingers gliding across it. The usual defiant satisfaction was missing but the significance of the gesture was not lost on Verona. This was one of her sister's biggest triumphs against John's absurd pride.

Des had bought the dresser secondhand, coming across it battered and forgotten in a junk shop. On the Saturday when it was delivered, John had been horrified, taking the flaking blue paint, with the splintered, discoloured wood showing beneath, as a personal insult.

'So now you want the world to see I can't provide for you, eh?' he had accused before the front door was properly closed behind the delivery men.

Overhearing them from her room, Verona was glad the

children had gone swimming. Lyn especially was unsettled by the rows they always seemed to be having since John went to work at the railway.

'It's not so bad,' Desiree coaxed. 'Once the paint's stripped and sanded, I can put a bit of varnish on it and it'll look good as new.'

John snorted. 'No junk can be as good as new. What you trying to do to me? Don't I get enough shit out there without coming back to this?'

'John, I wish you'd stop thinking I'm against you,' Des had countered. 'It's not true.'

Obviously making an effort, he said: 'I know things aren't easy just now, but bear with me, will you?' There was a silence and Verona knew he was trying to get round her sister. She wished she could close her ears to the conversation, but she was right above the kitchen.

'Let's get rid of this junk and look about saving to get something for that space,' John suggested hopefully.

Desiree's voice was sharp: 'I don't want anything else, I think this is going to be nice enough.' Verona could imagine the look of battle on her sister's face and was not surprised to hear John capitulate:

'Well, I want nothing to do with it,' he said, storming out of the kitchen. Hearing the front door slam, Verona shrugged. That was John's answer to everything, to run away, but at least he was not a beating man.

It had been hard work stripping away the layers of paint. Verona had volunteered to do it, feeling a secret pleasure at getting at John. Fumes from the paint-stripper hung in the air and made her feel light-headed and sick. But she had stuck at it, sanding the pale wood smooth before staining it a rosewood colour to match the trim of the kitchen units.

John had made no comment, but she often surprised him looking shamefaced at it, and when his friends came over and compared it to the expensive versions in the shops he visibly swelled with pride, refusing to divulge where he got it from and how he could afford it.

The sound of running footsteps told Verona that the children were racing for the bathroom. The mood Lyn was in, there would probably be a fight if Carol won. Sometimes Carol's love of mischief got a bit out of hand, and Verona wished the younger child was more like her sister, at least where it came to showing a bit of consideration for her mother's constant state of pain. *I suppose she wouldn't be Carol if she was any different*, she thought wryly. As a wail of anger from Lyn split the air, Verona marvelled at how dissimilar sisters could be.

# Two

She stared helplessly into the compelling depths of the strange grey eyes, feeling little quivers of nerves in the pit of her stomach as he moved forward with grim determination. 'How can I let you go, chérie?' The husky words startled her, betraying as they did . . .

Verona shifted to a more comfortable position on the sagging mattress as she came to the end of the page and turned the leaf slowly. She was lying face-down, head propped on one arm, free hand holding the novel against a tendency to close.

'Believe me, Rosemarie, I have tried but I cannot let you go.'

She wrenched her eyes from the almost hypnotic quality of his gaze, steeling herself against the pain threatening to swamp her. There would be time for that later; right now she had to be strong for both of them . . .

'V – telephone.'

The earlier trauma of the day temporarily forgotten, Verona was totally immersed in the role of the beautiful blonde heroine, her whole being transported to the French countryside and the tall, dark, handsome count.

'Verona!' Desiree's voice came from far away and the rap of her fingers sliced the web of fantasy. 'V, you awake?'

She closed the book, pushing it guiltily under her pillow. *I oughta get another bookshelf*, she thought, stepping over a pile of half-read novels and the latest consignment, still held securely in the brown-paper wrapping.

'*Verona!*' Impatience had crept into her sister's voice.

'Hang on, I'll be down in a mo.' Verona stretched in the middle of the room. 'I must have gone off to sleep for a bit.'

The telephone was lying on the stool in the darkened hall. The teak chiming clock – a free gift from a catalogue Desiree had joined – showed ten minutes past eleven. Who could be calling at this time of night? Picking up the receiver, Verona eased herself gingerly on to the spindly-legged stool.

'Hello?'

'Verona?' There was relief in the male voice on the line.

'Guy!' She glanced nervously at the slightly open sitting-room door, expecting Desiree to appear at any moment. 'I thought I told you never to ring me at home.'

'I had to, love,' Guy said placatingly. 'The wife wants me to take her round the mother-in-law's tomorrow night – so we have to make it another time.'

Verona scarcely heard him, ears straining to detect any sound from the sitting-room. 'Did you think my sister was me?' she asked on an urgent thought, remembering they were supposed to sound alike on the phone.

'I didn't let on anything – honest, love. You know me better than that, specially as you said she's a bit funny with white blokes like me.'

Verona relaxed a little; she had forgotten telling him that. It was the only way to prevent him coming round. Des would be furious if she knew.

At fifty-five, Guy still considered himself a charmer, unaware of how ridiculous he looked in the bright orange shirts and Teddy-boy outfits he favoured when not working. He was the youngest and most persistent of the men Verona had dealt with, and she could imagine her sister's anger and disgust were she ever to find out. As far as Des knew, Verona's interest in things sexual was limited to the romances she read so avidly. But how could Des understand the nightmares that still haunted her, or that out-of-control feeling that younger or more aggressive men – black men – gave her?

She realised that men like Guy were fascinated by her skin, finding the colour and texture alien and exotic. They were flattered by her attention. With them she was in control and could indulge her fantasy. She needed that control. It was her second line of defence, along with her huge size; and at the end of the day the men went home to their wives and nobody got hurt.

'I don't want you to ring me here again, ever!' she told Guy now.

The silence on the other end stretched for so long, she thought he had hung up. 'Hello? Hello?'

'I'm still here,' he said; 'couldn't get the money in the bloody box. Listen, love, why don't we meet Friday instead, make a night of it?'

Verona thought rapidly, wondering what excuse she could give her sister – which imaginary friend she hadn't stayed with for a while.

The sound of the front gate slamming brought her to attention. 'I'll give you a ring about it,' she said hurriedly.

'When?' he asked, disappointed. 'I'm out all day tomorrow and –'

'All right, Thursday.'

'It'll have to be first thing, before Mr Peacock gets in.'

She agreed impatiently, picturing the outline of John's tall frame, slightly stooped as if still unaccustomed to the height of his body after thirty-eight years of living in it.

'Anyway, love . . . nice talking to you,' Guy sounded a little awkward now. 'See you Friday, then.'

'Maybe . . .' Verona countered. 'G'bye Guy.'

John shut the door behind him, cutting off the sudden burst of icy wind swirling snow furiously through the porch. He shivered, clapping his gloved hands together to return the circulation, before pushing the safety chain home. 'Wha'appen, V? Don't tell me your tall, dark, handsome stranger finally come through.'

She ignored the mockery. 'Hello, John,' she kept her voice cold, getting to her feet to reinforce the hint that she did not wish to converse. 'There's a letter for you from Jamaica. It's on the dresser in the kitchen.'

Anxiety clouded the humour in his eyes, and Verona watched him curiously as he dropped his big black bag and rushed past her, making no attempt to take off the heavy snow-flecked overcoat he wore buttoned to the neck. It was pathetic the way he always rushed straight for any letter from Jamaica to check if it was from his grandparents. He doted on the old people and, like his brothers in Canada and the USA, would refuse them nothing. In the past, when he still had time for Desiree as well, Verona had thought his devotion to them exemplary. But now it rankled. Here was a case in point: his wife was sick, yet John couldn't pop his head round the door to see how she was before going for his letter.

Despite her disapproval, Verona lingered, curious to know who the letter was from. She hadn't been able to make out the writing when she had picked up the flimsy blue envelope in the morning.

John came back out slowly, head still bowed over the letter. Verona shifted her position and he looked up, as she had intended him to.

'It's from Delsey,' he volunteered, half to himself. 'It's about Granny Ruby operation.'

Verona showed no interest; John had been on about his grandmother needing an operation for months and she resented that concern when her sister was fading away right under his eyes.

'Maybe Des need an operation too,' she said pointedly.

He looked up with a flash of anger. 'Granny need this operation to walk, V!'

'Des might need one to live . . . if it ain't already too late.'

He gave her a helpless look. 'I ask her to go to the doctor a lot of time, what more you want me to do?' It was a plea for reassurance, and almost against herself Verona relented.

'I shouldn't worry about it. I'm sure Mara and me can think of something.'

He looked so relieved she felt almost sorry for him.

'How's things at work?'

John's face lightened. 'V, I have the promotion in here,' he paused in the act of taking off his coat to show her the palm of his hand. 'This time we going to be living life.'

Verona was unimpressed. 'I heard that before.'

'You might have heard about promotion but not living life.'

Sympathy for him was replaced by the usual impatience: 'Very funny, 'cept I ain't laughing.'

He sighed, abandoning the feeble attempt at humour. He seemed old suddenly, lines of tiredness and defeat ageing him prematurely. 'How was your work today?' He was polite now, making conversation as he hung his coat in the hall.

'Same as always.' Verona was glad the only light came from the sitting-room through the slightly ajar door. 'Desiree's in there,' she indicated with her head as an uneasy silence fell, 'and she ain't no better. Why don'tcha find out how she is?'

'Don't you want to know what else Delsey saying?' he offered hopefully.

Verona shrugged. There had been a time when she would listen eagerly to John talking about his family, feeling almost a part of it as he read out snippets of letters from Jamaica. He and Des would swap childhood stories and Verona used to sit in rapt attention, wishing with all her might that she could have stayed in the West Indies. She had envied John the warm, loving relationship he had with the grandparents who had raised him, admired the fact that all the years and distance hadn't dimmed the obvious love he had for them. But today she had no time for that. All she could feel was resentment. If John showed Des even a little of the care he had for the old people, things would be a lot better. As far as Verona was concerned, John's first duty was to his wife and kids, no matter how much his grandparents had done for him.

'You don't want to know what he saying?' John pressed on.

'No. Ain't my business, is it?'

John looked at a loss. 'How come you so unfriendly these days?'

The question was almost a plea but Verona gave him an icy

look, all her early sympathy gone. 'Go see Des and leave me alone, John.'

'Don't tell me what to do in my own house,' he snapped back.

'What's going on?' Desiree's faint voice floated out.

'Nothing, Des. John and me was just talking 'bout football,' Verona improvised.

John swore under his breath. 'The sooner you get out a here, the better,' he muttered. 'I mean, all you do is read them stupid books. When you last do anything for Des, eh?'

She knew he was lashing out in frustration, but perhaps he was right. Des had done so much for her, and what had she done in return?

'I'm going to my room.' Verona felt her dislike for him increase.

'Hey, V, sorry, you hear? I shouldn't have said that. Listen,' he added when she made to move past him, 'I know you think I take Des for granted and that I don't care.' He frowned. 'I trying, V. I mean, I did share my own dinner yesterday and didn't I wash up afterwards? What more you want me to do? If she don't go to the doctor, it can't be that serious, no true?'

Verona hissed air through her teeth. She should have guessed character would come look for him finally, and it was no use Desiree giving her that crap about frustration in his job. He should work as clerk for a couple of years, then he'd find out about frustration.

'Night, Des,' she raised her voice, before casting another look at John and heading for the stairs.

She had expected so much from Desiree's marriage. John had seemed different – not threatening like Ronnie had been, or sly like Leonard. John never looked at her in that uncomfortable way, he had just accepted her fatness as if it was normal. And he had been so considerate to Des. It was John who had persuaded her to leave her factory job and apply for a clerical officer vacancy at Social Security. When Des got the job, they had all gone out to dinner and John had been more excited than anyone, grinning all night as if he'd won the pools. He had been at Rathbourne's then, a skilled man earning a good wage. Maybe his going to the railway did have something to do with his moodiness and the quarrels he was constantly picking.

Pushing her door open, Verona moved about automatically, getting her nightdress and toiletries.

It was strange how much John had changed. There had been a time when he was always urging Desiree on with her studies, arguing with Verona in an attempt to persuade her not to leave school. Now he wouldn't even let her sister go back to work part-time. He was forever talking about the role of African women and how the children needed a mother. 'What about a father?' Verona was tempted to ask. Christ, sometimes he worked so much overtime the kids never saw him for weeks.

If only Des were like Mara, Verona thought, not for the first time; if she had more sense she would have left him long ago. She had been so proud of Desiree when she passed the exam, but what was the use of it when she sat in the house vegetating?

'No way I'm going to let no man do that to me,' she vowed, pulling back the covers and easing into bed.

The memory of her frightened fourteen-year-old self came to her, pushing through the layers of repression she hid behind. She could picture Ronnie vividly, the incredulity dawning in his eyes.

'Don't be stupid, I'm only going to kiss you.'

Verona had stared at him in shock. 'I don't want to do none of that . . . you said you'd help me with me homework.'

He had laughed, his face alien and mocking. 'You think I been coming round here just so you can learn maths?' Contemptuously glancing at the book in his hand he had thrown it to the ground.

She had stood frozen to the spot, stunned, unable to come to terms with this stranger who had taken the place of Desiree's gentle boyfriend. He had been coming to the house for months, helping her with her homework, staying to have dinner when her father and Des came home from work. Not once had she suspected that this other, ugly person existed.

Slowly, cautiously, she had tried to edge away, realising beleatedly that she was alone in the house with him. A glance at the star-shaped wall-clock showed it was four-fifteen, and her heart sank. Des wouldn't be back until six, her father even later.

She had wanted to make a dash for the door, but Ronnie was blocking her way and in the end she had burst into tears. Why didn't Des come? Why had she brought this horrible man into their lives? . . .

Verona frowned at the memory, impatiently pushing it away as the old, helpless fear threatened. She had broken out of that. She didn't need to wait for her sister any more. *If Des only knew how liberated I was!* she thought bitterly, her anger feeding on itself.

She picked up the book she had discarded earlier. One day . . . one day she would meet a man she could live with. A man so far removed from Ronnie, no echoes of her past would remain to prey on her and revive guilt or shame.

In the distance a pot lid clanged as John moved about getting his dinner, and fresh resentment flared in her. Who did he think he was impressing anyway, talking about helping by sharing his own dinner? When he cooked it himself, then he'd have something to go on about.

She fretted, unable to get into the book again, anxious for her sister. John should be able to get Des to go to the doctor. When he had been his old caring self, she always did what he asked, and anyway he would have made the appointment and gone with her himself – anybody with any sense could see that Des was scared of facing it alone.

Desiree sat stiffly on the settee, making no pretence of watching the late news on the television. She tensed at every sound from the kitchen, sure John was wrecking something in there. At least he no longer plonked himself in a chair and waited for her to put the food on the table. She heard water running and imagined the pool he would carelessly leave beside the circular sink. She would have to mop it up and put the dishes away before going to bed.

Her increasingly critical thoughts of him merged with a new wave of pain. Somehow all she noticed these days were his failings. Of course it wasn't his fault she was sick, yet she found herself blaming him because he couldn't understand. To be fair, he had tried to get her to the doctor, nagging at her every time they were alone, but her growing hostility eventually stopped him. She knew he was scared for her, but somehow that only made her resent him more.

Nevertheless he was a good provider, she reminded herself grimly, using the well-worn talisman against John's growing impotence, the hopelessness she dared not fall into for the children's sake. At least they never had to go without, even if the price was that he did work so much overtime.

She heard him leave the kitchen for the sitting-room and he entered hesitantly, pausing as if uncertain before coming to sit beside her. His weight depressed the cushion, folding the edges upward, and she flinched at the shuddering movement of the settee.

'How you feeling, love?' he asked, patting her hand clumsily.

'Fine.' She pulled her hand away irritably, then felt contrite at his lost and helpless look. She could see the tiredness in him, the way his shoulders drooped. Lines of bitterness, carved by years of disappointment and overwork, seemed deeper around his mouth. It was not his fault that she had so little of herself left to give after coping with her own survival.

'How's work?' She tried to sound interested, though the last thing she wanted to hear about was track-laying and maintenance. But she knew he needed to think she cared.

He perked up, newly animated. 'All right. You know that job – the one I was telling you about, for the supervisor?' She nodded, feeling dismayed as he added: 'I put in for it. I mean, I'm the most qualified electrical engineer there, and everyone reckon I'll get it.'

Suddenly she couldn't bear the thought of starting all that again. She had lost count of the times he had come home buoyed up with optimism. It was always the same. He would be full of hope, enthusing about yet another job opportunity – one with more prospects and responsibility, nearer to the level he had attained at Rathbourne's. Always he had been passed over, usually for a younger, less qualified, less experienced man – someone white.

'What if they don't give you it, eh?' she asked quietly.

'Don't be so negative, Des. Why I shouldn't get it?'

'John, all I saying is don't get up your hopes too much. You apply for everything that's come up, and they don't give you one thing in six years.'

'You don't have to tell me that!' he snapped. 'Why is it every time I try a thing, all you can do is go on like I not good enough for nothing?'

She knew better than to argue. She sank further into her seat and listened to the tirade with resignation.

'That's all I getting from the white man out there,' he continued, 'but I ain't taking it from you.'

She was seething silently; trust him to shift the blame to her. If only she felt better . . . She rested her head against the back of the settee. 'Is no wonder Mara left Winston,' she said under her breath.

'What's that?' he asked belligerently.

She gave him a cutting look. 'I'm going to bed,' she said, getting ponderously to her feet.

John was up immediately. 'Look, I'm sorry, you hear. I shouldn't take it out on you, seeing as you not well; but is work – it's getting to me, man. And with Granny Ruby needing this hip operation . . .'

Desire ignored him, moving to the kitchen.

'What you doing now?' he asked with renewed impatience, watching as she mopped the draining-board before starting on the dishes. 'I told you I'll wash up – why you always wiping everything down?'

'This surface is soaking wet, and it's dirty,' she answered flatly.

'You telling me something or what?'

'No, John.'

He sucked his teeth. 'I can't bother with this. If you want play martyr, you going have to play it by yourself. I tired.'

She turned to watch him go, relieved that she didn't have to put up further with his blundering, half-hearted attempts at being considerate.

*Maybe I ought to go see a doctor*, she thought, leaning against the sink as fresh pain hit her. If only she wasn't so sure it was cancer.

All at once she was too tired to bother with the dishes and she folded the tea towel back over its rail. Tomorrow she would think about the doctor again.

# Three

Verona was awake. The early morning light barely lifted the darkness as she struggled up from restless, unrefreshing sleep. The bedside lamp cast a dull glow and she felt a pang of self-reproach as she reached to turn it out. This made three nights in a row she'd fallen asleep leaving it on. It was freezing and she retreated under the covers hastily, then changed her mind and switched the light on again. She would read until the heating came on and the room warmed up. She picked up the book sleep had interrupted. She had been in the middle of the last chapter; she might as well finish it before getting ready for work.

Work! The thought crystallised the nagging feelings of unease that had populated her dreams through the night, yesterday's worry and fear rushing back to haunt the new day. There was a sick, fluttery sensation in her stomach, and she pressed her palm against it as she remembered the union men and the red Cortina.

She must have been mad to sign the piece of paper. Fancy admitting she had stolen that money when it wasn't her! She huddled further under the covers. Work would be a heavy trial today, what with everyone knowing. It was bad enough yesterday when she hadn't signed anything. *Least I've still got a job*, she thought dubiously. The men had assured her of that, but how was she going to cope now that she was branded a thief?

She had been at Stoneford's for twelve years – ever since leaving school – with not one day of absence against her name. Somehow that had always seemed important. It might not be the ideal job, working in the accounts department of a mail-order supply factory, but it was better than many, and she got on with the other women – well, most of them . . . most of the time. She couldn't imagine why anyone should want to do this to her. If it had been just after the 1981 rioting in Brixton, she could maybe understand. But that was six years ago, and the two women from packaging who had joined the National Front had both left to have babies. They had both been casuals and Stoneford's didn't guarantee jobs even for permanents.

She turned over on her back, tracing a hairline crack along the ceiling. Her mouth lifted in a slight smile as she recalled getting into a fight with one of them, a pasty-faced woman with a loud laugh and greasy brown hair. The woman had pushed her and called her a black bastard. Verona had grabbed at her, sending her crashing to the ground outraged that she had dared to touch her. They had both been summoned to see the floor manager; but either the riots had scared him or he was having an off day, for he simply muttered that he didn't want any trouble and ordered them back to work.

A vision of the riots formed in Verona's head. She had been shocked and ashamed at the reports on television. Mara and Winston were visiting, and the two men sat with attention riveted on the screen, one of them occasionally going to the phone to speak rapidly to someone. John had been a member of Black United Front then. He and Winston went to meetings regularly, and he could often be seen at rallies and public gatherings selling the organisation's newspaper, *Black Unity*. Verona never understood half of what they were saying; but she felt proud of what they were doing for black people and awed by the books on African history and culture they were always reading or discussing. That was until the riots.

She had been in Brixton getting some fresh bread for Desiree when it had started, but what she saw of it was mostly on the television, and that showed little enough. All she remembered was battling crowds and police behind riot shields, against a backdrop of sheets of orange flames and columns of thick smoke as cars and buildings went up in the destructive fire of years of frustration.

Afterwards she had gone to make sure the people she knew there were all right. There was an old lady she had started visiting from school, and she could have cried when she found out what the police had done to her. They had come to arrest her sons, neither of whom were in London, and when they couldn't find them their mother was made to pay for the loss of face and the fear of retaliation the police evidently felt.

Verona had been furious, empathising deeply with the youths whom before she would have dismissed as troublemakers. For the first time she wanted to be like John and Winston, wanted to do something to help out. When she heard about the public meeting, she had suggested to John that they go together.

He had been horrified. 'This ain't no joke, you know, not like something in them trashy white propaganda books. Is a uprising we a deal with. The youth need positive people.'

Verona had glared at him. 'You can't stop me if I want to go.'

'Look, V,' he said, a little nicer, 'you don't understand the struggle, yeah? So this ain't the sort of thing you want to get involved in, see?'

'No, I don't see,' she said stubbornly.

'Well, you ain't coming with me. I mean, is war we a deal with.'

'I don't care,' Verona said unruffled, 'I want to do something and you ain't stopping me.'

She had gone along, for once emptying her bag of the obligatory romance novel, feeling distaste at the cardboard unreality of it. What right had she to bury herself in white people's things when old black people like Mrs Fraser were being assaulted and insulted?

The meeting had started promisingly, and she had been all fired up as speaker after speaker demanded action and called for a public enquiry. Many gave graphic details of police brutality, a lot of it worse than Mrs Fraser's experience. Verona had really felt it when one speaker went to the rostrum and thundered: 'When they insult our old people, they insult us as well!' She had clapped until her palms stung as he finished with: 'We demand action now!' But by halfway through the meeting, she had begun to wonder, 'What action?' She had come to do something, to be involved in something, but all that emerged was talk; and then the insults started. She had watched horrified as black people traded accusations with each other, and she had wished she had the courage to voice her disgust.

Walking to the bus-stop afterwards, she deliberately avoided John and his friends. They were walking ahead, all of them on a high. She wanted to tell them that their revolution was simply in their heads – that it was wrong to use the frustration of the youths to make themselves seem big. They were like powerless defiant schoolboys and it made her feel ashamed.

After that she went to a few more meetings, but it was always the same. She wanted action, not political discussion. Yet all she ended up with was more fear of the police and the white laws used against black people . . . as if there wasn't enough to fear already. In the end, she had put her romance novel back in her bag and renewed her three subscriptions.

When the police had shot and paralysed a black woman in Brixton, Verona had been angry and scared – more so when she realised how unrepentant they were. There had been another riot, but this time she did not go to the meeting. What would have been the point? Even John had given up. Later, when the policeman walked free, she had felt the anger. But still she didn't bother. What was the use anyway, she told herself. It was all fine for Winston to say the judgment was a licence to kill black people, but what was new in that. All that it did was confirm what government was up to. They wanted black people out of Britain and didn't care how they did it.

The alarm went off, bringing her back to present reality with a start. She reached to click it off, forebodings of work weighing heavily again.

*If it wasn't for Des, I'd let them go to the flaming police*, she muttered inwardly. No, that wasn't true. The legacy of fear was too great for that. She knew too many people who had fallen foul of the police, only to end up confessing to things they hadn't done. On top of that, how many stories had been reported of black women raped and men murdered, seriously injured or brain-damaged in police custody? Even old Mrs Philley, the woman she'd met at the hostel where she'd stayed after the argument with John, had been arrested for causing a disturbance and beaten up after she had been robbed. What happened to the old woman still caused a burning anger in Verona – the anger and bitter fear of being exposed and vulnerable, so that she wanted to lash out and hide at the same time.

*Least I wouldn't sign the paper voluntary*, she thought ruefully, realising she had made a mistake in signing when there was no evidence of guilt. Des must never find out. She had made the mistake for her sister's sake and she must do everything to keep that knowledge from her.

'Is that you, V?' Desiree's voice sounded strained as Verona hurried down the stairs.

'Yes,' she responded, going into the kitchen. 'Here, I'll do that, Des.' She took the kettle from her sister, moving briskly to the sink. 'You sit down and rest. I bet you ain't had a cuppa yet.'

Desiree collapsed gratefully into the chair and Verona waited for the water note change to announce that the kettle was full.

'Shall I do you some toast?' she asked, taking the wholemeal loaf from the varnished pine breadbin.

'No, thanks, V,' she said listlessly, laying her head across her folded arms on the table, 'just some weak tea for me, eh.'

Verona felt helpless. 'Why don'tcha go doctor's?' she burst out in exasperation. 'Honestly, Des, you being real stupid! It won't make you feel no better if you don't find out what's wrong, ain't it?'

Desiree sighed, lifting her head. 'Don't start that again. We gone through it already and I said I'll go when I have time.'

Verona was in two minds about pressing the issue, but her sister's drawn face decided her. 'Look,' she said, 'I'll leave work early this afternoon and you can go doctor's then, yeah?'

'You know John coming early today.'

'So what?' Verona's voice was rising but she was determined not to quarrel.

'V, John tired when he come in, especially if he did overtime day before . . . and you know you won't cook for him if I not here.'

Verona bit down hard on her bottom lip; now was not the time to say what she thought of John. 'All right, what if I promise to get John dinner?'

'Let me think about it,' Desiree said finally. 'I probably wouldn't be able to get an appointment till next week anyway.'

Verona knew she was making excuses, but her sister's face looked so weary and pain-lined, she didn't have the heart to press the point. 'Well, think about it anyhow,' she said, suppressing impatience at Desiree's obvious relief when she heard the children's feet on the stairs.

The door crashed open as Carol burst in.

'Don't slam the door so hard, love . . . your father spend all weekend painting it.' Desiree didn't even bother to raise her head.

'Sor–ree,' Carol said, sounding anything but, as she walked over to hug her mother before going to give Verona an impulsive squeeze.

'Morning, Mum, hello, Auntie V . . . can I have my egg scrambled, please?' she finished, not pausing for breath.

Verona nodded, unable to resist the child's breezy cheerfulness.

'Can I butter the bread?' Carol asked wistfully, casting a wary eye at her mother's bent head.

Verona felt agreement burning on her tongue, but Desiree said:

'You know your father don't like you to do that kind of work.'

'Aw–ww,' Carol wheedled, 'Dad only said that 'cause he think we don't want to. But I do want to do things.'

Desiree didn't respond and the child persisted: 'When we go to Mara she let us and Charleen help you when she's here. Oh, go on, Mum, *please* . . . Tell her, Auntie V.'

'If your Dad don't like it, you better not,' Verona said firmly, realising that Desiree was in no state to battle with the child. 'Listen to what your mother says, Carol.'

'But it isn't fair,' Carol moaned, 'I *never* get to do anything. I'm dead fed-up. Anybody would think I was a baby or something.'

'Why don'tcha get out some plates and tell me what you want for your packed lunch?' Verona placated, successfully distracting the child.

Her good mood restored. Carol laid the table, setting everything out with the care children take over a rare treat.

The door opened and Lyn came in so quietly that if Verona had turned she might have missed her.

'Hi, Mum, are you all right?' the child asked, worry in her voice.

Desiree sat up painfully, giving Lyn a reassuring smile.

Verona picked up a grapefruit from the bowl under the window and sliched it in half.

'Just toast and marmalade with my grapefruit, please, Auntie V.' Lyn sat beside her mother and put a gentle arm around her shoulders.

Desiree met the enquiry in Verona's eyes with a frown. 'You should eat a proper breakfast, Lyn,' she said reprovingly. 'Is no good you scrimping on food, skinny as you are.'

'I don't want to get fat like Auntie V,' Lyn responded, sitting up and swinging her legs under the table, unconcerned.

'Lyn!' Desiree looked so shocked, Verona wanted to both laugh and cry at the same time. She realised the child meant no malice by her careless statement, but it hurt none the less.

'Some of the girls at school say you look like the Michelin man, Auntie V,' Carol informed her gravely, between mouthfuls of scrambled egg.

'Carol!' Lyn's voice was sharp with warning as she kicked her sister under the table. 'Stop lying!'

'I'm not!' Carol wailed. 'Mum, Lyn's kicking me.'

'Stop it, you two!' Verona said sharply.

'But it's true, Auntie V. Lyn pointed you out to them when you were walking past our school last week.'

Verona fought down her hurt at the child's cruel truthfulness.

'That's not what happened, Auntie V . . . honest,' Lyn said anxiously. 'Carol, you're such a liar, you are.'

'No, I'm not!'

'All right, that's enough,' Verona said sharply, realising that a full-scale argument was about to break out. She put the plate of hot toast in front of Lyn. 'Just eat your breakfast and get a move on, or you'll be late for school.'

It was still early after Verona started the kids off to school, and on impulse she decided to walk to work. Despite the brightness of the sun, it was a freezing cold day, typical of January. She huddled into her duffel coat, thankful for the sheepskin boots and gloves she had bought in the January sales. Right now she didn't care that she looked large and ungainly, wearing her woolly hat over ear muffs as if that was the height of fashion. She hated the cold, but, wrapped up as she was and with the sun sharpening the focus of the day, she could almost believe it was nearly spring.

She cut across the common – the most direct route – liking the pretence that she was out of the crowded rush of city life. The flat greenness was full of frantic activity: winter birds searching hopefully along the frozen ground for unwary insects, and a lone grey squirrel darting up and down a large sycamore for all the world as if it was not the dead of winter. It gave her a sense of freedom as she stepped on the short grass, glad that it had not frosted over the night before.

Her spirit lifted, her mind letting go of worry and shifting to her latest fantasy. Narrowly missing a spot where a dog had relieved itself, she moved reluctantly to the winding path. Still, she made believe it was a country lane. At the bottom she pictured a little cottage where she lived, its whitewashed walls wreathed with rambling roses. *Do roses bloom in January?* she wondered fleetingly.

The green fields drowsed under the blossom-scented heat of an imagined Spanish sun. It was a world away from the bleak reality of a South London winter and the endless struggle for survival. All she had to think about was the brooding mysterious stranger, following her with his eyes. She could almost feel him watching her, drinking in the graceful sway of her hips, the slender beauty of her legs under the wide gipsy skirt and the soft glow of her long blonde hair. She could feel the tension emanating from him, knew he wanted to approach her. Her nerve-ends tingled with a mixture of anticipation and excitement as she felt him undressing her with his eyes. There was something familiar about the set of his strong, stubborn chin, and the penetrating greyness of his eyes under the hawk-like brow . . .

'Hoi! Watch where yer going!'

The screech of tyres and the strident blare of horns brought Verona's dream world crashing into reality, and she looked up, feeling her stomach lurch. Her feet froze as she saw that she had wandered into the middle of the road, and the harsh angry noises were from cars surrounding her.

A man in a brown Mini had stopped inches from her and was leaning red-faced through the window, looking almost as scared as she felt, and screaming obscenities. He seemed about to get out and shift her out of the way himself. Fear galvanised her into ponderous movement and the next moment she was almost running full tilt into an oncoming car. She felt hot and embarrassed as the car swerved and its occupant leaned out.

'Bloody nigger!' he shouted, the rest of his abuse drowned in the roar of his passing.

She hurried along the pavement with her head bent, feeling marked. Everyone was surely looking at her, laughing at her; the mood of the morning was broken by the resurrection of her old fear.

Unhappiness took her feet into the newsagent's on the corner of the street where Stoneford's was.

'Morning, Miss,' the Asian man behind the counter greeted her as the echo of the shop bell died away. He was a friendly man of indeterminate age; but his usual smile of recognition failed to elicit an answering spark today.

'What can I do for you today?' he asked, undaunted. 'Same as yesterday, or do you want the big box instead?'

Verona hesitated, Lyn's words coming back to her with a painful sting. She felt miserable, fat and unlovely.

'Give me two boxes of the assorted and a pound of

peardrops,' she said defiantly. To hell with it, she might as well get something out of life.

'Anything else, love?'

*Well, why not? I can only put on two pounds a day maximum anyway*. 'Yeah, let me have a bottle of cherry cola – no, not that one, the big one beside it – and two caramel bars.'

The man smiled uncertainly. 'Something to celebrate?'

'You could say that,' she muttered, stuffing her purchases into the roomy canvas bag which carried her books, then holding out her hand for her change.

The crisp sunlit morning had dissolved into cloudy drizzle, bringing with it an icy wind, by the time she turned into the heavy-gauge factory gates. Hardly anyone was about yet, just a few stragglers from the warehouse dashing towards the main office block.

Verona pulled her coat close at the top, fastening it under her chin, and headed for the dull glow of artificial light spilling into the gloom from an open doorway. Pausing only to shake water drops from the worn cardigan, she hurried along the silent corridor, praying that she meet no one before she reached the relative safety of the locker-room.

The room was empty and she sighed with relief as she unbuttoned her cardigan and hung it on a peg. There were only a few coats, so she knew she was one of the first in. Not many people liked to work at the earlier end of the flexi-time system.

Anticipating the whispered comments and snide remarks of the day ahead, she wished she had phoned in sick. She could have pretended she had caught something from one of the children . . . and then just spent the day in the library. She put the idea firmly out of her head. Today was only Wednesday, and there would still have been the rest of the week to face; there was just so much you could skive.

At least she herself knew the accusation was untrue, whatever anyone else might say. She hadn't taken the money. She wondered who had, or if it had been taken at all. Stoneford's did not go in for long-term staff, and if they were in difficulties they wouldn't want to pay her the redundancy she was due after her twelve years' employment.

'It will come back on them,' she told herself with conviction. 'One day they going to see.'

Not that she would blame any of the women if they had taken it. Working at Stoneford's was a thankless task. The company only managed to turn a profit by cutting corners and exploiting its workforce. Apart from the management, only office staff and supervisors were given permanent contracts and they were not encouraged to stay too long. In fact Verona was one of the longest-serving members of staff, and with all the talk of staff cuts she was grateful they had not used the excuse of the missing money to sack her.

*I should have stayed at school and got some exams*, she thought despondently. She regretted her impulse to leave more bitterly with each year that passed. She had tried night classes, but somehow she just didn't have the determination. The least excuse, or a good book, was all she needed to drop out. Well, it was no good crying over spilt milk. She picked up her bag and before putting it in her locker took out one of the Caramac bars.

She didn't notice the official-looking envelope until her hand was almost on the camouflaging brown of the locker. Her heart skipped a beat, and her hand shook as she took out the envelope. It had already been opened, torn with careless disregard for the PRIVATE written above her name in the floor manager's neat, precise handwriting.

It was a short note, brief to the point of curtness. Mr Dorkings wanted to see her as soon as she arrived and before she clocked in. There could be only one reason for that, she realised.

*I should never have signed that paper*, she thought morosely. God, she should have guessed it was a trick. She would never get another job.

She sat down on the bench beneath the bank of lockers, blindly ripping off the chocolate wrapping and chewing on the crumbling sweetness. It steadied her nerves a little, eased the shaking that seemed to start deep within her stomach.

Mr Dorkings was sitting behind his wide desk, a big, florid-faced man with thin grey hair that had long ago migrated from his crown. Worry had etched permanent lines across his forehead, and his frown of concentration deepened them when Verona knocked and walked in. After a last look at the charts he was studying, he turned his attention to her.

'I'm sure you know why you're here, Miss Harris,' he said, elbows on his desk, fingers forming a bridge on which to rest his sagging chins. His eyes slid away from the directness in hers. 'The general manager considered your case and felt that, given the seriousness of the situation, there was no alternative but to terminate your employment without notice.'

She had expected it, but that did not stop the sick desperation that gripped her, the sudden breathing difficulties that made speech laboured.

'Th-the union reps s-said if I s-signed the paper I weren't gonna get the sack,' she almost whispered.

Mr Dorkings shifted uncomfortably on his chair. 'They had no authority to make that kind of promise,' he said, with less firmness than earlier.

'I don't believe you!' The words jerked out, betrayal burning angrily inside her. 'You got the union blokes to say that so you can kick me out. It's the redundancy thing, isn't it?'

He flushed to his hairline. 'If I may say so, Miss Harris, this attitude is hardly helping your case.'

'Sure, and what's that, Mr Dorkings?' she said sarcastically. 'To think I was mug enough to believe anything you lot said! Walked right into it, didn't I?'

Undeterred, he continued with his prepared speech: 'We are taking into account the fact that you have been with us for twelve years –'

'It's the redundancy, ain't it?' Verona pressed.

'That's nonsense,' he said hastily, 'and I would advise you against spreading that kind of talk, Miss Harris. We have your signed confession of guilt – but, as I was saying . . .' He paused, losing his thread. 'In the circumstances, and because you have cooperated, the company will not be calling in the police.'

'Big of you,' she muttered, scuffing her toe against the brown carpet.

He ignored her remark. 'You'll be given a week's pay in lieu of notice, plus wages for the whole of this week as well as an additional week for long service. Any holiday entitlement will also be included, less any amounts owing the firm, the usual deductions and of course the money you stole.'

*Cheap at the price*, she thought bitterly. She didn't know much about redundancy, but it would definitely have been a lot more than two weeks' pay, and they would have had to give her notice.

'Will I get a reference for another job?' she asked, knowing the answer.

'I'm afraid the company is unable to give you one.' He ran a hand through his thinning hair. 'An accounts clerk has to . . . well, deal with money –'

'I know. I been doing it for twelve years,' she said with heavy irony. To think she had liked Mr Dorkings, had gone out of her way to be pleasant to him, sorry for him because his wife had left him and everyone laughed at him behind his back. Well, she should have saved herself the bother.

Her bravado lasted until she quit the building for the last time. The day stretched bleakly ahead, endless hours to fill between now and the time she could even contemplate returning home. That was when it hit her. She had lost her job. All she had to show for twelve years of her working life was two weeks' pay and no prospect of other employment.

Her feet dragged as she wandered the street in aimless indecision. The rain had stopped but the wind, if anything, was worse. It cut through the thick layers of clothing she had cocooned herself in, making her shiver. A high of forty-two degrees Fahrenheit, the radio weatherman had said that morning, but she was sure he had over-estimated. It was bitterly cold and no doubt the rain would come again, judging from the heavy clouds hanging in opaque masses across the skyline.

She considered a walk in the park, but rejected that. It would be sodden and bedraggled now. Her hand plunged instinctively into the canvas bag on her arm, fingers rummaging inside one of the paper bags to emerge with a dusting of powdery sugar and a peardrop.

As she sucked the lemon-flavoured sweet, she toyed with the idea of going home. She could lie in the warm cheerfulness of her buttercup room and lose herself in the champagne world of Rosemarie and her brooding Frenchman. It was tempting, and only the image of Desiree's worried face dissuaded her. She had got into this mess through trying to protect her sister. It would destroy all that to turn up right now.

In the end she settled for the library, crossing the road to where it stood, modern and awkward against a backdrop of sunken gravestones in the older part of the cemetery. The building was like a hollowed-out square, single-storied and open-plan. The middle was a beautifully paved courtyard, where you could sit and enjoy the nature garden creeping across the stones in spring, or watch the antics of the ever-increasing bird-population when they came back from their winter holidays. Verona always found it soothing, liking the soporific effect of droning bees and rustling pages on a summer afternoon. At this time of year she loved to see the way the variegated ivy had begun to fan out along the courtyard stones, starting a new season of growth, in defiance of the wintery chill.

She found a quiet corner against one of the wide, full-length glass doors to the courtyard. Getting comfortable in the cushioned black chair, she arranged her four romance novels in a neat pile on the floor and stared pensively at the dripping ivy outside.

*How am I ever gonna keep this from Des?* she wondered unhappily, making no attempt to start the book on her lap.

'V! What are you doing here? Aren't you supposed to be at work?'

'Mara!' Verona's heart thudded with guilt and shock as the tall, lanky frame flopped into the seat beside her. 'What a surprise! Fancy seeing you here,' she tailed off lamely.

'Yes, isn't it?' Mara answered, evidently failing to notice the tension in her features. 'How's Des? She been down the doctor's yet?'

Verona shook her head, concern for her sister pushing to the surface of her mind. 'I did offer to mind the house while she went . . . but, if you want the truth, I think she's scared she's got something real bad.'

Mara nodded sympathetically. 'Mmm, that figures: I felt just like that – remember the time when I got that lump and thought I had cancer because I had that gallstone as well?'

How could she forget! No one had ever seen Mara in such a panic, not even when she was coming off Valium after leaving Winston. She had rushed around to everyone, looking far from her normally neat self, extracting promises that her children would be cared for. Everyone had really pulled together, supportive and full of willingness to take the 'burden' from her. Verona had marvelled at her bravery, sure that she herself would not be able to be half as calm if she had so little time to live. No one knew that Mara hadn't actually made it to the doctor yet. When she did, she had been shamefaced and embarrassed to discover that the lump was no longer there. It turned out that Mara had begun examining herself a few weeks before, after seeing a video about breast cancer, but had forgotten to make allowances for pre-menstrual changes in her breasts. Noticing these happening she had panicked, too scared to have it looked at in case it confirmed her fears.

'Mara, I wish you'd talk to Des,' Verona urged with emotion. 'If you see her . . . she's in ever so much pain, and it's getting worse.'

Mara nodded, unsmiling. 'Girl, I going to do more than that. I rang up her doctor and got her an appointment for Friday, and if I have to stand over her, she going.'

Verona looked at her admiringly. 'Why didn't I never think of that?'

Mara's cheerfulness resurfaced: 'Maybe because you're as big a coward as Des when it come to doctors.' She leaned over and picked up one of the books from the floor, raising an eyebrow at the title.

Verona tensed. The guilt of her situation returned and she felt on edge and defensive, her scalp prickling as Mara replaced the book.

'V, is everything all right? I mean, generally – things fine at work?'

For one panicky moment Verona thought Mara had somehow found out she had been given the sack. 'Yeah . . . I've just got a few days off, and since Des ain't so keen on having people underfoot right now I thought I'd kill some time.' She prayed that Mara would accept her hastily concocted excuse and not question why she was a bus ride away from the library close to home.

Mara gave her a hard stare, then shrugged. 'Well, I got to go. I came in to organise some books for a thing the youth club is doing.'

Verona watched her leave with mixed feelings. Mara always lightened her mood; but at the moment Verona only hoped she had managed to quiet the suspicion in the other woman's eyes.

# Four

The ring of the front-door bell sliced sharply through the soothing voice of the radio announcer. Desiree jumped, nearly dropping the plate she was drying. Thoughts of the past week's events scattering from her head, she straightened laboriously from the sink.

The telephone shrilled out when she had nearly reached the passage. Irritated, she ignored it to answer the door. Wasn't it always like that – peace and quiet for hours, then everything erupting at once?

'Mara!' she greeted the cheerful woman at the door with surprise. 'You not working today?'

Mara shook her head, then motioned towards the phone: 'You better answer that. I'll put the kettle on while you're talking.'

It was a wrong number and Desiree resisted an urge to vent her frustration on the hapless caller. When she came into the kitchen, her friend was stacking the breakfast dishes away.

'Girl, you might as well go put your feet up.' Mara turned to fill the teapot as the kettle boiled. 'I'll bring this in a minute.'

Desiree accepted gratefully, already exhausted despite the early hour.

'V back at work?' Mara asked, sipping her tea and relaxing back into the deep comfort of the settee.

Desiree's hands were unsteady as she lowered the mug on to one of the Jamaica coasters John's brother had sent them the previous year. 'She was never off. Why?' she asked cautiously.

'She ain't take last week off?'

'Not that I know,' Desiree frowned. 'She tell you she was going to?'

Mara was about to say something but changed her mind. After a pause she asked: 'What did the doctor say? Weren't the results due today?'

Desiree stiffened. She had tried to blank out her visit to the surgery, had not yet discussed with anyone what the tests revealed.

She had been terrified when Dr Lightfoot insisted she go straight down to Casualty at the hospital, and she was almost sorry that Mara had taken time off to spend the afternoon cooking dinner for John and the kids. It denied her the usual excuse for not going to the doctor and it made sure she had no reason to back out of the visit to Casualty.

They had been expecting her at the hospital and that had scared her more. You usually had to wait around these days, so being sent right through after she gave her name at the huge circular desk had to mean that something serious was wrong with her. She had really been sweating by the time she took off her clothes and struggled into the embarrassing no-back robe and dressing-gown they insisted she wear.

There had been so many tests, one after the other, and Desiree had felt pain ripping through her when the doctor insisted on giving her an internal examination. She still felt sick disbelief whenever the incident forced its way into her mind. She had known she wouldn't like what she would be told . . .

Mara's urgent voice broke the silence: 'The doctor, Des – what he say?'

'I have to go into hospital,' Desiree said distantly, trying to calm her tone. 'They're going to let me know as soon as they have a bed.'

'But what's the matter?'

Desiree hadn't wanted to cry, thought she was too sensible to let something like that bother her. After all, at least it wasn't cancer – the fear that had stalked her for so many months – and she did have two children. Mara's arms came round her and she leaned against her friend, grateful for her strength.

'I sure is going to be all right,' she comforted herself in a muffled voice, pulling away from Mara with grim resolve. 'You know,' she sniffed, 'when I used to hear of women with children losing their womb, I did think they were making a song and dance about nothing.'

Mara was very still. 'You have to have a hysterectomy?' she asked, not managing completely to keep the horror out of her voice.

Desiree's smile didn't quite make it, as she nodded, tears forming again in the corners of her eyes. 'You don't think I is stupid?'

'No, Des, just normal,' Mara reassured her quietly. 'Look, don't try to bottle up how you feel or pretend it's no big thing. That way you ain't going come to terms with it. But . . . you sure they don't have no alternative?'

'You think I didn't ask?' Desiree said with self-mockery. 'I kept thinking: *God, they've got me mixed up with someone else. It can't be me, I not even thirty-three* . . .'

Mara nodded encouragingly, giving her her full attention, letting her talk.

'All this time I sitting there thinking I was dying and that I couldn't cope with finding out, and now' Desiree's voice wavered – 'I wonder if this isn't worse.'

'The thing is, Des,' her friend said gently, 'you *don't* have something terminal and you *do* have two great kids . . . oh, I'm not saying it's going to make the loss less real, just that it really *could* have been a lot worse.'

Mara stayed a couple of hours, moving around the kitchen with her usual efficiency, cooking John the oxtail Desiree had started in the morning. Desiree was grateful for her practicality, realising that she felt a lot better. The thought of the operation still scared her but at least she could contemplate it logically now.

For the first time since learning the results of the tests she didn't feel weepy, even managing to smile when Mara told her about an ongoing feud she was having with a couple of the people she worked with. Being the only woman in the project, she had immediately antagonised her fellow workers by starting up a girls' night. A lot of the kids coming wanted to do things like darts and snooker, and the male workers were always complaining that girls couldn't handle the equipment properly.

'You know what they say,' Mara complained. 'The other day, one of them drop a weight on his toe, nearly mash it off, and hop around saying is because we touch it.'

'What, girls do weight training? But they must look real awful when they get all muscly.'

'Shame on you, Des! Listen, I been doing it for two years now and I never felt fitter.'

Desiree eyed her slim form enviously. 'No wonder you looking so healthy. You still jogging?'

'Mmm. I'm hoping to get a place in the marathon.'

'You mean the London one?' Desiree was impressed.

Mara grinned. 'But you'll never guess what . . . or I should say *who* entering.'

'Who?'

'Winston, my dear! I saw that new woman of his – what she name . . . Paulette? – and she told me he doing some sponsorship thing.'

'Oh, that must be the thing for Ethiopia. I'm surprised, didn't think he'd get involved. No BUF saying is reactionary?'

Mara made a face. 'Maybe they finally decide to work up some sweat for a change. Sure beats theory.'

'You think he going finish the course?'

Her friend threw back her head and laughed. 'Well, I was never a one to say miracles couldn't happen, but the way Winston like his food and his television I think he'd need a new lifestyle. I mean, Sunday football is hardly going to get him fit, is it?'

Desiree smiled at the image of Winston, complete with prosperous belly, huffing along in front of the cameras.

'Paulette must be doing him some good,' Mara observed cynically, 'though what she see in him is nobody's business.'

'I hear they thinking of getting married.'

A shadow crossed Mara's face, gone almost immediately it came. 'I hope she don't give up her job like I did,' she said heavily.

'She's doing accounts or something, isn't she?' Desiree asked, curious.

'She works in some firm down Kennington and she studying to be a chartered accountant – and you know how Winston 'fraid of competition.'

'Is that how come you stop working?'

Mara agreed half-angrily. 'Girl, I was real dumb . . . really thought he was doing me a favour when he didn't even want me to finish the A-levels.' She laughed mirthlessly. 'Just goes to show how women turn fool over man.'

After Mara left, the house seemed strangely quiet and Desiree felt depression coming back. It was all well and good to talk rationally about her operation with Mara's understanding optimism there to buoy her up, another thing to deal with the dread and sense of impending loss that were conjured up in solitude.

Her thoughts turned to Verona, worry lines deepening on her forehead. She had tried to find out why Mara thought Verona was on holiday, but her friend could be so tight-mouthed when she chose, no doubt trying to protect her; but it simply added to Desiree's anxiety to suspect that Verona was skipping work. Was it to do with the two men who had come round that day? She was certain that Verona was hiding something from her, and it occurred to her that her sister had acted like this before.

It had been about three months after Desiree started going out with Ronnie, just before Verona had run away. Funny how V had suddenly taken a dislike to Ronnie. That had upset Desiree, even though she herself had begun to go off him; his insistence that she have sex with him had become quite ugly at times. Had her uneasiness communicated itself to her sister? Verona had liked him up till then, badgering him to help her with her schoolwork or plying him with food and cups of tea.

One thing about Ronnie, he had always had time for Verona, treating her with a respect and patience that did her fourteen-year-old ego good. He even took to dropping by to help her with her homework, and Desiree supposed that was why she had let the relationship limp on as long as it did.

'You can't have everything,' she mused, knowing that she could never have become too serious about the other man. Whatever John's faults, he was not a beating man, and nobody could say he was irresponsible.

She wondered what had happened to Ronnie. He had broken with her just before V ran away – come to think of it, V had become . . . almost scared of him.

Desiree felt a nagging sense of having overlooked something important.

Why had her sister run away? Their father's explanation about it being growing pains now seemed nonsense. When they had found Verona she had been so withdrawn and unlike herself. But she had come out of that, falling instead into eating as if she needed food as a shield to hide behind.

Desiree felt a familiar guilt. She had tried to get Verona to talk to her, but then had come the car crash. With their father dead, there was enough to do just trying to stop them taking her sister away. Social Services had tried to insist that Desiree was too young to care for her, using the fact that Verona ran away to argue their case. Desiree had been determined. She and V were family, all the family she knew, and she had to hang on to that at all cost. In the midst of everything, somehow she had shelved Verona's problem, and now she felt the old guilt as once again she realised that Verona was in trouble and she was failing her.

The sound of the children coming in interrupted her train of thought.

'Hi, Mum.' Lyn popped her head round the door. 'Are you okay?'

Desiree nodded, sighing as she heard Carol stomping up the stairs.

'Carol's in a bad mood cause her teacher told her off,' Lyn volunteered, putting her lunchbox at the door and coming to hug Desiree. 'Look, Mum, why don't I get our tea? Dad doesn't have to know.' John had always been insistent that no child of his was going to grow up accustomed to doing what he saw as menial work; they were destined for something better out of life.

Desiree's heart went out to the child. Lyn was so considerate. It was a temptation to accept the offer. Nowadays she was always so tired and weak.

'Please, Mum!' Lyn begged. 'Dad only says we mustn't do housework because he thinks we won't want to, but I *like* doing it, honest. I do it loads of times at Mara's. And Auntie V says we have to do more things for ourselves while you're sick.'

Desiree finally conceded. 'All right; just this once, mind.'

Lyn's face broke into a smile. 'Oh, thanks, Mum,' she said, hugging her again. 'Shall I make you a cup of tea first?'

'That would be nice.'

'I'll make it just like Auntie V does,' Lyn promised.

Desiree listened to the children's muted squabbling in the kitchen as she drank the tea while half-following a quiz show on the television. She glanced automatically at the clock when she heard a key in the front door. *V's early*, she thought with a frown, schooling her face as the door swung open and her sister looked in to say hello.

'How was work?' Desiree asked.

'Tiring as usual.' Verona grimaced, making to withdraw.

'Don't go, V. Come and talk to me,' Desiree said impulsively.

Now it was Verona's turn to frown, her expression wary. 'I'll just get a cuppa,' she said, unbuttoning her jacket.

Holding a brimming mug that threatened to spill its contents, Verona soon subsided on the settee. 'I can't stay long,' she warned. 'Me and some of the girls from work are going to see a film.'

Desiree bit back a question just in time. Verona had been going out a lot lately and something told her the darkened car she sneaked out of when she came home did not belong to any of the 'girls' at Stoneford's. On top of that she was always vague about the films she said she had seen and even about the pubs her circle of friends supposedly used. But Desiree judged it best to let it pass for now; there was something far more urgent to probe.

'Why did you tell Mara you were on holiday last week?' she asked. Her heart sank as the mug shook in Verona's hand, spilling some of the tea. She was right: there must be something she hadn't been told.

Verona brazened it out: 'That must be when I saw her down Norwood library last Wednesday. I did a couple of hours flexi-time and was just killing time.'

'So why you couldn't stay here? I could've well done with some help, especially seeing as I had all the washing to do.' She hadn't meant to lash out, but Verona's lack of confidence in her was hurtful.

'I just wanted a bit of time to meself, all right?'

Desiree was taken aback to hear the sharpness in Verona's voice. This wasn't at all like her. She was usually quite even-tempered – unless she was hiding something.

'V, is something wrong at work?'

'No, should there be?' Verona's voice was unnaturally high, her expression challenging.

'Verona, you don't have to hide anything from me. You know I'll do anything I can to help you if you in trouble.'

'Oh, for Christ's sake!' Verona exploded. 'Just back off, will you? I'm fed up with you going on at me. Why can't you give me some credit for knowing what I'm doing just once, yeah?'

Desiree felt the prickle of tears at the back of her eyes and she ducked her head to hide her pain.

'I'm sorry, Des,' Verona said contritely. 'I shouldn't have said that. Look, I *know* how much you care, and I do appreciate it . . . but I'm twenty-seven and if I don't start doing for meself soon I ain't never gonna.'

'Sorry, V, I suppose you right,' Desiree agreed with a strained smile. 'I just so into the habit of looking out for you.'

Verona's nod acknowledged that she was letting her irritation pass. 'Did you get the results from the doctor?' she asked with concern.

Desiree put down her half-empty mug as steadily as she could. She tried to pick her words carefully, fingers locking together:

'I have to go into hospital,' she said.

'Des! What's the matter?'

'It's to do with my womb . . . they say is not in the right place and that causing it to pain up so much.' She hesitated, adding: 'They say they can't do nothing and, as it getting worse, they have to take it out.'

'Well, it could've been worse,' Verona responded lightly, obviously relieved.

'I suppose it might have.'

'Des, are you . . . I mean, d'you feel very upset about it?' Verona said, sounding surprised, as her sister's unhappiness registered on her.

Desiree nodded, staring at her hands.

'Yeah . . . well, I'm sorry,' her voice reflected her embarrassment, 'I just thought that, as you had Lyn and Carol . . .' She trailed off, realising that she was making things worse. 'When you gonna tell John?'

Desiree shook her head sadly. 'I just don't know. I'm hoping he gets that promotion he's after, then he might be more able to deal with it.'

'Des, sometimes you really make me mad, you do. Honestly . . . here you are, real sick, and all you can think about is what going to suit John. He really saw you coming, didn't he?'

'You don't understand,' Desiree protested.

'Oh, I understand all right. All I can see is John wiping his foot on you, and you just sit there. I mean, I'm not a feminist and that, but what I can't understand is how you take so much crap from him when you won't take it from no one else.'

'John is a good provider.'

'Yeah, and he'd be an even better one if he wasn't so afraid you'll go back to work and end up earning more than him.'

'John face a lot of racism at work. You don't know half of what he has to put up with, and you must admit he is being passed over for promotion.'

Verona grudgingly agreed. 'But I don't see why he don't take them to court or something. Wasn't they saying on telly that you could do that, remember? In that documentary programme.'

'It's not as easy as that,' her sister dismissed.

'Yeah, it's easier to take it out on you, ain't it? God, anyone would think you never face no racism in *your* life. I mean, nobody tell him to stay there – what's wrong with finding another job?'

Desiree opened her mouth to protest, then closed it again as the idea registered. She hadn't thought of that before.

'Auntie V, can you help me with my maths?'

Neither of the women had heard Carol coming in, though judging by her expression the child had not picked up any of their conversation. Knowing how much the children adored John, the last thing Verona wanted to do was pass on any of her own bitterness to them.

'I ain't sure I can,' she teased now. 'This new maths business is a bit too hard for me.'

'Oh, come off it, Auntie V,' Carol laughed, 'you always say that, then you know how to do all of it. Anyway, you're always helping Lyn and she does harder sums than me.'

In truth, Verona liked to help the girls. Maths was her strongest subject, the thing she would most like to do if she ever went back to studying, and she often regretted not having taken the chance to go further when she had it. The more she thought about it, she felt it was because no one had really had the time to encourage her. Desiree had had so much on herself, what with working, looking after her, and everything.

'Come on, then,' Verona acquiesced, getting to her feet. 'If I'm going to help we better get a move on. I'm going out later.'

Carol giggled. 'Is he nice-looking, Auntie V?'

'What?'

'The bloke you're going out with,' the child persisted.

'And what make you so sure it's a bloke, then, eh?' Verona asked half-teasingly. Lyn was getting into boyfriends and presumably that was where Carol got her ideas from.

'Oh, I saw you get out of his car yesterday. I didn't like him though,' she added with youthful candour, 'he was old.'

Desiree's eyes sharpened their focus on her sister.

'That wasn't my boyfriend,' Verona said evenly.

'I'm glad,' Carol said. 'I told Lyn you weren't that old.'

Desiree thought she saw her sister breathe with relief when the child let the subject drop.

# Five

'Why don't you turn it off . . . he's not supposed to be working late tonight, is he?'

At Mara's words, Desiree looked up unhappily. She lifted the lid from the shallow pan, sighing as she saw how dried out and curled the fish was beginning to look.

'If he comes in and the food not hot, he liable to get into one of his moods . . . especially if he just have a hard day.' She felt tears burning the back of her eyes. 'I don't think I can stand it today.'

'Des, come and sit down,' Mara was firm. 'I'm going to make you some tea and you're going to relax.'

There was a crash above their heads, and Desiree closed her eyes, trying to suppress her misery.

Mara swore under her breath. 'What you lot doing up there?' she shouted.

'It's Charleen,' Carol's voice floated back. The noise intensified.

'I'll go and sort them out.' Mara got to her feet.

When she returned she was smiling smugly. 'They're doing their homework now. I just told Charleen she couldn't come over again this week, and we won't have Lyn and Carol for the weekend,' she explained in answer to Desiree's questioning look, busying herself with the tea.

Desiree nodded without comment.

'Look, Des,' Mara said, sliding the cup in front of her and sitting in the chair opposite, 'I know how you feel, I was there once, even if it's five years now and I wasn't ill . . . but things not going to change once you feeling better. I don't forget how it was with Winston, you know; and whatever else you say about John, he ain't no Winston.'

Desiree ignored the last part of that, her interest caught by the reference to Winston. She had often wanted to ask the other woman how she had managed to leave . . . what had driven her to such a desperate act. Mara used to be such a shadow. In fact, it wasn't until she left Winston that Desiree was forced to take a good look at her, liking the new Mara so much they soon slipped into a pattern of friendship.

'How you manage to cope with the kids?' she asked hesitantly.

'The same way you're coping with your three.'

'Mara, is not any joke I making. You know I only have the girls.'

Mara was unmoved. 'Really!' she exclaimed in mock surprise. 'So why you walking around agonising about John's dinner when your whole life falling down around you?'

Desiree was puzzled: 'I don't get you. You know how John is about his food.'

'Tell me something,' Mara asked gravely. 'Would you be worrying yourself like this if it was V's dinner?'

'Well, no . . . but you have to understand –'

'I know,' Mara interrupted, 'V isn't you child, even if you treat her so most of the time.'

'John is a good provider,' Desiree said, not even convincing herself this time with the defensive litany.

'Mmmm, and I suppose all you do is add to his burden . . . and there is he getting all that shit out on the street.' She shook her head. 'Des, I've been there! I've heard all the arguments.'

The words gave Desiree a jolt and she realised with a sense of shock that she had no idea why her friend had left her husband. Everyone had been stunned. Somehow Mara and Winston always seemed so permanent. Not that the marriage was a particularly happy one; indeed, Desiree used to harbour a secret contempt for Mara and the way she allowed herself to be reduced to the level of Winston's personal servant. It used to make her so angry to see the way he took Mara for granted – the way he would hold out his empty glass without a sideward look or a pause in speech and expect it to be filled. In those days Mara had little confidence, her whole world wrapped up with Winston and the children.

Then one day she had just disappeared, taking the children with her. Desiree had been shocked, feeling guilty for not taking more interest in the other woman, and concerned that anyone so timid could be wandering around London with three children.

Before long, Winston started coming home with John to eat. Desiree felt as if she was being disloyal to Mara by feeding him and she found it difficult even to be civil to him. But it was when he started bringing round his dirty clothes with the football kit for the team that she had put her foot down, telling John she was not prepared to clean up behind his friends. John had been annoyed, but Desiree wouldn't budge: if Winston wanted his clothes washed, he could get himself another woman or do it himself. He had a perfectly good washing-machine at home.

When Mara had simply turned up on her doorstep a few months after leaving home, looking tired but satisfied, Desiree had been so surprised she had let her in. They had talked, warily at first, skirting round issues, careful to avoid any sensitive nerves . . . How could she have known this woman for almost six years and yet never know how much there was to her?

She put down her half-empty cup. '*Why* you up and leave Winston so? Everyone did well surprise, specially as you all was so . . . content together.'

Mara laughed at her attempt to be tactful, 'Don't you mean I seemed to be so under his thumb?' she corrected bluntly. 'Oh, I was,' she admitted, humour still lacing her voice, though she sobered as she added: 'at least . . . he thought I was. Don't get me wrong, Winston was a good provider – just like your John. Better even, because he earn more money.'

To Desiree, that made it all the more puzzling. 'What made

you leave him – especially to go to that refuge place? Did he beat you?'

Mara pulled at her short, cropped hair, not in the least put out by the question. 'No, Winston didn't beat me. But then again, that's not the only way man oppress woman.' She nodded her head in self-agreement, adding almost to herself: 'Winston just made me feel moronic . . . like I was some kind of burden he was struggling around with.' She warmed to the theme. 'You know what he used to tell me?'

Desiree shook her head as her friend continued.

'He used to say how lucky I was that he provided for my children. Can you credit that? I mean – when did women start self-fertilisation!'

Desiree was uncomfortably reminded of the many times she had talked to John about going back to college . . . back to work – the way he made her feel ungrateful and like a weight he could hardly shift under. But then, John *was* Winston's friend.

'But you got out,' she said almost to herself.

'Yeah, but that wasn't why. I suppose things are a bit different with you and John. At least John is only trying to protect his role in your life. But there wasn't much chance of me earning the sort of money Winston was getting . . . not down Woolworth's anyway.'

Desiree made a non-committal sound, and Mara nodded vigorously. 'It's true, Des. I'm not trying to defend John, but I bet he only started on this thing about you not working since he don't get promotion down the railway.'

Desiree couldn't deny her friend's words. She just hadn't thought of it that way before. 'Is true,' she admitted reluctantly.

Mara shrugged, a self-derisive smile on her face. 'My dear, you don't know the half of Winston and me. I was doing the A-level when we met, you know. Well, he wouldn't even let me take the exam, kept telling me all that crap about women should support their men . . . and me like a fool sat there believing it.'

'I suppose he get that from BUF.'

'What came first?' Mara joked.

'Eh?'

'The chicken or the egg . . . remember? Des, Winston *is* BUF.

The way he tie those men in knots, is a good thing your John get out.'

'I would prefer he in BUF than reading the *Sun*,' she sighed. 'Remember when he used to talk about the struggle, and sell *Black Unity* down Brixton?'

'I remember all right. Winston used to sit on his backside at home holding court with Longers, and that girl from Hammersmith . . . Patsy.'

Desiree shook her head. 'You not to let the way you angry at Winston blind you, Mara.'

'I ain't angry at Winston. I wouldn't even have minded him reading the *Sun* if he did care for the children like John does Lyn and Carol.'

Desiree was horrified. 'I don't understand you. Winston is positive . . . and at least he still in the struggle.'

Mara shrugged. 'You condemn John through he out of the struggle . . . Tell me something, Des, you know what the struggle is?'

Desiree looked at her in surprise, her mind a momentary blank. 'Is the struggle for black people liberation,' she said finally.

'You sure it's not the black struggle for Irish, Palestinian, Tamil and every other thing but black liberation?' Mara mocked. 'Don't get me wrong; I know a lot of positive people struggling for just that. But they not in BUF. They out there struggling, whether it's in Africa, the Caribbean or right here in Britain.'

Desiree groped around for what John used to say in justification of BUF. 'Just because black people make common cause with other oppressed groups don't mean they not positive.'

Mara laughed. 'I never say that! But just think for a moment: when BUF making these common cause, which black people you know getting the benefit? Know why they bring in this thing about "politically black"?'

Desiree couldn't hide her ignorance. 'What's that?'

'The next step from fighting other people battle. It just say that black is oppression, so anybody who feel oppress can get black people to fight their battle for them by voting to be black . . . then when they not oppress any more they just vote themself back to whatever colour they were before – instant promotion.'

'But that not right! Why nobody doing something?'

Mara shrugged. 'Because organisation like BUF so top-heavy with tadpoles from the white left trying to turn big fish.'

'You shouldn't be so hard on them, Mara. At least they're trying to do something for black people.'

'Girl, I not saying there isn't people in them that sincere, but you have to admit, people like Winston use them to feel big.'

Desiree thought that was a bit harsh, but she kept it to herself. Right now she wanted to get back to why Mara left Winston. 'Just tell me about your marriage, eh.'

'Mmm, I was telling you about me moving out . . . You know, when I started disliking Winston I used to feel real guilty and disloyal. I mean, there was he working all hours down the law centre, and me only having the little part-time job out at Freeman's – and he wasn't too bad about money either. Yet I'd be there finding all kinda fault with him in my head.'

'Is that why you left him?'

'Hell, no. The way I was them days that was nothing . . . naw, it was the children.'

Desiree's ears pricked up. 'What – did he beat them?'

Mara shook her head. 'Jay started beating on the girls . . . and you know how that Charleen is such a madam. Well, I didn't like the way she was starting to act. You know how she always like mathsy things . . . well, she decided it wasn't the kind of thing girls should do.'

'They must have really resented you when you took them away from their father though,' Desiree sympathised, looking at her with open admiration.

Mara chose her words carefully: 'You know, that's the funny thing. It wasn't Winston they were vex about, it was the house. I tell you, they hated the refuge, especially Jay; I think he felt crowded out by women.' She grinned. 'There was me waiting for all this hassle about their father, when all the time they'd seen so little of him he was a near stranger.'

'You mean Winston just let you walk out?'

'What! I tell you, girl, he was furious, threatening all manner of things. I used to sit on that lumpy little bed and bawl my eyes out.'

'Is he all right about it now . . .'

The slam of the front door cut across Desiree's question and she tailed off as she heard John's heavy tread.

'Tell him about the operation!' Mara urged in a whisper. 'Give him a bit a trust, share it with him.'

Desiree shook her head wordlessly as the door was pushed open, and she gave Mara a warning look when she saw the light of battle in her eyes.

John looked tired and out of sorts, but his eyes lit up at seeing Mara.

'Wha' happen, Mara!' he greeted, dropping into the seat beside her. 'I hear you thinking of working for that women's centre down Stockwell – mind you don't catch something, you know.'

Mara's welcoming smile faded. 'What's the matter, John . . . why does women doing for each other scare you so much?'

He laughed uneasily. 'It depend on what it is, don't it?' Then on a note of bravado: 'Mind you, you too sweet-looking to get inna none of that.'

Mara gave him a killing look. 'It's not even worth having an argument with you, John.'

He shrugged, getting back his confidence. 'Seen Winston lately?' he asked slyly. 'That man must have been weak to let woman like you go. Now if that had been *me* . . .'

Desiree felt something curl up inside and she quelled a sudden spurt of anger. The irony was that John never used to have any time for Mara. He and Winston used to get together on Saturday afternoons, watching sport on television before going down to the pub.

They had been at school together, Winston going on to do A-levels at college while John did electrical engineering. Desiree knew John had thought Winston could have done better for himself than Mara.

'I'll get your dinner,' she said quietly, wanting to hold back the bitter words burning on her tongue.

'No need,' he responded breezily, 'I ate down Saunder's place earlier.'

'So why you never tell Desiree, instead of letting her cook and keep it warm?' Mara asked indignantly.

'Des don't mind, do you, girl?'

Desiree realised that his performance was for Mara's benefit, but suddenly it was all too much for her. Here she was struggling to keep herself together from one day to the next and he couldn't even have a bit of consideration. She said nothing. Moving awkwardly to the frying-pan, she uncovered it, looking at the fish with distaste.

There was no firm intention in her head, just a burning anger inside her. John must have sensed her mood, and the look he gave her stayed her hand as she held the pot over him. She wanted to cover his complacent face with the ruined fish. Instead she slammed it on the table in front of him.

'Is you want fish for the little brain in your head,' she said bitterly. 'From you make it stick, you clean it out!'

Mara looked as if she was going to choke. 'Well, now you know if Desiree mind,' she mocked.

John was livid. He sat there breathing hard as if he had been running a race, then burst out: 'What the bloody hell's the matter with you now?'

Desiree leant against the sink, fighting a wave of sickness. Folding her arms, she ignored Mara's anxious gaze. 'You tell me cook fish for you tonight, John; the least you could do was tell me you was eating out.'

He gave her a baleful look, mindful of Mara. 'I told you we were up at Saunder's about the football,' he muttered. 'Flaming heck, what am I supposed to do if you don't answer the bloody phone when I ring?'

'You were going down to Saunder's tomorrow,' she retorted, undeterred. 'I'm not taking it, you know, John, you not going treat me like this no more, you hear me?'

He looked surly. 'I sure everybody else can as well.' Then to Mara: 'Is you, yeah? Telling Des all sorta crap . . . why don't you keep your bleeding nose out of other people's business and go back to your man?'

Mara's smile widened. 'It'll be harder to clean the pot when it's cold, John,' she said sweetly. 'Shouldn't you scrape it out before it set?'

'You think you smart just cause you go to college . . . well, I can tell you this, the way you are now you not gwine find one man to put up with you.'

'That's their loss,' Mara shrugged indifferently, the grin staying on her face as she watched him stalk through the door. 'Good for you, Des,' she said before it even closed behind his retreating figure.

Desiree sobered. 'I shouldn't have done that,' she said, picking up the frying-pan, wiping the table where bits of overcooked fish had spilt over.

'Why not?' Mara challenged. 'Des, since you been ill, John's just started to take all sorts of liberties . . . and don't think I don't know he was acting big to impress me.'

Desiree couldn't deny it. Everything Mara said was true. What was it about John that made him afraid to show consideration when other people were around? Mind you, since she got sick, he had been taking advantage, hassling and nagging her, knowing that most of the time she was too tired to do anything about it.

John looked subdued when he came back half an hour later, giving Desiree a wary look to see if she had calmed down. The women had moved to the sitting-room, and he slumped morosely into his favourite chair when they both ignored him.

'I don't suppose I can even ask for a cup of tea,' he muttered sulkily, eyeing the pot on the tray with longing.

Mara poured him a cup and handed it over silently. He relaxed visibly.

'Did Des tell you about the job I'm after?' he said eagerly.

Mara shook her head, sipping her tea, one eye on the television.

'Yeah, it's more money and I'll be doing a lot more supervising. Might even think of moving from this dump.' He scanned the room with distaste.

'What if you don't get it, John?' Mara asked quietly, giving him her full attention now.

'You mad or something? Even my supervisor say I'm the man for the job.'

'But suppose they don't give it to you, are you going to take it out on Des as usual?'

John and Desiree were equally taken aback at Mara's directness.

'What she been telling you?' The tension was back in John's large frame. 'Whatever she say isn't true – she know full well I don't hit women.'

Mara hissed air through her teeth, giving him an impatient look. 'Desiree never told me nothing. You forgetting I was married to Winston, and the two o' you favour kissing cousin when it come to how you think.'

'You trying to tell me Winston *hit* you!'

Mara looked angry at the tone of his voice. 'Don't try to intimidate me, John,' she said coldly. 'Is a long time since I care one way or other what man like you and Winston think.' And as he made to protest: 'No, Winston never hit me. But is like I was saying to Des earlier: there's more than one way to beat on a woman.'

'Woman is always complaining about one thing or another,' he said uncomfortably. 'Cho! You don't can find nothing better to do with your time?'

'You mean like football and cricket?' Mara asked with mock innocence.

'What's wrong with football and cricket?' he challenged. 'At least black blokes have a chance to make a bit of money and get somewhere.'

Mara shook her head and sighed. 'Arguing with you is like running round a circle. I've got to go.'

She raised her voice, yelling for Charleen, getting to her feet as she heard the children on the stairs.

'How old is Jay now?' John asked, stretching his back tiredly.

'Seventeen,' Mara responded.

'Left school yet?'

'He's down at Vauxhall doing a BTec in electronics.'

John brightened. 'You should send him round sometime so I can help him out,' he said enthusiastically. 'Not having a boy, I don't really get the chance to do that.'

'You have two children, John,' Mara said. 'What's wrong with encouraging one of them to get involved with electronics?'

'You telling me you want Charleen to do something like that?'

'Why not? Listen up, Jay's been helping Charleen with her physics for ages and, for your information, she wants to join Telecom as an engineer.'

John had no chance to comment, since Charleen had entered. She was a smaller version of her mother; Mara could never deny her, Desiree thought with sudden amusement.

'What's Lyn and Carol doing?' Mara asked her daughter suspiciously.

'They say they're going swimming tomorrow and they're getting their stuff together.'

Her mother looked sceptical but didn't comment. 'I gone, you hear, girl,' she said to Desiree instead, checking that Charleen had not forgotten anything. 'Send them round after swimming tomorrow, will you?'

After the echoes of Mara's departure had died down, Desiree sat worrying at her bottom lip. John had changed the television channel several times before resorting to a football video. The way his body shifted about in the chair with the action irritated her and she wished she could just tell him to keep still. *That's what Mara would do*, she thought, dissatisfied. She felt a real sense of envy at her friend's ease and confidence. To think that she had once despised Mara's submissiveness! Sometimes she could hardly believe this was the same woman and wondered if she too couldn't do with one of those assertiveness courses Mara was always raving about.

Not that she didn't stand up for herself; but when John came in full of tired disappointment, she tended to let him get away with trampling on her, however bad she was feeling herself. She knew it was going to have to stop, had known it for a long time, if the truth was told.

'John, I want to go to college.' The words stunned her and she was sure her expression must match his open-mouthed disbelief.

The sound from the television was suddenly too loud.

'Go to college? You?' his voice was shocked, scandalised, and there was fear in his eyes. 'What make you think you can go college, eh? What wrong with you? You can't even look after your own house and you talking 'bout college.'

She was not going to lose her temper, was not going to give John the satisfaction of brushing her aside again. It was always the same whenever she mentioned college or work, and she resented being treated as if she was incapable, or worse.

'I been thinking about it for a while,' she persisted. 'I thought I could maybe get some A-levels . . . and then, who knows?'

John was clearly shaken. 'Desiree, you can't do that, man!'

'Why not?' It was hard to understand why he had become like this, discouraging and destructive in his attitude to her, and she added bitterly: 'I was doing it before I met you; and anyway, I thought you liked me studying. You was the one always encouraging me to do more.'

'That was different and you know it. You got me and the children to look after. I mean, when you going to find time to bother with no studying?'

She ignored that. 'John, tell me something. You admire Mara, don't you?' she asked quietly.

'What you trying to suggest?' He was immediately on the defensive. 'If you want say something, Des, you better just out and say it one time, hear.'

'Mara went and took the A-level that Winston never want her to sit for, then she did that access course and even went on and do the degree . . . John, Mara is really doing well now.'

John's nervousness was obvious in the way he shuffled about on the sofa.

'Mara leave Winston,' he pointed out suspiciously.

'I know that, John,' Desiree's voice was neutral, 'but that was before she go back to study. Is the people at the Refuge that encourage her, though is Winston drive her out.'

'What you saying to me, Des?'

Desiree ignored the plea in his voice. She had dropped her barb and she wanted it to sink in. 'I can go on what they call a flexible learning thing; and if I don't feel the A-levels right for me, I can always do the access thing – like Mara did, but a different subject . . . maybe something like Law.'

John was desperate now. 'Look how I do so much City and Guild and even the Ordinary National Diploma and the Higher National subjects – all right, so is not O-level and things, but you have to study a whole heap of subjects in engineering and the exams just as hard. I have all the certificate them, and none of them do me no good.'

Desiree could feel no sympathy this time. 'Mara did a degree, John.'

'Is that what you want? You want to feel better than me, is it? Look how she start look down on Winston through she have degree and he don't?'

'John, we talk about this so much time I lose count – you already know what I want; and as to why Mara do what she do, is she and Winston business.'

He shook his head unhappily. 'I don't know about this college thing. I gwine have to think about this some.'

He was stalling for time, but she had no energy to push him any more.

'I tired. I think I'll go upstairs,' she said flatly.

She lay in bed battling with the pain and her unhappy thoughts. It was at times like this that depression really swamped her, and more than ever before she knew she had to make a stand for independence if anything was to change. *God, soon I won't even be a whole woman no more!* She pushed the thought away with an effort, holding on to Mara's steadying words. Thinking about it, she supposed she had spent too much time doing for everyone else. She wanted to go to college more than anything, and inside the determination was growing – to go out and do it.

The bed depressed as John climbed in. Her back was towards him and she stiffened as she felt his palm smooth over her hip. She had taken two Codeines earlier, to ease some of the pain, but his heavy hand brought it alive like a raw, exposed nerve.

'Des, you awake?'

She felt angry with him. He knew she was sick, yet all he could think of was satisfying himself. At times like this she almost wished he had a wandering eye.

'Des?' he persisted. 'Look, love, I know you not feeling too good right now, but . . .'

She wasn't listening, her mind closed against him as he continued stroking her with clumsy concern. All she could hear was the whispering against her ear, and she held hard against letting her irritation spill out. He knew how much she disliked anyone breathing in her ears, and yet the minute he felt the urge he would be there sounding like some old brucksy-up steam engine.

'Des, I want to help,' John said despairingly, sliding his arm around her to try and pull her close. She resisted, hardening her heart to the plea in his voice.

It was a relief when he finally gave up and rolled away from her, and she was glad to have been spared another confrontation.

Feeling wide awake and miserable, she wondered where Verona was. She had been out till all hours in the past few days, and Desiree dared not imagine what she might be up to. She knew it wasn't really her business what her sister did; Verona was an adult after all. But she couldn't get the thought of the man Carol had seen out of her head.

# Six

'V, don't tell me you out again tonight?'

Verona looked over to where her sister was turning from the window and lowered her head when she saw the concern in the older woman's eyes. 'It's that new Clint Eastwood film,' she muttered, feeling a little better for the fact that it wasn't a lie, only a half-truth. She was going to see the film, but not with the girls from work as Des thought.

'You got a boyfriend, V?' Desiree asked quietly.

Verona fiddled with the handle of the bag she had been hunting through. 'Why d'you ask that?' she countered, playing for time.

Desiree moved to sit on the end of the bed. 'You been acting so strange lately. First you start cutting work, now you out almost every night . . . with your girlfriends.'

Verona ignored the jibe. 'I wanna live a bit a life,' she said, hoping her sister would drop her questioning about work. Des was always on about it these days, and Verona was so terrified of her finding out she had been sacked that she had not even signed on the dole. She had tried looking for a job, but always there was the knowledge that if she was offered something and they took up references, she would be nowhere.

'V, is not that I don't think is a good thing you getting out . . .'

'So let's leave it, shall we?' Verona cut in hurriedly.

Des looked bowed and defeated. Then she said: 'They want me to come into hospital Monday.' Her attempt at casualness was spoilt by a tremor in her voice.

'Next Monday! Isn't that a bit soon? I mean, today is Wednesday.'

'Seems it work like that sometimes. The letter came this morning and I spoke to Dr Lightfoot . . . he say it could get worse if they leave it too long.'

'What does John have to say about it?'

'I don't tell him yet.'

'What!'

'I never have the opening to talk to him.'

'Des, you mad or something? You know he's gonna have to take time off to look after the kids.'

Desiree was sceptical: 'How much you betting he won't want to do it?'

'Des, this is serious!' Panic was growing inside Verona. The thought of hospital always filled her with dread. For her it was a place of birth and death, and it was the death that haunted her. Apart from when Lyn and Carol were born, the only times she had ever been to hospitals were when her mother and her father were dying. *Don't be so selfish*, she admonished herself. *At least you're not the one having the operation.*

'When you gonna tell John?'

Desiree sighed. 'I was going to last night, but he got another letter from his grandfather and was looking really upset.'

Verona suppressed her quick anger. She knew the resentment she felt towards John's grandparents upset Desiree and she tried to hide it. It had been hard lately, though; not a week had gone by since Christmas without a letter from Jamaica. 'Did he say what's wrong?' She forced herself to sound interested.

'He saying Granny Ruby in pain and need the hip operation bad. You know, V, something keep telling me they wanting her to come to us.'

Verona snorted. 'Yeah? Well, they can't expect you to pay for it. You and the kids do without a lot already.'

'V! Papa bring us up better than to disrespect old people. Whatever John faults, you must admire the way he love his grandparents. How much people always make sure and send something for their people back in the West Indies? Even now things so hard John never once forget to send the money end of the month. You know is them raise him.'

Verona was unrepentant. 'So they bring him up – is you

looking after him now, ain't it? And he don't do nothing back for you. No, everything is Granny Ruby this, Grandpa Clifford that . . . Des, you know I get on with old people, but I ain't sacrificing my family for them.'

Desiree changed the subject. 'Anyway I thought I'd wait till Friday night to tell him about the hospital.'

'Why not before? I mean, he had the day off today, ain't it? And I bet he's spent all of it in that stupid garden. I'm sure he'll be in a better mood now than after he been working all day.'

Her sister nodded, pausing as the sound of fork against earth came clearly through the window. This was the time of year when John came to life, digging frenetically in the garden and planting every variety of flower and vegetable seedling he could cram into the tiny square of land. He would have his garden lamp out there, squeezing the last hours out of his day off, even though daylight was long gone. This was the only time he didn't complain about the cold, and for an unreasonable moment Desiree felt he valued her less than their small garden. Pushing the thought away with determination, Desiree came back to her sister's question.

'Friday is when they going to say who getting the supervisor job, and from what John been saying I think he might get it this time.'

'Des, not you as well! Is 'cause he have to look after the children, ain't it?'

'Well, you know how he feel about what he call women's work.'

'Them is as much his children as yours. Is no wonder I ain't ever want to get married.'

'Leonard would have made a good husband,' Desiree said nostalgically, remembering the shy, quiet youth who used to follow Verona home when she first started work at Stoneford's.

'Leonard wasn't nowhere like you think. Anyway, me and him wasn't no boyfriend and girlfriend.'

'Why? What was wrong with him?'

Verona shrugged; what was the point in trying to explain? 'He just wasn't my type.'

'So what's your type?' Desiree asked provocatively. 'Somebody white?' She looked around the cluttered room with distaste. 'That's why you always reading these trashy books, isn't it? So you can pretend. What's the matter with you anyway? What's wrong with a black man?'

'I ain't gonna argue with you, Des,' Verona hid her hurt with difficulty. It was no secret that Desiree disapproved of the books she read, but she'd never been so blunt before. It was easy for people like Des to condemn, though her own life was nothing to boast about. If it hadn't been for her bringing Ronnie into their life . . . She squashed the thought; it was a dangerous road to go down. How was Des to have known what he would be like? Verona had never told her about that night Ronnie had caught her on her own . . . it was all so unreal. Verona still felt cut off, padded around by her romance and her fat.

Desiree sighed. 'Look, V, I sorry. I just feeling so on edge of late.'

Verona forced a smile. 'It's okay . . . and you know you ain't got no worries 'bout the kids while I'm here.'

'I don't want to burden you down with them –'

'It ain't no burden.' She was already doing most things for them anyway, taking over most of the washing and acting as a buffer for Desiree whenever she was there. She loved her nieces and had never had any trouble getting them to listen to her.

Desiree smiled, grateful: 'Thanks, V. Look, I don't want to make you late, but maybe tomorrow evening . . .'

'You mean I never tell you I was off tomorrow?' Verona said impulsively.

Desiree turned, eyes shadowed with alarm. 'V, is something the matter?'

Verona cursed herself for falling into the temptation her sister's worried face had opened up. She needed something to do, to get away from the idleness of lurking in one library after another, worrying about her money running out. Even her daydreams and her novels had begun to pall as a constant daily diet, left her feeling jaded and a little bored with them.

'Dentist,' she said, scrabbling for the first thing that came to mind. 'I lost a filling and was thinking I better go 'fore the hole get any bigger.'

'What time you going?'

'Early. Why?'

'I was wondering if you could make Lyn an appointment; she was saying she had toothache this morning.'

Verona nodded. She wasn't exactly lying; she had lost a filling eating a toffee on Monday and she might as well get an appointment for herself.

She listened as Desiree shuffled slowly along the hall, before turning back to her bag. Sweeping her hand carefully across the bottom, she let the jumble of sweet wrappings and old receipts slide through her fingers. 'Ten pence more,' she muttered as her fingers emerged with the silver coin. She shifted herself in the hollow of the bed and rummaged underneath her bottom to bring out a handful of assorted coins, counting them carefully before putting them on the bedside cabinet. Three pounds twenty. Verona frowned, toying with the idea of tipping the bag upside down, changing her mind as she took another look at the jumbled mess inside.

She wandered over to her coat on the back of the door, searching each pocket. The top one yielded two pence and a crumpled bus ticket. *I'll just have to walk*, she thought morosely, *no point wasting seventy pence on bus fare*. She had promised herself a chocolate bar and some peardrops . . . and she could almost taste the sweet comfort in her mouth.

She wasted another ten minutes looking for a five-pound note she was sure she had hidden in a pile of books, and by the time she left the house, there was only five minutes to spare for the bus.

'Hello, love, how's your sister?'

Verona stiffened in dismay, wishing she could disappear in the folds of her duffel coat. Mrs Evans was there talking to Angela Brownleigh, their next-door neighbour, her small brown eyes avid with curiosity and looking like hard little buttons in the sallowness of her thin face.

'Fine,' she said abruptly, eyeing the large Alsatian the

neighbour was holding. Thankfully, the dog had a large stick firmly clamped in its jaw. Verona hated dogs, but this one she was also afraid of, particularly of the way it hurled its huge body at the door with frenzied purpose every time anyone paused outside its front gate.

'Has she got cancer or something, love?' Mrs Evans asked with her usual tactlessness, as Verona made to walk away.

Verona made no attempt to hide her irritation. Mrs Evans, middle-aged and with nearly grown children, had too much time on her hands. Her husband was a heavy-goods-vehicle driver who spent most of his time ferrying loads to the Far East, and Verona secretly thought this was because of his need to escape his wife.

'You have to ask her,' she responded, knowing the woman was too wary of Desiree to ever approach her.

'Shame though, ain't it, love? You must all be ever so worried.'

Verona gave her a cold look. 'I have to go, I'm already late.'

'Meeting your fancy fellow again, are you, love?'

Verona froze. What the hell did Nosy Dora know about Guy?

'Bit old for you, ain't he, love?' She turned to the neighbour: ' 'Ere, Angie, he don't half remind me of your Stan – bit thinner on top, but same eyes.' Angela Brownleigh looked furious and Mrs Evans shook her head hastily.

'Naw, couldn't be. He don't like dark . . . oops, sorry, love, no offence, you know . . . but it's a free country, ain't it? Not that I'm colour prejudiced, mind –'

Aware of the neighbour's angry interest, Verona gave Mrs Evans a killing look, cutting her off in mid-flow. Fortunately, Desiree did not get on with the Brownleighs and was always arguing with this one about the noise the dog made when it was let out in the garden.

Verona started walking rapidly, hot and uncomfortable despite the coldness of the day. God knows how many other people in the street had seen her with Guy.

She looked into the shop windows as she walked, in two minds about the bus. She was still irritated with Mrs Evans, blaming her for how late she was now running. *Nosy bitch*, she thought in annoyance. The cold was seeping into her bones, an icy wind cutting through her clothes, and she wondered if she really wanted to walk all the way to Streatham.

In the end she compromised: if the bus didn't come soon, she'd buy herself a Caramac and start walking. A glance at her watch told her she would be late if she walked, and she considered getting the sweets and going back home. She could pretend she had changed her mind and spend the evening with Des instead. It was a long time since she had done that, being afraid that if she stayed in too much her sister would somehow find out the truth about her job. There was no denying that Desiree suspected something; often she asked so many awkward questions, Verona would put on her coat and just go out walking, sneaking back in when Desiree was in bed or John got home.

It was only the fear of Guy phoning that stopped her going back now. Des was bound to recognise his voice, and after what Carol had said it would not take her long to fit everything together.

The bus was chugging down the road as Verona turned the corner, and she made a dash for it, blessing London Regional Transport for always being late. *I can always get Guy to buy me some sweets*, she consoled herself as she waited in line to board. It was a one-man operated bus and she fumbled for the right change, wishing they would bring back the buses with conductors. She always felt nervous and self-conscious on these ones. All the people already boarded seemed to be watching her, mumbling impatiently when her tardiness caused other stragglers to reach the bus and the whole slow process had to start all over again with them.

'Bleeding bus goes from bad to worse,' a woman said loudly as Verona squeezed past her on the way to the back.

'It's since they took the buses from the GLC,' the man beside her volunteered.

'Too right,' another muttered.

They lapsed into silence as the bus lurched away from the kerb. Verona breathed with relief. She always felt personally to blame when she didn't have the right change and was last on the bus.

Guy was waiting for her outside the usual pub, waving madly as the bus sped past to the stop a few yards on. Verona felt a sudden revulsion, wishing she hadn't agreed to meet him today. No doubt he'd expect her to spend some time with him away from the eyes of other people. She felt depressed as she noticed his sagging trousers and overflowing stomach.

'Hello, Verona.' He put an arm around her shoulders and gave her a squeeze. As he bent to kiss her, Verona averted her face, so that he caught her clumsily on the cheek. He smelt of beer and she wondered how many pints he'd had already.

'We've got half an hour before the film starts,' he said. 'Why don't we have a drink?'

She agreed reluctantly. She hated the Green Man pub he insisted on using. It made her feel conspicuous and embarrassed to be the only black face in there, especially the way the others stared. Once or twice, when Guy had gone to the toilet, someone would sidle up to her and she would tense, feeling the hatred emanating from them.

'What you drinking, nigger?' they'd sometimes ask, and she would stiffen, pretending that she hadn't heard.

'Ain't he too hot for you?' one man asked her on another day. 'Mind you, I suppose you spades like it hot.'

She had wanted to walk out; and only the hostile looks and the remarks kept her in her seat. When Guy came back, she told him she didn't want to stay. She felt boxed-in and choked by the hate and the smoke that made visibility hard. They had left that time; but occasionally he still insisted on going in, especially if she had kept him waiting. He no doubt thought it gave him stature in the other men's eyes.

The smoke and noise hit her almost immediately, and suddenly she didn't feel like coping with it. There were hardly any other woman about and the men looked at her in a way she knew meant trouble.

'I've changed me mind,' she shouted at Guy above the din, 'I don't want anything to drink.'

He looked put out, following her retreating back angrily.

'What's the matter now?' he demanded.

'I just don't feel like a drink, all right?'

'No, it's not all right.'

'Listen up, Guy, I've had a hard day; now if you want I'll go home, but I ain't having you sulking on me.'

She watched his face cave in, feeling a vindictive sense of power. He'd do what she wanted, all right; men like Guy always did. He was the sort who had spent most of his life doing all the right things, and now he saw her as a challenge, something forbidden that could earn him credibility and excitement.

Her eyes fell on the sweetshop across the road and her earlier craving returned.

She leaned closer to him, avoiding the wispy grey hairs that made no attempt to cover his scalp, and steeling herself for the slightly unwashed smell that always clung to him. 'Can you get me some sweets?' she asked pleadingly.

'Sure,' he agreed, eager to please, 'anything for my girl. What do you want – chocolate mints?'

'Let's see what they got first, ain't it?' she said, the abrupt manner coming back.

'Is something the matter, love?' he asked tentatively.

'No – why d'you ask?'

'Naw, forget it. It's just that you don't seem yourself today.'

What was *herself* anyway, she wondered unhappily? She never seemed to know from one day to the next who she was; and she sometimes thought her many lives would catch up on her, and it might not be such a bad thing. Normally she would pretend Guy was one of the heroes in her novels and she was an innocent blonde-haired virgin. She would walk along feeling special, then she would catch a glimpse of their reflection in a shop window and depression would descend. It would be such a shock – the fat black woman looking squat and untidy, and the old leathery-skinned white man. But still she would continue the charade, hiding her disillusionment.

The film was good and she was soon caught up in the action, her eyes glued to the screen. She felt Guy's hand moving along her thigh and had to steel herself against the irritation that made her want to push him away. Instead she twisted in her seat, turning slightly away from him. No wonder he always preferred to sit at the back. She had not once been to the cinema with him without having to deal with his podgy, groping fingers.

The funny thing was that they had met at the Odeon. She had gone to see a rerun of *Sahara* and by chance had sat beside Guy. She would not normally have sat at the back but she had been late and it was the only available seat. He hadn't spoken to her until the interval, but after that he had spent the rest of the film whispering to her. She was flattered by his attention, and when he had invited her for a drink afterwards she had accepted.

Sometimes she wondered why she sought out men like Guy. He was not the first older man she had allowed to pick her up. Indeed, she preferred them. She wasn't stupid; she knew why they went for her. They saw going with a black woman as adventure and had probably tried a good many before they succeeded with her. Strangely, that didn't bother her. In a way, both she and they were living out individual fantasies, and if all she got was the odd outing and a lift home, at least she had her books to sink back into.

He took her for a burger afterwards, sitting squashed up beside her at a corner table in the McDonalds up the road from the cinema.

Verona ate hungrily, disliking the way his eyes followed her every move.

'We could go for a drive,' he suggested hopefully as they got to the car.

She knew what he meant by that. Guy was never subtle. She nodded – why not? The idea of going out into the country, watching the dark ribbon of road swallowing up the headlights as they moved, was appealing.

'Hello, V.'

Verona turned, heart sinking at the quiet voice, all her worst fears coming true at the same time.

'Mara . . . hi.' Lost for words, she gave the other woman a guilty smile.

Mara looked attractively elegant and her companion did not

bother to hide his distaste as he looked from Guy to Verona. She felt rumpled and sordid.

'What you doing up here?' Mara asked.

Verona felt angry at the way the man with Mara shifted away as if he didn't want to be contaminated. Who the hell did he think he was anyway? What business was it of his or Mara's who she went out with? She glanced round at Guy, instantly wishing she hadn't when she saw his vapid smile and the way he was eyeing Mara as if hoping his luck might change.

'We just been seeing that Clint Eastwood film,' she admitted unwillingly. 'What about you?'

Mara grinned. 'Oh, this is Olu. We've just been to see *Woza Albert*, and we're off to get something to eat.'

'Have you seen the play?' Olu asked, making Verona feel inches tall.

'I don't go to no theatre,' she said almost belligerently.

'It's about South Africa. You should see it if you can,' Mara added.

Verona nodded, not sure she wanted that. There was always so much about South Africa on television, and it only made her furious and depressed. She wished Guy would stop gaping and get on with opening the car door, and she wanted to throttle him when he suggested:

'We could all go together like, in the car.'

'No, we can't,' she said vehemently, seeing the horror on the other two faces. 'Guy's only joking,' she assured them, 'we just eaten.'

'Well, we don't want to keep you,' the man said pointedly.

Verona avoided Mara's eyes as they took their leave. She had seen the disbelief in the other woman's face and knew this was not the last of it. *How come I'm always bucking up on her?* she wondered in irritation, thinking about the incident in the library. She had managed to avoid Mara since then, terrified that the other woman would confront her and somehow find out about her being sacked. It wasn't that Mara would be likely to tell Desiree, just that Verona couldn't stand the idea of another lecture. The last thing she needed was someone to confirm how silly she had been.

When Guy finally opened the car door Verona slid gratefully in, belting her seatbelt tightly.

'They weren't very friendly,' he remarked, turning the key in the ignition.

'Guy, I don't fancy no drive. I just want to go home, if you don't mind.'

He muttered: 'It's them, isn't it? Who is that bird anyway?'

'Me sister's friend,'

'That's torn it!'

'Yeah, it has, ain't it?' Verona agreed sarcastically.

'Don't take it out on me, love, it ain't my fault if they got a problem.'

She ignored him, feeling anger against the world but especially against the man Olu. The way he had looked at her as if she didn't count, as if she had done something reprehensible. She knew what it was, of course. Black men like him were all the same: making a big thing about black women going with white men. She bet they didn't make the same noise about the men who had white girlfriends. Most of them had done it anyway, especially if they'd been to college. They thought they were too good for the black girls; yet women mustn't do the same as them.

*At least I have good reason*, she thought defiantly, *look what a black bloke done to me. Even Mara had left Winston because he treated her bad*. Verona sighed. She should be used to it by now; she had heard it all before. Well, at least Olu hadn't been openly rude, like a lot of others.

'Something the matter, love?' Guy asked.

Verona looked at him sidewards, feeling suddenly tired. 'Just take me home, will you?' she said.

# Seven

The whine of the television penetrated Desiree's sleep fog and she sat up slowly, wincing as the movement jarred her stiff joints. Her eyes felt glued together and gritty as she forced them apart. She shifted her legs and lowered them gingerly to the floor. She hadn't meant to drift off to sleep when she curled up on the settee, just to rest until John came home.

The clock was showing 12.15. She flicked from channel to channel on the television until she found *Into the Night* on ITV. She eased back against the settee, feeling the blood circulating painfully round her legs. Her head ached and she closed her eyes against the overhead light, too tired to switch it off.

The sound of the front door brought her eyes open again. At last! She sat up, half-apprehensive. *He must have got it*, she prayed, *please let him have got it*. He had been out so long . . . he must have been celebrating.

'John?' she called tentatively as she heard his shoes dropping one by one on the carpet.

She felt his anger before the door came crashing in on itself, and her heart sank when she saw that he had been drinking.

'You didn't get it.' It was more for something to say than through any real need for confirmation.

'No, I didn't,' he snapped. 'I suppose you satisfied now.'

She hadn't seen him like this since he had last failed to get promotion. It was the usual pattern; only this time she had been so sure. On previous occasions he would come in grim-faced, sit morosely in his chair and work his way steadily through their small stock of alcohol, before collapsing into bed to sleep it off. His ego would be fragile for a few days, but in the end he would pull himself together, adding the new bitterness to the rest of his stock. This time had been different. He had not rung to say he would be late, and she had convinced herself he had been carried away by his success.

'Is people like you bad-mouth me all the time,' he grumbled, flopping down into a chair. 'Is not you keep telling me I wasn't gonna get it?'

'John!'

'What you mean "John"? Is true, ain't it? You and the white man them is all the same, always putting black man down.'

She was silent. What was the point in remonstrating about the injustice of his remark? In this mood John's tongue was razor sharp and she didn't want to be on the receiving end of it.

He pulled a copy of the *Sun* from under his arm and opened it defiantly at Page 3.

'Where's my dinner?' he snapped, catching the look of distaste on her face. 'Man can't even expect a decent meal in his own house.'

Reluctantly Desiree slid off the settee. Part of her wanted to curse him for bringing a prejudiced paper into the house, but the other part just wanted peace. She wished she could believe what Mara was always saying about John caring for her, but when he was in this mood, it seemed too far-fetched.

She wondered how she was going to broach the subject of the hospital, shied away from doing it. Better to feed him first, especially since she felt so worn out and disappointed herself. Without realising it, she had let him convince her that the job was his, and she had pinned so much on it. She sighed, moving out of the room. She should have known better. From what she gathered, he was one of the most qualified and experienced in his section and they liked his work; he was always deputising for his supervisor when the other man was at other sites. Yet he had been passed over for promotion four times. She shouldn't have expected them to have a sudden change of heart.

Desiree's heart sank as she lifted the lid of the frying-pan and saw how dried and curled up the fish was. For the past four days John had insisted on white fish for dinner after reading somewhere that it was good for brain development and was less fattening than meat – not that it would make much difference to his girth. Desiree sighed. He would have a brainstorm when he saw the state of the food. With a resigned sigh, she added a bit of milk, before giving the peas and carrots in the other pot an extra stir. She would have liked to do more – at least warm up some corn; but the set of his face told her that would bring down further criticism on her defenceless head.

She kept her back to the door as she heard him come into the kitchen and drop heavily into a chair. He was slumped over the table when she pushed the plate at him. He raised his head slowly, his eyes filling with disbelief.

'What you call this?' His lip curled at the dried-out food. 'This ain't fit for a dog.'

'It been ready hours ago,' Desiree responded, determined to keep her temper. 'I had to keep it warm because I didn't know what time you were coming back, and I know you don't like –'

'Don't gi' me that! You think that's why I earn good money, so you can treat me like a pig?'

'Oh, don't be so stupid! If you'd come back when you say you was coming, the food would have been all right.'

The plate hit the side of her face, bouncing and spinning to land near the dresser as she started to turn away. It slapped painfully against her ear, hot food scalding and stinging as it slid to the cushioned lino.

Desiree stood very still, fighting the tears clogging up her throat and burning in her eyes. 'If you don't like what I cook, why don't you do it yourself?' She breathed deeply. 'I know how hard it is for you, John, I know you should have got the job; but you can't blame me when you don't, it isn't me stopping you, you know. Why don't you get at them instead of me?'

'So you saying I accuse you of stopping me getting the job . . . that what you telling people now?'

'That's not what I'm saying, John, and you know it. Look, I know how hard it is for you, but is nothing I can do. If you want to get at somebody, why not try the blokes that didn't give you the job?'

'What you suggesting by that – you saying I 'fraid of white people?'

'You were doing all right at Rathbourne's and if it hadn't been for the recession you mightn't even have gone to the railway.'

'Yeah, five years ago I was earning nearly the same as now.'

'At least you're earning something . . . millions aren't.'

'Shut you mouth!' John hissed. 'You don't know nothing.'

'You think you the only person ever stop from getting what he deserve?' she asked wearily.

'I going to give you what you deserve in a minute. Since I meet you is pure trouble, yeah? Why don't you take that good-for-nothing sister and get out of my house, stead of sitting round my neck like some brick?'

'My sister pays her way . . . and as for it being your house – you better look at them mortgage papers again, John.'

He gave her a killing look. 'All a you just looking for somebody to live off. Why you don't do something useful and cook me some dinner instead?'

The sound of a key in the front door cut the tension, pulling her back from the brink of temper.

'I going to bed,' she announced decisively, not even bothering to clear up the spilt food.

'What?' John looked alarmed. 'Who going to get my dinner, then?'

'I don't know and I don't care,' she said dismissively, leaving him staring open-mouthed after her.

As she emerged from the kitchen, Verona was just sneaking up the stairs. 'How was your evening?' Desiree asked, ignoring the other's guilty start.

Verona turned. 'Oh, hi, Des,' trying to sound surprised. 'I never want to . . .' She tailed off as she noticed the bits of food and white sauce clinging to her sister's hair and face. 'What happen?'

Desiree was walking up the stairs with her. 'John got a bit annoyed –'

'What! He chuck food at you?'

'Let's leave it, shall we, V?' she said tiredly. 'Let me just clean meself up before you start.'

Verona walked with her to the bathroom and watched

silently as Desiree washed the remnants of John's dinner from her skin, before pulling off the soiled dress with awkward movements.

'I'm fed up at the way he treat you, Des,' she muttered angrily. 'What happen this time – he change his mind about brain food?'

'V, stop it,' Desiree warned. 'John didn't get that job.'

Verona tossed her head in exasperation. 'You surprised? Honestly, Des! You really think he would get it? You know what them people down the railway stay like.'

Desiree nodded, her face betraying her.

'Oh, Des,' Verona said, relenting, 'look, I'm sorry John never get the job, but you *know* they never gonna give him nothing . . . You look awful – why you don't sit yourself down for a bit?'

Desiree followed her into her room and sank down appreciatively. 'I still don't tell him about the operation.'

'Des, you're mad! You said you'd tell him. I mean, you're going in come Monday.'

Desiree looked defeated. 'I was going to tell him tonight, but he in such a mood, he not going to listen.'

'I know,' Verona soothed, 'but there ain't time to keep putting it off.'

'V, will you come with me? If I go down and tell him now?'

'Course. I could tell him for you if you like.'

'No, I'd better tell him myself. I just want you to be there – you know, like moral support.'

John was watching a football video while eating some kind of sandwich. Verona sat in the vacant chair and he grunted acknowledgment at her hello.

Desiree perched on the edge of the settee, looking ill at ease. She began nervously: 'John, I've got something to tell you.'

He glanced up impatiently, sinking right back into the game. 'Can't it wait?' he asked bad-temperedly.

'No, John, it can't wait!' Verona burst out before she could stop herself. Desiree gave her a warning glance and she subsided, ignoring the look of menace John flashed in her direction.

'I could make you some fish and chips,' Desiree suggested.

'I've got some battered haddock in the freezer, and some french fries to go with it.'

'Yeah, all right,' he said with ill grace, 'and get me a beer while you in there, will you?'

Verona followed her, fuming. 'Why you doing this for him, Des? The worse he treat you, is the more you do for him.'

Her sister gave a tolerant smile. 'How else do you think I'm going to get him to listen?'

Verona nodded half-heartedly. 'Here, let me do that.' She took the fish from Desiree, putting it down while she set up the chip fryer. 'You sit and rest yourself and I'll put the kettle on.'

The kitchen was soon full of the warmth and smells of cooking, and Verona joined Desiree at the table.

'I told you I'd look after the children, ain't it?' she said. 'Surely John can't make no fuss about you going if it don't cause him no bother?'

'V, I don't want to impose –'

'Yeah, you never do,' Verona cut in. 'Let's don't make a song and dance 'bout it, I'm just saying the offer is there . . . and is up to you.'

Desiree smiled gratefully.

They drank their tea silently for a while, listening to the sizzling noise of the fryer and the occasional spit of hot fat from the fish under the grill. A faint rustling from the sitting-room told them that John had resumed his paper, no doubt back to Page 3 again.

There had been a time when Desiree would never have thought to see him reading the *Sun*. Not when he used to be so full of pride in black people and doing all those things for them. She felt ashamed of the way he had changed, hated to see the anti-black hysteria he now read without a single comment. There was a time when he wouldn't even buy the *Mirror* because he said it was subsidising racist crap. 'Black people who read them racist papers must really hate themselves,' he would say, angered by another biased headline or twisted story. 'Why don't they boycott it? So much of them go in and buy it, I'm sure it would make a lot of difference, you know.'

She wondered if he remembered those conversations,

evenings spent curled up together on the settee when they both came in from work. In those days he had been active in BUF and she had been proud of him. She had sometimes gone with him when he sold the group's newspaper in Brixton market. It had been great the way people recognised him and stopped to talk. She liked it when other group members came up to ask him about 'the struggle'; it didn't matter that she never really understood the concept. Her John was a *real* black man, not like those he was always criticising, the ones he would dismiss as 'coconuts' – white on the inside. She used to think the expression clever, joking about it with some of the other black women at work . . . now she wondered what she would find if she scratched below John's surface.

Despite Mara's scepticism about BUF, Desiree refused to let go of her ideal. If John had stayed with 'the struggle' she was sure he would have been all right. He was frustrated at work, but so were lots of people; and, whatever his frustration, there was no need for him to read the *Sun*.

Desiree thought back to how things had been. The change had been so gradual she had hardly noticed at first: his excuses for not helping out around the house, no longer going to BUF. It had all started after he had been at the railway for two years – long enough to realise that his skill and merit were getting him nowhere. She had watched him change so much. The only thing that had remained constant was his love for his grandparents. No matter how poor he was, John would always find something to send them.

It was only that characteristic, and his love and care for the children, that made her hang on to the life they had once been so happy with and try to contain her dissatisfaction.

Verona was laying the heaped plate of steaming fish and chips on a tray with the remains of yesterday's coleslaw from the fridge, salt and vinegar and a cold beer. As she lifted the tray, Desiree got to her feet.

'Let me take it, V,' she offered half-heartedly.

'No, just shove open the door for me.'

John glanced up, grunting, when she put the tray on the coffee table and pulled it up to him. He discarded his paper, starting hungrily on the food.

Desiree watched him for a few moments, pressing her hands to her stomach in an automatic gesture as the pain rose up again. Suddenly she wanted to confide in him again, to share her worries as she used to when he worked at Rathbourne's and their future still seemed secure. He was always there for his grandparents and the children . . . surely he could be there for her again.

'I have to go into hospital, John.' There. It was out now.

John continued eating, his eyes never leaving the screen.

'Is about the swelling in my belly,' she persisted, determined to finish now that she had started. 'The doctor say I have to get my womb out, cause is what causing the trouble.'

John looked up in alarm. 'You have to stay in hospital?'

She was surprised when he spoke; it hadn't seemed as if he was listening, but now she wanted to make the best of the attention while she had it. 'Yes, the doctor said it would be about ten days.'

There was a long silence as he searched her face anxiously, his eyes hunted and frightened, and Desiree started to relax, sensing concern in him.

'What happen if you don't come back? What you going to do about the children? Who's going to look after them while you gone?' he asked, shattering her illusion.

'I suppose you going to have to,' she said without sympathy, aware of Verona shifting restlessly on the other chair.

'You've gotta be joking! What about football, or have you forgotten that the season don't finish for two weeks? When they want you in anyway?'

'Monday.'

'Christ almighty! If you're off from Monday, who going to wash the kit? Don't forget it's your turn this week.'

'Des don't play football, John.' Verona could hold her tongue no longer.

'Who's talking to you anyway?' he rounded on her. 'Can't we ever have a bit a peace from you? Why you don't go and read a book or something?'

'Go on, V,' Desiree advised, before her sister could explode, and Verona rose reluctantly, giving John a baleful stare as she left the room.

'V is right,' Desiree said, determined not to let him browbeat her, 'I don't play football, is your team and your kit, John.'

'What d'you mean by that?' He was belligerent now. 'Anyone would think it was some big deal – all you have to do is put them in the machine and do a bit a sewing here and there.'

'In that case you do it!' she virtually shouted. 'If is simple as you say, you can do it yourself in future.'

'All right . . . but don't expect me to look after your children as well.'

'They your children too, John. I didn't ask to need this operation.' The worry pushed aside her growing anger, the need to be reassured strong in her. 'To tell the truth, I'm real scared –'

'I don't want to know! There's always something or the other wrong with you. You know what you are, you're a bloody hypochondriac!'

That was rich coming from him, she thought bitterly. All he ever did was feel sorry for himself, forcing her to listen to his complaints about what white people did to him. She had spent weeks coping with pain, afraid something was fatally wrong with her and that there would be no one to care for him and the children. Now she felt scared for the kids . . . afraid that something might go wrong and they would be left with him. How could he look after them when he was such a baby himself?

'You know I been ill a long time, John,' she tried again.

He looked at her, cooling down, his eyes sliding away guiltily. 'I know, Des. Look, I sorry, y'hear. I shouldn't take it out on you like this . . . is just that I feel bad about the job, you know.'

It was always the same; whenever disappointment hit him he took it out on her. What she felt didn't count, only his hurt mattered. Here she was about to go into hospital, about to lose her womb, and all he could think of was a flaming job that if he had any sense he'd have known he wouldn't get.

'How'll I manage on my own?' he asked almost plaintively. 'I can't take time off work, Des . . . anyway I wouldn't know what to do with the kids.'

'You won't be on your own,' she retorted, determined not to

be made to feel guilty. 'The children old enough to fend for themselves, if you give them the chance, and V will cook for them.'

'And who going to cook for me, eh? Who going see if I'm all right?'

'John, I'll be gone for ten days, that's all. I have to go whether you like it or not, so you just have to cope.'

He sucked air through his teeth. 'Go on then. You think I care?'

She gazed at him, stunned. His callous words underlined her isolation, resurrecting her fears.

'Well, if you don't care about me, why should I care?' With an exaggerated movement, he rewound a goal kick he had missed. 'Anyway, I thought you were going to bed.'

'Yes,' she said sadly, moving to the door. 'Goodnight, John.'

He didn't answer, and somehow it didn't matter. What was the point in telling herself he'd had too much to drink and too many disappointments? She didn't need excuses, she needed a partner to confide in.

# Eight

Verona came awake through layers of sleep, the ticking of the clock penetrating her dream world and merging it with reality. There was a shrill noise in her head and her chest hurt as though someone had been beating on it. The nightmare came rushing back as she lay blinking owlishly, trying to re-orient herself within her buttercup room.

She listened, ears straining. Why did she think someone was calling her?

Silence. She relaxed, feeling clammy and sweaty, the

nightmare still on the edge of her consciousness. It was the dream she had been having ever since Ronnie . . . Her subconscious added new twists to it as fresh fears materialised. It was funny how, under stress, she only remembered the bad things. Yet her childhood memories were mostly good ones – of sunny days spent sitting in her grandmother's yard listening to old-time stories, eating Metagee, going into the bush with her greatuncle.

She thought she heard another sound, but once again there was nothing. Her mind drifted back to her nightmare.

It seemed to be when she was staying with her uncle far away from Georgetown, in a place whose name she could never recall. That one trip which she had made by herself was the only image of Guyana she ever dreamed, muddling it with later images after her father's death, and her deepest fear.

As always, there was the schoolyard with its bleak construction, set in the deep bushland she could hardly remember, and there were the steep steps to the tiny flat her sister got them from the council after their father died. Verona always thought of it as her National Front dream. That was what brought the fear. Demon people, with punk faces and skinhead haircuts, stomping through the house in Doc Martin boots. Flames licked greedily at the carpets, while the swastika-carved faces of hate leered as they cowered behind the belching smoke streaming up from the settee. All of them were there – Des, the children, even John – all huddled underneath the bed while the fire crept closer and closer. There was blood everywhere, and Verona was never sure who had died . . . her eyes glued to the bloodcrazy people, whooping and screaming like bad American film cowboys.

But that was only half of it. There was the other thing as well, strands of frightening memory from early childhood weaving through the second half.

The walk through the steaming undergrowth of the early morning gully . . . the smell of growth and decay making her want to gag. The jumbled events moved too quickly to be more than an impression; yet it was so agonisingly slow, her feet barely moved in front of each other.

There were three of them who escaped the fire, two boys and a girl. They were walking single-file . . . Joey Gardener, yes, that was his name! Joey Gardener, leading the way with childish arrogance. She couldn't remember what they were going for, just that it was summer and morning moisture hung fresh on the still air and penetrated her socks through the thin plastic sandals.

They came across it suddenly: black candles burning. Joey stopped short, the others bumping into him. Overhead a bird screeched and took off in noisy flight. The children jumped; she cried out as they turned. Then she was running, running, running . . . sometimes at the back, other times clawing her way through to the front.

Everything was a jumble from then. The gaping handbag, the woman's body lying in the buttonfront dress, eyes gazing serenely at the wispy traces of cloud melting in the face of the morning sun . . .

They were back in school and the heavy climbing-frame was shuddering while she stood rooted to the spot, horrified yet fascinated. It shifted, groaning slightly. Then it was falling, moving slowly, then gathering speed as it sliced through the air. She was struggling to get away, tugging at legs held fast by unseen hands of panic. She closed her eyes as the metal glinted in the strengthening sun.

The cold bite in her flesh never came. Instead it swept past with a whoosh, shuddering through the ground with a massive clang and a sickening thud. Dust billowed up in clouds, but when it settled it was Joey Gardener who lay helpless, pinned to the ground by the heavy iron bars. She stared at him, inches from where she stood, watched in horror as his eyes rolled back, body twitching, mouth open in a silent scream.

Away in the distance was the sound of running feet, never getting closer as the heavy bar sank further into khaki-covered belly.

Sweat kept dripping into her eyes, blinding her, and she was splashing down blood-reddened stairs, heart pounding when she realised the blood was coming from her, and he was behind her, closing in, shouting. If only her feet were not so clogged . . .

'Auntie V!'

Verona jumped, yanked out of remembered nightmare.

'Auntie V, Carol is crying and she says her belly is hurting her . . . and Dad's gone already.'

Verona burrowed deeper under the covers, feeling unnerved. She didn't want to face another day just yet, wished she could ignore the high, insistent voice.

'Auntie V!'

'Yes, Lyn, I hear you,' she called back when it was obvious that the problem wasn't going to evaporate. She hoped it was nothing serious. The children had been so miserable since Des went away, and she was beginning to feel a real failure at her inability to calm their fears. Not that it was all bad; she allowed them to do a lot more, showing Lyn how to pick and wash rice, letting them wash up. Her heart warmed as she saw how important and busy they looked. She hoped she could persuade Desiree to let them continue once she was out of hospital.

The children were careful not to let their father catch them at it, knowing that would spell the end of their treat. Verona felt impatient with John's attitude. She realised he thought he was trying to protect the children; but that was no justification. She was only glad they were so sensible, refusing to see housework either as something they were born to or something to be avoided until there was no choice.

Verona felt out of her depth as she saw Lyn's hopeful face staring trustingly at her. Sitting blearily on the side of the bed, she blinked rapidly, trying to ease the grittiness from her eyes. Carol lay huddled under the cheerful pierrot quilt in the bottom bunk. The child was moaning softly, her body tense as she cried into her pillow. Verona moved the covers aside, laying a gentle hand against the small forehead, feeling relief that it was cool.

'What's the matter?' she asked softly.

'It's my belly, Auntie V.' Carol's sobs become louder with the sympathy. 'It's hurting.'

'Hush, it's all right. Come on now – it'll be better soon as I get something for it,' Verona promised, with more certainty than she felt. She could guess the cause of the problem: Carol had gone to a friend's party the day before and, judging from what she said, had eaten too much cake and ice-cream. Thinking back to how Desiree usually dealt with such a situation, Verona realised she would have given the child something the night before.

'Lyn, get me the Milk of Magnesia from the kitchen, will you?'

Lyn trotted off obediently, eager to help, and Verona was yet again struck by her resemblance to Desiree. At ten she was far too responsible, too much burdened by the role of second mother to her sister.

Lyn was back in record time, hovering anxiously as Verona gave Carol the medicine. She looked as though she might stay there all day, and Verona had to almost stand over her to get her dressed and out of the house in time for school.

By the evening, Carol had recovered and the three of them shared the washing-up.

'Tell us about you and Mum in Guyana, Auntie V,' Lyn cajoled as she shook excess water from a cup before placing it gently in the open tea-towel. 'We're doing a Caribbean project at school and we're supposed to ask our parents about when they were young.'

'Yeah, tell us!' Carol joined in eagerly. She had been trailing her hand through the soapy water, but now she looked appealingly at Verona, bringing an involuntary smile to her aunt's face. 'Dad never tell us about Jamaica,' she moaned, 'he keep saying we're British and mustn't bother about the West Indies, 'cause no one can make us go there.'

'I want to go,' Lyn said wistfully. 'I want to see how it was when you and Mum and Dad were children.'

Verona kept her face blank. She had made it a rule never to encourage the children to criticise their father; but this time she agreed with them and wasn't going to defend him.

'I can't tell you much,' she warned. 'It's better if you talk to your mum. I was only seven when I came over.'

'What's going on here?'

They had been so engrossed in their conversation, none of them had heard John come in, and Verona's heart sank as she faced his disapproval.

'Dad!' Carol launched herself at him, hugging him despite his attempt to avoid her soapy embrace. 'I didn't go to school today . . . I had a tummy-ache and Auntie V had to give me Milk of Magnesia,' she giggled. 'She said it's because I was a pig at the party.'

John's face softened. 'Do you feel all right now?' he asked gently.

'Oh, yes, and I was so hungry she had to make me some soup before Lyn got back.'

'Auntie V was just about to tell us about she and Mum in Guyana,' Lyn inserted, before Carol could launch off again.

'And getting you to do her work for you while she's at it,' he grumbled.

Verona bristled with frustration. She wanted to tell him there and then what to do with himself, but the presence of the children restrained her.

'I can see how women can kill,' she muttered under her breath.

'What's that, Auntie V?' Lyn asked, curious.

'Nothing. You and Carol go upstairs and start your homework . . . Carol, you can do that reading you were supposed to do yesterday.'

'Aw . . . it's not fair,' Carol wailed.

'I'll come and go through it with you later,' Verona promised, and the child's face cleared instantly.

'Oh, will you! Great – you always make me laugh when you read with me.'

'Dad, could you look at my maths with me?' Lyn asked quietly, and Verona's heart went out to the child, knowing she had asked in order to stop John feeling left out.

'I don't have time for that,' he said irritably, and hurt showed in Lyn's eyes.

'Don't worry, love,' Verona comforted, 'I'll go through it with you after you finish. Now off you go. Your father's tired right now.'

As soon as the children were out of earshot, Verona said: 'Let's get one thing straight! I ain't no kitchen bitch, and cleaning your dirt ain't *my* work.' She had a flash of Stoneford's, and quickly suppressed it. Now was the wrong time to think of the mess her working life was in. Better to wait until Des was back on her feet.

'You're supposed to take Des's place while she is in hospital,' John challenged. 'The jerseys don't wash and we need them for tomorrow.'

Verona pressed her hand against her temple, feeling as if her head would lift off with the force of her temper. 'I did agreed to look after the children,' she said with slow precision, forcing back angry words with an effort; 'now if I can't do it my way, I suggest you do it instead.'

'Me!'

'Yeah, you!' Verona said forcefully. 'If you did have your way, Lyn and Carol would be dead selfish and spoilt. Des might be too tired to do anything 'bout it, but I ain't.'

John's eyes narrowed. 'Don't push your luck, woman.'

'I am not your woman, John!' she snapped. 'You just like all them others, ain't you? All that talk 'bout how you love and respect your African sisters.'

'If I never love and respect my African sisters, you think you could park your fat backside on my settee night after night, and still come cuss me out?'

She was damned if she was going to let him know she was wounded by his words. 'Yeah! Since you have so much respect and love, how come you only see Des in hospital once? Tell me that!'

He was immediately uncomfortable. 'Des understand, she know I don't like hospital.'

'Can't you think about anybody but yourself.'

'What you want me to do? She look so sick and everything, suppose she get worse? Suppose she don't get better?'

'How you going to find out if you don't go? And, for your information, she *is* getting better, though the doctor says it'll help if you spend more time with her.

John looked upset. 'I would, you know, V, but . . . well, is work, you see. Is already February and what with Granny Ruby and Grandpa Clifford –'

'John! Des just lose her womb.'

'So? What's the big deal? She already have children, don't it?' He was angry now and he gave her a bitter look.

'Yeah, well, all I can say is I hope the kids ain't like you when they grow up.' Verona shook her head wonderingly.

'My children are going to get somewhere,' he said with conviction. 'They not going to work in no factory or clean no white man floor . . . and they going to have the education to get married to the right people.'

'John, nobody want them to work in no factory, but you ain't doing it right. You just can't expect us to wait on them, it ain't healthy.'

The shrill ring of the phone cut off her flow, and she moved swiftly to the door, wanting to end the oppressive conversation.

'V? Is that you?' Mara's voice came clearly down the line.

'Oh, hello, Mara,' Verona said without too much enthusiasm, as she remembered the last time she had seen the other woman. She had managed to avoid Mara since, knowing that she would demand some form of explanation for her presence in Streatham with Guy.

To her relief, Mara made no reference to that night. 'What's the matter?' she asked instead. 'John giving you a hard time?'

Verona relaxed a little, smiled. 'You can say that again – how did you guess?'

'Stands to reason,' Mara responded, an answering smile in her voice. 'Listen, why I was phoning was to find out if you need a hand. I've been a bit busy or I'd have been in touch before. We always just miss each other down the hospital.'

Verona felt uncomfortable, knowing she had deliberately timed her visits for well before Mara finished work. 'I wouldn't mind some help,' she said cautiously, 'specially with them wanting homemade bread. I can't make it like you and Des.'

'I was thinking of coming over. Charleen wants Lyn to come round for the night, so if we came by in, say . . . an hour's time, would that be all right?'

'Fine.' Verona was relieved not to have to put up with John on her own for the rest of the evening. 'The girls will like that.' She replaced the receiver on its cradle with a smug smile. Let that idiot John continue, she thought with relish, Mara would soon put him in his place.

She felt a glow of satisfaction as she moved towards the kitchen, but the phone rang again when she had taken only a few steps and she turned back impatiently.

'Yeah?' she enquired unhelpfully, expecting it to be one of John's football team phoning about the kit.

'Is that Verona?'

She almost stood to attention as she recognised the thick English voice. 'Guy! I thought I told you not to call me!' she hissed down the line, glancing nervously at the kitchen door.

She had not seen him since their ill-fated encounter with Mara, ringing him to tell him she would be busy for a few months. He had been upset and put out, claiming that it was because of Mara and Olu. Verona had denied it, but it was partly true. She had felt ashamed and soiled, aware for the first time how she must really look to other black people. She had been shocked by the meeting, never expecting to meet anyone she knew like that. Somehow it all seemed a dangerous, pointless game, and she realised that it was only a matter of time before Des found out. *God knows how I've got away with it this long*, she told herself after coming home that evening. She couldn't face the prospect of her sister's hurt and shame and was determined that this time she would stop it altogether. True, she had said as much before – once when the man had come in panic, telling her his wife had found out and knew that she was black; and another time, when she had nearly stumbled into John in Woolworth's in Camberwell –

'... You didn't get in touch for a whole bloody week,' Guy was complaining.

'I told you I'd be busy, ain't it?' She didn't bother to hide the impatience in her voice. 'If you can't understand that, find someone else. In fact,' she added, 'I ain't in the mood for your nonsense, so maybe you should find someone else anyhow.'

'Don't be like that, V,' he wheedled. 'Look, I won't ring you again, if you promise to phone me at work in the week.'

'I *told* you,' she started, 'I can't –'

'Bloody hell,' he cut across her, 'look, I've got to go, love, the wife's coming.'

The click of the phone disconnecting was followed by the dialling tone, and she gave it a baleful stare before replacing the handset, all her earlier equanimity evaporating.

'Who was on the phone?' John's voice was loaded with suspicion as he came to the kitchen door.

'No one you know,' she responded rudely.

He looked suddenly concerned. 'Is somebody bothering you, V? 'Cause if they are –'

'I told you it's none of your business.'

'V, I know we don't always see eye to eye, but you and Des is sister, and no way I'm letting no man bother you and don't do nothing about it.'

Verona shrugged off the implied offer. 'There's dinner in the pot, why you don't eat it or something?'

'Why you always so unfriendly, man?'

' 'Cause you treat my sister like dirt, ain't it?'

'Hey, I ain't taking that. Just watch what you saying, hear!'

She sucked her teeth. 'I'm going upstairs,' she said, turning away.

Verona was sitting on the floor in the children's room, helping Lyn with her maths homework, when the doorbell rang.

'That must be Mara,' she exclaimed, looking at her watch. 'Have I been up here that long?'

'Do you think Dad might look at the rest for me?' Lyn asked, and Verona felt bitterness at John as she saw the hope in the child's face.

'Your father's real tired right now,' she hedged, 'it ain't been easy for him, what with your mum sick, and him having to go to work.'

'Auntie V, why don't Dad go and visit Mum in the hospital?' Carol asked, looking up from her book. She sat cross-legged on her bunk, while Lyn lay on the Paddington Bear rug, a present from Verona in better days.

Hearing a child's feet on the stairs and Mara talking to John downstairs, Verona seized the interruption as a lifeline. 'We'll talk about that later,' she said. 'Mara's come to help me do a few things.'

'Can I help?' Carol asked.

'When you finish the book we'll see,' Verona said. 'Hello, Charleen,' she said, as Mara's skinny daughter came in.

'Hi, V,' the child said, stepping aside for Verona to leave. The other two girls immediately discarded their work and mobbed her.

Charleen was truly Winston's child, though to look at she was all Mara and there was nothing visible of her father. She had many of his mannerisms, although they were temperamentally so different. Verona often marvelled at how laid-back the child was.

When Verona reached the hall, Mara threw her arms around her with characteristic expansiveness: 'How are you, girl?'

Verona hugged her back. 'I'm fine. Things was a bit hectic yesterday being as Des had them tests in the morning, but the girls been great.'

'Des is lucky,' Mara said, making a face when she heard the familiar football on the television. She raised her voice: 'What you watching this time, John?'

'FA Cup Final 1985,' his reply came back, and Mara shrugged.

She followed Verona into the kitchen and, the door securely shut behind them, asked: 'Who was that man you were with up Streatham the other night?'

Verona stiffened, her face guarded. 'That was Guy,' she said warily.

'Is he your – ? That is . . .'

Seeing Mara at a loss for words made Verona feel equally uncomfortable. 'We go out together now and then,' she said unhelpfully.

Mara sighed. 'Why so old, V? Couldn't you at least pick someone younger, or, better still, black?'

'I don't tell you who to go out with,' Verona said stonily.

'You're right,' Mara placated. 'Look, let's not quarrel. I'll keep my big mouth out of your affairs.' She paused. 'V, I do care about you . . . and, well – if you have any trouble, you know I'm there.'

Verona nodded, thankful for her tact. She considered telling her about work but decided against it. Mara was Des's friend and it wouldn't be fair to put her in that position.

The appetising smell of new bread warmed the kitchen as the two women sat sipping cups of tea.

'Shouldn't we make John a cup?' Verona asked hesitantly.

Mara laughed. 'Don't worry, as soon as he smell this bread he'll be out here with his long belly, you wait and see.'

Almost on cue, they heard the sitting-room door open and moments later John came in. He looked a little more relaxed, and Verona wondered if he had been reading the *Sun* for light relief in the interval.

'Mmm, something smell good.'

'It's bread for the children,' Mara said pointedly, getting up as the timer went off.

John sat in the chair she had just left, watching as she removed the loaf. 'Cut me a slice while it hot, noh,' he told her as she put it on the cooling-rack. 'Verona can make some tea to go with it.'

Mara looked at him in irritation.

'I told you I ain't no kitchen bitch.'

'You supposed to look after me while Des in hospital.'

'What you take yourself for?' Mara snapped, arms akimbo. 'You just one renking man – don't even know you taking poison when you reading your trashy newspaper. It reach so bad, you even treat black woman like they is dirt.'

'Don't get so personal,' John said defensively. 'The only reason I read the *Sun* is for the bingo.'

'And the half-naked white women,' Verona sneered.

John kissed his teeth. 'The minute I win the big prize, I going write to the editor and tell him what to do with his paper.'

Mara gave him a killing look. 'John, when you gon visit Des?'

Abashed, he said: 'I been to see her when she had the operation, ain't it?'

'That was a week ago.'

'She did seem all right. Anyway, Des understand that hospital make me nervous.'

'John, she just lost her womb!' Verona exclaimed, horrified at his selfishness. Des was struggling to come to terms with things, but there was no denying she was taking it badly.

'You could go and give her some support,' Mara suggested, 'I'm sure she'd cope better with your help.' She sighed. 'John, it ain't too late to save what you and Des have, but you have to make it give and take. You think hiding your head is how you going to keep her? Well, I tell you this: that is the way you sure to lose her.'

A haunted look was in his eyes, and for a moment his guard dropped. 'If I only did know what to do.'

'Go and see her, and talk about it with her, share what she going through. Just find some time for her.'

As if regretting his momentary lapse, he shrugged with feigned nonchalance. 'All right! All right,' he conceded. 'If Des feel a way I'll do it. Why you women have to make so much fuss about everything?'

'One day somebody going to take off that useless thing between your legs, John,' Mara exploded, 'and I hope I get a ringside seat.'

'Cho, Mara, I don't know what biting you, man! I may as well go if all you can do is attack me.' He got up petulantly.

'Yeah, you do that,' Verona taunted, 'we don't want to keep you from Page 3 too long.'

He hesitated, but it was Mara he was looking at. 'I don't read the *Sun* for none of that,' he insisted, eyes almost imploring as they met her gaze.

Something passed wordlessly between them, a plea, a recognition, before John moved awkwardly to the door.

'Do you want anything on the bread?' Mara asked quietly.

He turned back at once, his face full of gratitude. 'Just some butter, please,' he said, coming to the table with an eagerness that was pitiful.

Verona looked from one to the other, sure that she had missed something, her face puzzled as she continued to drink her tea.

# Nine

'In't your work going mind you taking so much time off?' Desiree asked, looking up with troubled eyes. She seemed sharper and more clear-headed than she had done in a long time. The pain was gone, though she still felt sore and weak.

Verona looked apprehensively across at the drawn face. She had been bracing herself for this question since her sister came home yesterday. Desiree had been too tired to ask then, staring listlessly out of the taxi and slipping gratefully into bed when they arrived. Until now there had been no mention of the topic and Verona had been thankful that she had not yet needed to use the little lie she had rehearsed.

'I left,' she said bluntly; it was at least halfway to the truth.

'You *what!* Verona, why you do that?'

'They wouldn't give me the time off, ain't it?'

'But that's the most fool thing I ever hear, you still have most of your holiday to take, and they never stop you before.'

Verona's heart raced so that she had to breathe deeply to control her nervousness. 'Look, they was just being difficult,' she explained. 'One of the women from Personnel says they was having money trouble and they want to cut staff. So they told Mr Dorkings I never give them enough warning and if I take the time I shouldn't come back.'

'V, why you don't say something? There ain't no sense you losing your job because of the kids.'

'Yeah, well, I was thinking of leaving anyhow,' Verona said hastily. 'I'm dead fed-up of clerical, thought I might do something different . . . might even go to college.' The last suggestion was calculated to throw her sister off the scent. She knew how much Des wanted her to go back to studying, and in fact it was an idea worth considering; at least it would give her a reference from somewhere.

Desiree was silent for a long time, worry scarring deep lines into her forehead. 'V, did you lose your job?' she asked quietly.

'Why d'you think that?' Verona responded with a question of her own, playing for time.

'Since the two men come from your work, you acting strange.'

Verona gave a nervous laugh, wondering if she looked as guilty as she felt. 'If I lost my job, you'd be the first to know, ain't it?'

'Is long time the men come to see you and you don't tell me why,' Desiree challenged and Verona sighed inwardly. There was no denying Des was on the mend.

'I *told* you, they was doing that new system for people what need to –'

'I know what you told me, but is not the real truth, is it?'

Resentment bubbled over in Verona. 'I never need to look after your kids!' she said. 'I must be a real idiot. Yeah, I did feel responsible for them and John weren't going to give up his holiday to look after them. Well, if that's all the thanks I get, I ain't sticking my nose in again.'

Desiree held out a placating hand. 'V, I'm sorry. I grateful for what you did. Truth is, I feel responsible for you too.'

Verona felt terrible. She had confessed to stealing to protect Desiree in the first place and she was determined not to add that to her sister's conscience. 'I know,' she said, avoiding the other's eyes. 'Listen, I'll go make you some soup or something. Anything you fancy?'

Desiree grinned, sounding like Mara as she joked: 'After that hospital kitchen? Girl, I could give you a list as long as your arm.'

Once she had gone, Desiree lay back against the pillow, the cheerful front slipping away from her. She felt weak and useless, the familiar feeling of failing Verona sharpened by what Mara had told her about seeing her at the library. She was convinced her sister was lying about leaving work because of the children. V had always been terrified of losing her job. In fact, though she regretted leaving school at sixteen, she was too afraid of not getting another job to walk out of this one, even to go to college.

'Look how much of them people with O- and A-levels still can't get no job, and some even have to work down at us,' she often pointed out, when they talked about going back to studying and getting qualifications.

Desiree frowned, hunting for an explanation of her sister's secrecy. Then she remembered Verona telling her some of the women in the warehouse had joined the National Front, and she wondered if this had anything to do with it. No, that couldn't be it. V would almost certainly have told her about that. There had to be something else behind it, something much worse.

She blinked back involuntary tears. If only Mara were here. Mara had kept her sane in the hospital, bringing her food every day and sitting quietly, listening while she poured out her feelings. But for Mara, she would be deep in depression now, like that young woman on the ward who had been referred to a psychiatrist by the counsellor that came to see her after the operation. Desiree had been terrified the same thing would happen to her, especially at the beginning when she didn't seem able to stop crying. Not that the counsellor hadn't been sympathetic, probably too much so; she seemed constantly tired and harassed, face showing signs of overwork.

Desiree too had wanted to talk to someone, to weep on a shoulder . . . but she could never have exposed herself to anyone white. She needed a black woman who would really understand. Anyway, this white woman seemed to have enough on her plate already. She obviously cared a lot, judging by how hard she tried with other women on the ward; but how could she possibly relate to a black woman abandoned and alone, without her womb?

John had come to see her after the operation, and again about a week later. She was sure his second visit was at someone else's prompting, though neither Verona or Mara would admit to it. Even so, she had begun to warm to him again. He was almost as he had been before Rathbourne's closed, attentive and soothing, gentle and sympathetic.

So much for that. Her mouth tightened as she remembered yesterday. It wasn't so much that he had left it to Verona to collect her from hospital, or that he had refused to miss his customary Wednesday night at the local pub with his friends – though those were bad enough failings. No, it was afterwards. He had rolled in at his usual eleven-thirty, smelling of drink and sweat, and she had wanted to push him away when she felt him slip into bed beside her. Her eyes had widened in disbelief as she felt his hand slide across the back she presented to him.

'You feeling better now, Des?' he asked, his voice not quite sober.

Desiree felt angered by the crude suggestion she was sure his words contained. To him, this was just another Wednesday night. It had been like that for years now, John's night of recreation: a few jars with the boys, then home for some sex to round the evening off. She refused to credit the concern he voiced, preferring to attribute the uncertain tone to his attempt to get what he wanted. It was months since they had slept together and she knew John well enough to realise that he would not have gone to anyone else.

'They only let me out through they need the bed.' Desiree's words were pointed. 'The doctor said I not to exert myself.' The doctor had said no such thing, but she was damned if she was going to let John use her tonight.

There was silence and he took his hand away abruptly. 'Des, what you trying to suggest?' he asked, indignant. 'You think I is some kind of animal, you think I don't know you just come from hospital or something?'

Desiree made no attempt to hide her resentment. How dare he try to make *her* feel guilty? He was the one with the one-track mind. That was John all over, though; catch him out at something and he went on as if it was her fault. But she wasn't fooled by him; as far as she was concerned, John had long ago forgotten about mutualness and sharing in his need to get his way.

'John, my belly have one big, big cut and the whole thing

paining bad . . . how you expect to do that now?' She refused to let him off the hook. Not this time.

He hissed through his teeth. 'I never say you should do that.' He rolled away from her with a grunt, muttering bad-temperedly under his breath.

She had lain awake most of the night, his snoring keeping her company, all the good feelings about being home oozing away with the long, lonely hours.

Her thoughts were interrupted when Verona came into the room, balancing the tray carefully as she pushed the door shut. 'Here you are. Tomato soup and a roll. It ain't much, but the kids and me is cooking something special this evening.' She put the tray down carefully across Desiree's lap, chatting away as if the earlier altercation had never happened.

Desiree smiled, wishing that she didn't have to risk reintroducing unpleasantness; yet she needed to know how things were. 'What are you going to do about work?' she asked cautiously.

'I'm going down to Social Security tomorrow, and then I suppose I'll just keep signing on till something come up.'

'How about this college thing – shouldn't you check out courses?'

'Yeah . . . well, I'm going to do that, but that ain't till September.' She paused. 'What I was thinking of is one of them twenty-one-hour things – the ones that don't affect your dole.'

Desiree relaxed a little. Verona had obviously thought about it to know that much.

'What about those access courses like Mara did?' she asked, voicing what she had half-decided on for herself in the hospital, after she had confessed to Mara her fears about having to do A-levels with a bunch of kids.

'That's exactly why I went for the access,' Mara had confided. 'I never think I could deal with that kind of studying.'

'But isn't it harder than the A-levels?'

Mara nodded. 'Yes, and a lot of the people in the college looks down on you when you go the access route, but you don't let that bother you, hear.'

The more Desiree heard about the access course, the more convinced she was that it was what she wanted to do.

'Let we do the course together, eh?' she suggested now to Verona. 'You know . . . be company for each other.'

'John ain't never going to let you,' Verona said realistically. 'You always talking 'bout this an' that and when it come to it you can't go 'cause you have John and the kids.'

'John can't stop me from doing what I want.' The response was stung out of Desiree. 'I tired of being stuck in this house. The kids not babies no more. I been thinking about things a lot in the hospital this ten days.'

'Yeah, but what if John don't cooperate? With both of us at college, what'd you do 'bout the girls?'

Desiree lifted another spoonful of soup to her mouth. 'Mara said they could come down the after-school club by her.'

'You've really thought it out, ain't it?' Verona said in admiration.

Desiree nodded, satisfied. 'Oh, yes, I had plenty time to do that in the hospital.'

The sound of the children home from school broke the silence.

'I'd better go,' Verona said cheerfully, 'I did promise we'd make a cake special for you today.'

Desiree looked surprised. 'John know all a this?'

'Yeah, he does,' Verona assured her drily.

'And he don't mind?'

Verona smiled wickedly. 'Put it like this, his belly mean more to him than that stupid rule.'

'Auntie V! Mum! We're home,' Carol yelled, clomping up the stairs, Lyn close behind.

Desiree looked past Verona eagerly as her daughters opened the door. She had been asleep when they came in the night before and had only seen them briefly before they went to bed. Though they had visited her daily in the hospital, she still felt they had been away from her for weeks.

She put the tray on the bedside table as they came into the room and surrounded her, kissing and hugging, both talking at once.

'We were real worried,' Lyn said, ' 'cause you were just sleeping all the time since yesterday.'

'I all right now,' Desiree assured her, 'and the pain nearly gone.'

'You are all right, aren't you, Mum?' Carol asked anxiously, refusing to move from her side, as Lyn fussed around, straightening the cover and fluffing the pillows.

'Carol, move!' Lyn exclaimed. 'She'll be more all right when she feel comfortable. I know what you need,' she said to her mother, gathering up the tray importantly. 'I'll make you and Auntie V some tea before we start the cake.'

'Cake! Yeah, we're making you a cake for your coming home,' Carol said excitedly.

Desiree winced as she bounced off the bed. It was good to be home, she thought, as she watched them leave with fond eyes.

'Can I get anything else for you, Mum?' Lyn wanted to know later when they came for her empty cup. 'You can borrow one of my books if you like.'

'No, borrow one of Auntie V's,' Carol disagreed. 'They're not silly really, and she says they cheer her up.'

The thought wasn't appealing, but Desiree didn't have the heart to refuse. She found romantic novels boring, disliking the set-piece plots and the caricature of reality. She flicked through the books without enthusiasm, finding the style too bland for her liking. She put them down on the bedside table.

Her mind returned to John, but the resentment and sadness she still felt made her want to think of other things. Maybe V was right: maybe it was best to stick to a hero in a book. At least you'd never have to wash his dirty underpants, or grit your teeth when he rolled on you grunting like a pig because that was how he ended his evening out. She shook her head; it might be selfish but she didn't see why she should suffer because someone else made John suffer . . . as if she had no suffering of her own. Familiar depression crept up on her, and tiredness made the back of her neck ache.

With a sigh, Desiree slid further down into the bed, listening to the murmur of voices and the clatter of activity from the kitchen. She would feel better later. Her eyes felt weighed down, and she closed them to relieve the tension in her head, drifting off into an uneasy doze.

Verona looked at the clock on the wall, stretching slowly before drying the last spoon. It had been a good evening. Under her guidance, the children had made a cake for Desiree, and suppertime had almost turned into a party. It was nice to have Des back, a relief to see the genuine pleasure and enjoyment in her sister's face. She had been worried that John's thoughtlessness might have affected her more, but Des seemed determined not to let it get to her. Even so, Verona was still angry with him. She had told him about the girls' treat for their mother, asking him to be back in time; and he had promised, saying what a good idea it was. Since Desiree went into hospital, he had changed his mind about the children helping out. At first he had blustered about them not doing it if they didn't want to, but nowadays he seemed to have abandoned his objections. Verona shrugged the thought aside, her mind returning to the irritation of the moment. She should have guessed it was all talk. He was no different from other men when it came to it; character always came to look for them, forcing out their true colours.

She picked up the book she had left open in readiness on the kitchen surface, her mind plunging eagerly into it. She would read for a bit and then go to bed, she told herself, heading for the sitting-room.

> She was curled up on the sofa, her eyes still sleep-dazed, and she blinked uncomprehendingly up at him, feeling her bones melt at the slumbering fire that burned in his golden eyes.
>
> 'I . . . I must have fallen asleep,' she said huskily, appalled at how unsteady her voice was.
>
> He didn't answer, walking purposefully towards her. Leena shrank further into the yielding leather fabric, the tip of her tongue touching nervously against suddenly dry lips . . .

Verona wriggled back against the settee, uncrossing and crossing her legs as she turned the page.

His eyes fastened on the betraying movement. 'Don't do that,' he muttered hoarsely, coming down beside her, his powerful length trapping her slender form against the chair.

'No, Alberto,' she gasped.

'Yes!' he bit on an edge of violence.

Something quivered to life inside her . . .

The front door slammed shut, jolting her abruptly out of the story.

'Verona!'

She frowned. He would wake Desiree if he was not careful.

'Verona, where the hell you is? I hope my dinner ready on the table.'

She snapped the book shut, animosity boiling up in her. Who did he think he was flaming yelling at?

'What d'yer want, John?' she asked ungraciously, pretending she had not heard his shouted demand, as he came into the room.

'You know what I want . . . I want my dinner.'

'Where'd you leave it?' she asked innocently.

He looked as if he wanted to hit her, and she glowered defiantly at him. Let him try it, let him just try.

'Don't come it with me, you!' John almost shouted. 'I work all day and come here to find you clap on your backside and my dinner not cook . . . and is not the first time either.'

'I told you, John, I ain't no kitchen bitch . . . I did ask you to get back early and you agreed, so when you didn't come I never bother save nothing.'

'So what you suggest I do?'

She shrugged, unmoved, still resenting the interruption to her book. 'What other big people do, I suppose,' she said with indifference. 'Look after yourself.'

'What you saying to me?'

'John,' she said patiently, 'I agree to look after my nieces, as my sister ain't too well. Now and then I do a little something for you from kindness . . . but right now you could drop dead, see if I care.'

'This is my house you living in and you can't even grateful,' he blustered.

'For what? If I never look after the kids, you'd have to . . . and anyway, it's my sister house as well.'

He gave her a sour look. 'Is that what she been telling you? Well, let me just say this, is only one name on the mortgage papers.'

She knew he was trying to bluff her, and she shrugged again, getting up and moving past him to the door.

'The sooner you get moving, the sooner you get what you want, ain't it,' she said unsympathetically.

'I could beat you,' John yelled as she reached the stair.

Verona turned in amazement. 'Beat me!' She had to breathe hard to stop herself exploding. 'You lay one finger on me and I'll have the law on you so fast you won't know what hit you.'

He deflated visibly. 'Look, V, I'm sorry. I shouldn't have said that. Is just that things been real bad at work, and with Granny Ruby sick and needing this operation.'

Verona's mouth tightened and any compassion she might have felt evaporated. Granny Ruby again! The same old irritation came at her. If he wasn't doing one thing for his grandparents, it was something else; and to think that Mara practically had to shame him into visiting Des in hospital the second time. John had to accept that he had his own family now and couldn't keep expecting them to give up things in order that he could keep the old people.

'I don't want to hear no excuse,' Verona snapped, squashing down sympathy at how tired he looked.

John controlled himself with obvious effort. 'I wish you wouldn't be like that,' he coaxed. 'You used to like hearing about Granny Ruby and Grandpa Clifford – you'd like them, you know, especially Granny Ruby. I'm sure the two of you will get on well.'

'I ain't never going to get no money to go to no Jamaica, and if I had that money to burn I'd just as cheap go to Guyana anyway,' Verona dismissed.

'V,' his voice was hesitant and unsure, 'what if they was to come here?'

She gave him a speaking look. 'You needn't think you gonna dump no more dead weight on my sister.'

He sighed. 'Don't let we argue, no, and could you please get me some dinner?'

Verona hissed air through her teeth. 'No.'

'How come you such a bitch all of a sudden?'

'Yeah, go on, call me names,' she muttered angrily. 'Des was a real fool to marry a deadbeat like you. And I tell you this for nothing: you want food tonight, you get it! Goodnight, John. I'm off.'

She stomped angrily up the stairs, muttering all kinds of curses. He had totally ruined the mood of the evening as always. She had intended to have a good read, then a nice long soak in the bath, and John had to spoil it all.

'Men!'

Her mind turned to tomorrow. She was signing on in the morning, and on top of that she had to get rid of that god-awful old man. She shrugged resignedly. She wasn't going to think about that now; she would just finish reading her book while she waited for John to go to bed.

Verona popped her head around the kitchen door, pleased to see Desiree laughing and joking with Mara like old times.

She let herself out of the house, almost squaring her shoulders at the thought of Guy. Trust him to make life difficult. Why couldn't he just take no for an answer and leave, like all the others?

She had gone off Guy completely since the incident in Streatham, fobbing him off over and over in the hope that he would get the message and go. In the end she had told him outright, ringing him up after his third call in as many days to tell him it was over. Guy refused to accept it, phoning her almost daily, and in the end she agreed to see him, terrified that Desiree would start to realise what was happening.

She had arranged to meet him after signing on, at the usual place at eleven-thirty. She told him she was taking the morning off to go to the doctor's, not wanting him to know she had lost her job.

The queue at the benefit office seemed longer than ever and Verona shuffled along, tense and impatient, feeling the usual shame at being part of the shambling row. It was all very well to talk about three million unemployed, but she hated being one of the number. It seemed an age before the man on the other side of the glass partition found her papers. She scribbled her signature on the form, thrusting it back at him and almost snatching back her UB40. Her bus was rounding the corner and she puffed to the traffic lights, feeling thankful when they changed to red and she could scramble on.

He was standing by the bus-stop, looking cross.

'Sorry I'm late,' Verona said breathlessly, alighting before the bus had quite stopped. 'My doctor was running late.' She looked around cautiously, mindful that someone might more easily see her in the crowded daytime street.

'It's all right, love,' he said, relieved. 'I know what doctors' surgeries are like. How are you anyway?' He looked her over with approval. 'Did you know you've lost a bit of weight?'

She shrugged, recognising that he was trying to humour her. She bit down her irritation as he squeezed her tightly round the waist.

A black couple was coming towards them and Verona had to step closer to him for them to pass. The woman gave her a look of utter disdain, while the man regarded her in much the same disparaging way as Olu had done; then they were gone, and Verona pulled away from Guy.

'What's got into them?' he asked in annoyance, noticing the exchange of scornful looks. 'You done them something?'

'You could say that.' Verona's voice was full of irony. She felt shame that the unknown couple had seen her like this, and she hated them for the way they had summed her up and dismissed her as beneath contempt.

'Where would you like to go?' Guy asked cajolingly.

'Nowhere,' was Verona's blunt response. 'I just came to tell you I don't want you to keep ringing me no more.'

'You don't mean that, love,' he said confidently, hand moving back to her waist.

Verona pulled away brusquely. 'Guy, I'm warning you, you keep ringing my house and see if I don't tell your wife what kind of bloke you are.'

His jaw dropped, colour seeping into his face. 'You bleeding well won't,' he said finally, anger matching hers.

'You keep ringing my house and you'll find out,' she promised evenly.

He gave her a look of bitter dislike. 'It's them other Blacks, ain't it? It's just 'cause they don't like to see none of their own with Whites. You niggers are all the same, always stick together, ain't it?'

She wanted to hit out at him but realised the futility of it. 'At least it never cost you much, ain't it, just the odd meal and hotel room.' Her voice was still cold and even, hiding the well of revulsion she was feeling both for herself and Guy.

She watched him walk away, feeling that a weight had been lifted off her. 'Never again!' she vowed with the conviction she always felt at the end of a relationship. *I suppose in future I best look for somebody I don't have to feel too shame to be with.*

Her eyes fell on the sweetshop across the road and she decided on impulse to treat herself to some peardrops. Why not? Right now she needed something to take her mind off the unpleasant morning she had spent.

# Ten

'You sure I got enough onions in this?'

Desiree stretched her legs under the table and leaned back as Verona turned round, lowering the bowl of mince for her inspection.

'Yes, is how John like it.'

Verona's mouth thinned. 'Yeah, well, I ain't doing it for John, is just through the girls have to eat.'

Desiree half-smiled, eyes drifting back to the college prospectuses she was studying. 'Think I don't know?'

'Why you don't lie down for a bit?' Verona suggested, eyeing her. 'The doctor said you was to rest and take it easy, ain't it?'

'That was over two months ago, V. I'm fine now, honest.' She was beginning to be irritated by everyone's kindness. Even John was going out of his way to try to be helpful.

'Yeah, but you been really strung out since you did that exam and it's two weeks now. Anyway, I thought you said the exam went all right.'

'When I just finish it that was how I feel, but now I not too sure.'

Verona shrugged. 'You can take it again, can't you?'

Desiree nodded, feeling unconvinced. The Vauxhall exam had been worse than the one at Brixton. Not that it was any harder, just that she wanted Vauxhall badly. Her application to the college had initially been an act of defiance after yet another row with John and she had not really expected a response. When she had been invited for tests and interviews, she had nearly lost her nerve. It was Mara who had strengthened her determination.

'What you have to lose? Better get on while John think you still sick and he prepared to be reasonable.'

Surprisingly, John had been reasonable. Mara had spoken to him and, though she refused to tell Desiree what went on, his attitude changed from hostility to a patronising tolerance. Despite that, Desiree doubted she would have turned up for either of the exams if her friend hadn't gone with her. The Vauxhall exam had been in the afternoon and, dismissing her protests, Mara took the time off work to drive her there.

They had driven down in silence, Desiree becoming more tense and rattled the nearer they got to Vauxhall. The cold March winds didn't help her mood, rattling the car and chilling them despite Mara's inadequate heating. Desiree huddled further into her duffel coat, feeling more depressed as it started to rain. By the time they reached the college she was visibly shaking, the imposing annexe of South Bank Polytechnic dwarfing the site and making her feel small and insignificant.

'Nervous?' Mara asked as she parked outside the council estate at the end of a dead-end road.

Desiree nodded, swallowing hard. 'I can't do it, you know,' she confided shakily.

'Girl, don't talk nonsense. We have an hour, so you have plenty of time to pull yourself together.'

Mara refused to allow her to panic, dragging her off to a friend's house and plying her with coffee and biscuits. By the time she went in to the exams she felt a lot better, but she had been glad that Mara was waiting for her when it finished.

Desiree sighed, forcing her mind back to Verona and the meat; at least the activity had kept some of her depression at bay. She was so terrified of failing, and so on edge with the waiting for the result, there was little time to think of anything else.

The phone rang and Verona turned and looked around helplessly, hands sticky with seasoning.

'I'll get it,' Desiree said, moving towards the door.

It was Mara.

'Talk of the devil,' Desiree joked, 'I was just this minute thinking 'bout you.'

'Des, you can come over?' Mara's voice sounded tearful and strained, and Desiree stiffened in alarm.

'Mara, what's happened? What's the matter?'

'It's Jay. He been arrested.'

Desiree nearly dropped the phone. 'Arrested! What for?'

'I'm not sure . . . they ain't say, and they ain't let me see him either. I'm trying to get hold of Winston but he ain't in work.'

'Don't worry,' Desiree reassured her. 'I'll come straight away.'

'Can you get a taxi?' Mara's voice wobbled, then strengthened: 'Don't worry about the cost, I'll pay for it.'

'No, you won't, but I'll do that anyway.'

She put the phone down, surprised to see that her hands were shaking. *Jay arrested!* The words went round and round in her head. Mara's son was one of the nicest young people she knew. At seventeen he was small for his age, fine-boned like his mother, his eyes always thoughtful in his sensitive, intelligent face.

'Who was it?' Verona asked as she came back to the kitchen after dialling the local mini-cab firm.

'Mara,' Desiree answered, shrugging into her coat. 'The police done arrest Jay.'

'Jay! What for?'

'She don't know, they won't tell her.'

'Yeah, I bet is just from he's black, ain't it?'

Desiree gave her sister a thoughtful look. 'We got to get him out,' she said quietly. 'He got exams next month.'

Verona nodded. 'Listen, don't bother 'bout getting back, I'll see to the kids, and I'll make John his tea.'

There was a lot of traffic on the road, and Desiree fidgeted impatiently as the taxi slowed to a crawl at Crown Point. It edged slowly along, and she breathed with relief when they turned down Crown Lane. She was worried for Mara, impatient to get to her, stories of other people taken into police custody making her feel nervous and impotent.

Mara lived in a ground-floor conversion with three bedrooms and a garden in West Norwood, on one of those tree-lined streets near the main road that would not have been out of place in a more suburban setting. Desiree had gone with her to view it when she had been house-hunting, but for once the memory did not raise a smile.

Neither of them had been in Norwood before, having to find it on John's *A to Z* map. Mara had not long passed her driving test and was still at the stage when road signs often passed unnoticed, so they had lurched round the elaborate one-way system several times before stopping at the imposing new red-brick bus garage and asking for directions. Even so it had taken them several wrong turns to find the quiet residential street, so unexpected after the frenetic rush of traffic to Croydon and Crystal Palace. Mara had fallen in love with the flat, liking the large, marble fireplace, something she had always wanted, and the long, narrow garden with the glassless greenhouse at the far end. It had obviously been well tended once, and not even months of neglect could quite eclipse the striking display of the herbaceous borders.

Mara had been lucky with her flat, having bought it quite

cheaply just before prices started to rise. Desiree liked the street. There were several black families there, many of whom had moved from Brixton when prices there got too high; and most of them were friendly, unlike the sprinkling where she lived.

The flat was bright and airy, and Desiree envied Mara the African cloth prints on the walls. She liked the feeling of space and the soothing shadows after the bright glare of the sun.

'I rang the police again,' Mara said in a panic as soon as she opened the door for her. 'They say he mugged one old woman.'

'Come and sit down,' Desiree said. 'You look all done in.' She was shocked at her friend's appearance. Mara's usually bright face was puffy from crying, and her hair was a spiky mess where she had been pulling at it. 'Let me just put the kettle on; we can talk while you drinking some tea.'

She watched Mara drink the tea, glad to see that her hands weren't shaking too much.

'I shouldn't ought to be here drinking tea when they could be doing anything to my son,' Mara said distractedly.

'Rushing down there again won't do no good,' Desiree cautioned.

'What I going to do?' Mara asked. 'I trying to get Winston all two hours now but he ain't in work.'

Desiree felt out of her depth, searching her memory for what John used to do when one of the kids at the youth club got arrested.

'First we gon need a solicitor,' she said, trying to sound more positive than she felt. 'I'll ring the Law Centre and leave a message for Winston.' She was itemising things on her fingers as she thought of them. 'You got the number for Charleen and Meeli school?'

Mara rummaged in her bag for her address book, handing it over at the proper page. 'What you going to do?'

'I going to get them to tell Charleen that she and Meeli must go round our house. That way you don't have that worry. She got money?'

Mara nodded.

Desiree went systematically through her list, mentally ticking items off as they were done. She dared not think beyond those things, lest the feeling of being overwhelmed crowded in on her again. She wondered what they were going to do down at the police station. She had never been to one before, and the thought of it scared her.

The police station was crowded. As they sat together on the long bench in the ante-room, Desiree eyed the electronic doors suspiciously, feeling trapped and boxed-in when it was their turn to go through. To her surprise the man behind the station desk was friendly, listening politely as Mara explained that she was there about her son. The two women exchanged worried glances as the man disappeared into the main body of the station.

'Do you think Olu got in touch with they aready?' Mara asked anxiously.

'He said he going to get on to them straight away. I sure it will make a difference,' Desiree added with false confidence.

'I'm afraid he's still being interviewed,' the policeman said as he returned. He looked a little less friendly now and Desiree's heart sank.

'Can they do that when he don't have no lawyer with him?' she asked suspiciously.

'Who are you?' the policeman wanted to know.

'This is my sister,' Mara said promptly. 'Look, can we at least see him?'

'Sorry, miss, we can't allow that.'

'Why not?' she asked desperately. 'You know he innocent . . . it's through he's a black youth, isn't it?'

The man flushed a painful red, looking young and spiteful. 'Hey, watch what you're saying. I might just bleeding arrest you too.'

'Come on, Mara,' Desiree said apprehensively, putting an arm around her friend, 'you just playing his foolish game.'

The man looked angry. 'Is there anything else?' he asked shortly, all pretence of politeness stripped away, leaving naked contempt.

'Has he got a solicitor with him?' Desiree asked.

'Yeah . . . real hard that one; wouldn't say anything till his brief came.'

He made Jay sound like a seasoned criminal and Desiree forced back angry words as she saw the look of challenge in the hard blue eyes.

'Can they just keep him lock up in there like that?' Desiree burst out when they were on the street again.

Mara shook her head mutely.

'At least Olu is in there with him.' Desiree attempted to be consoling. 'And Jay had enough sense not to talk to them on his own.'

'I taught him that, you know,' Mara said distantly, sounding shell-shocked. 'But I never think it could happen to Jay. Des, he so quiet . . . why they want to do this to he?'

Desiree had no answer. 'Let we go back to my place,' she said gently. 'You can stay for a bit, and then see how you feel.'

Mara pulled herself together with a visible effort. 'No, I got to see Winston. He in with BUF – they must do something.'

Desiree agreed, eager to go along with anything positive.

Winston was on the phone when they arrived, sitting behind the reception desk and lolling back with accustomed ease. He looked up abstractedly, waving them to the moulded grey plastic seats in front of the desk he was manning.

Desiree looked around, noticing with interest the cramped, badly decorated room and the various leaflets on the overflowing wall rack. She had never been to the Law Centre before and she wondered if other people found its cheerless bleakness as depressing as she did.

'What's this about Jay?' Winston asked sharply, his face serious as soon as he came off the phone.

'The police done pick he up,' Mara said tonelessly.

'Have they still got him? Did they say why?'

Mara's voice was wobbly again: 'They said he mugged an old lady and stole two hundred pounds from a house.'

Winston looked stunned. 'Is the Territorial Support Unit up in Norwood?'

Desiree felt as blank as Mara looked.

'Is the police arrested he,' Mara repeated.

Winston shifted his skinny frame, scratching his scalp through neat shoulder-length locks, his free hand stroking his well-trimmed beard. 'Where is he,' he asked with brisk practicality. 'Gypsy Hill or Streatham?'

'Neither,' Mara answered. 'He was on his way down Oxford Street to get that leather jacket he was saving for.'

'Have you been to the station?'

'We just coming from down there but they wouldn't let us see him.'

'Has he got a solicitor?'

Mara said: 'Olu is down there with him.'

Winston nodded. 'Right.'

Desiree cleared her throat, sensing that he had come to the end of his questions. 'You sure you can't do something?' she asked hesitantly. 'Can't BUF take it up . . . do something?'

Winston had been frowning as she spoke, but now his face cleared. 'You know, that idea not bad,' he said with slow consideration. 'The Babylon been downpressing the youth them a long time, but this new wave of criminalisation is something man haffe stand and fight.'

'I don't want no meeting or no march,' Mara said flatly, blowing her nose. 'I just want my son out of there 'fore they kill he.'

'Don't be so backward,' Winston said impatiently. 'Is through we don't stand and fight why they do these things, you no see it? We have to stand up as united and show them they can't do these things, seen?'

'What the use in that if they brain-damage him like they did that little youth last Christmas?' she asked tearfully.

Desiree was surprised by Mara's lack of enthusiasm. She was usually the first to encourage action, hating the idea of too much talk. Yet here she was actively discouraging Winston from taking up something that could stop what was happening to kids like Jay.

'Of course, I'll have to take it to the party first and see if they want to take it on.'

'What?' Desiree couldn't prevent the exclamation. 'I thought you –'

'There's a lot of other important struggles,' he interrupted. 'You have to realise that we can't use up our energies on just anything, Des.'

Mara gave a disgusted sniff. 'Yeah, what with the Palestinians and the Irish question still burning issues,' she said bitterly, 'wouldn't do to put too much energy into a couple a kids getting brutalised, would it?'

'Come off it, Mara, I think that's bloody unfair.'

'Ain't that always the case? Oh, come on, Des, we got to get back in case Olu ring.'

'What skank you pulling now?' Winston asked, aggrieved.

Mara gave him a disparaging look, heading for the door. 'You go have your meeting, Winston, I going to get my son out of that place.'

Desiree had forgotten her house keys and Verona let them in the front door.

'Some bloke phoned for you, Mara, said he think he can get Jay out the police station,' she reported anxiously.

'Did he give his name?'

'Yeah, but I never catch it. He sounded African but I ain't too sure.'

'Where are the kids?' Desiree asked, registering how quiet it was as she gently prodded Mara forward.

'The big ones are upstairs doing homework, and Meeli is in the kitchen driving me bonkers and reading her story book. She's real good at reading, ain't it? Can scarce believe she's only six.'

'Jay teach her,' Mara said absently.

Verona's eyes were sympathetic. 'Tell you what: you go in the front room and I'll make a pot of tea,' she suggested, helping Desiree to usher Mara in the right direction. 'The kids ain't no trouble.'

Desiree was grateful for her sister's tact in taking Mara's coat and leaving them together. 'You must try and take your mind off it,' she told her friend gently as soon as the door closed.

Mara nodded like an automaton, sitting stiffly on the edge of John's usual chair.

Desiree felt herself faltering after introducing yet another subject to discuss and watching it peter out because of her friend's lack of interest. She searched for something to take

Mara's mind off Jay, for a short time at least. When the front bell rang, she sprang to her feet as though reprieved, yelling to Verona that she would get it. She needed a little break from the tension around Mara. Her head was aching and her belly still itched at a spot where the wound hadn't fully healed.

The man at the door was tall, with a cool ebony complexion that attracted a second look and undeniably Nigerian features. He seemed tired but triumphant, moving aside to let the slim youth step in front of him.

'Jay!' Desiree hugged the startled youth before he could protest. 'Thank goodness! Come let we go see your mum – she going be real pleased.'

Hearing her exclamation, Mara and Verona came out, Mara stumbling forward to hold her son tightly, Verona watching with relief in her eyes.

Mara wiped away her tears with the back of her hand. 'Oh, Des, you ain't met Olu, have you?'

'No.' Desiree smiled a welcome. 'Come in, you must think we don't have no manners.'

He gave a courteous denial, accepting her invitation with gratitude.

Verona froze as the light fell full on his face. This had to be her worst nightmare coming true. Her heart pumping, she retreated hastily into the kitchen, praying that Olu had not recognised her, that Mara hadn't mentioned she was Des's sister that day they had met her with Guy.

'That's all I need,' she muttered to herself, frowning as she contemplated Meeli's neatly plaited head bent studiously over her book.

The little girl looked up solemn-eyed. Darker than Mara, she had inherited most of her features, with the smooth skin texture of her father. 'Can I read my *Popples* comic now?' she asked appealingly.

'When you finish the book.' Verona's mind was only half on the child.

'I finished already.'

Verona blinked at her. 'Yeah, all right, but make sure you put your books away neat.'

The child nodded vigorously, her voice rising on a well of generosity now that she had got what she wanted: 'I'll put them all away neatly, and I'll never, never be naughty again . . . and can I eat one of my sweeties?'

'Yes!' Verona sighed with resignation. God, she could talk! Meeli hadn't stopped until she sat her at the kitchen table and thrust the book in front of her, after rescuing the older girls from her constant chatter.

'And can I play with my Care Bear after, and do some cutting-out?'

'Tell you what, Meeli,' Verona said with forced patience. 'You read your *Popples* comic, and we'll wait and see how good you are, ain't it?'

'Can I have something to eat? Some Mr Men cheese and –'

'We don't have Mr Men cheese, ain't I said that? You can have grated cheese and biscuit.'

'I don't feel hungry again,' the little girl said, getting off her chair just as Desiree came in.

'Hello, Meeli.'

'Auntie Des! Is my Mummy here?'

Desiree nodded.

'And Jay is?'

Verona heaved a massive sigh when the child ran out eagerly. 'Does she always talk like that?'

Desiree grinned. 'Meeli can out-talk anybody, but she really sweet with it . . . Well, you coming in, then?'

'I thought I'd make us all another cuppa,' Verona said quickly, moving to fill the kettle. 'What happened?'

Desiree leaned against the work-surface. 'They give him bail, but he have to go to court.'

'Yeah? You mean they charged him?'

'Yes: assault and burglary.'

Slow anger started inside Verona, the frustration that always came when she saw how black kids were treated. 'But he never did nothing, ain't it?'

'I got the feeling they didn't business with that. Is just through the money he had on him,' Desiree said.

'What money?'

'About a hundred and fifty pounds. Mara say he been saving up for a leather jacket in his building society, and she ask him to buy her a pair of shoes she saw in the sales. Jay said they just came on the tube, pull him off. When they see the money, they just start to abuse him. Look, they still discussing it in there. Why you don't go in and I'll make the tea?'

Verona wanted to refuse, but she couldn't without raising Desiree's suspicions. 'I'll just check on the girls first,' she tried.

'No, leave them; they not causing trouble – is best not to disturb them.'

Verona pushed the door open with trepidation, wishing she could slip in without being noticed.

'V, thanks for looking after them,' Mara said as soon as she entered. Meeli was on her lap, head buried in a comic, lips moving over the words she was reading.

'That's all right,' Verona murmured, sidling to the far end of the settee, not daring to raise her eyes. 'They weren't no problem. Charleen always make the other two get on with their homework.' Glancing at Jay, she noticed his glasses were missing. 'You all right?' she asked awkwardly.

'They broke my glasses,' he said in disgust, 'and they took my money.'

'Jay's been charged with burglary and assault,' Olu said evenly, forcing Verona to look at him. She steeled herself, expecting the same contempt as in Streatham, her heart hammering at the thought that he might refer to it.

'Yeah, they kept saying I been mugging old ladies and breaking into houses,' the youth said, offended, fear and uncertainty also in his voice.

'Did the policeman beat you up?' Meeli asked into the silence. 'Charleen say they kill black people like in South Africa.'

Mara looked horrified. 'Meeli, I want you to go and stay with your sister,' she ordered sternly, 'and don't go bothering them.'

The little girl nodded obligingly, sliding off her lap. 'And don't let the policeman trouble Jay again,' she ordered importantly, before trotting out of the room.

'That child hears too much,' Mara sighed.

'Maybe it doesn't do any harm for her to know what kind of place she's growing up in,' Olu suggested.

Desiree came back with the tea, and Verona was relieved that no mention had been made of her date with Guy. She sat listening with increasing anger as Jay recounted how he had been kicked and punched, and how the police had told him they wouldn't let him go until he confessed.

'I didn't tell them nothing,' he said triumphantly. 'I remembered what Mum and Olu says about not talking to them if you don't have no solicitor.'

'Now we need to do a few practical things,' Olu inserted calmly. 'Jay, those two friends you were with, did you say they were going to get names and addresses of witnesses?'

'Yeah, they shouted out they'd do that.'

'Good.' Olu was writing in a notebook. 'Can we get in touch with them?'

Jay nodded.

Verona couldn't help admiring the solicitor's efficiency. He seemed to know exactly what to do, and her earlier resentment of him faded a little. *Maybe if I knew about people like him, I wouldn't have signed that paper*, she thought wistfully.

'Right, I'll get on to this lot,' Olu said, standing up. 'I'll see you tomorrow, Jay, and we can work out details of what to do. Desiree, will you and Mara chase up those kids?'

Desiree nodded, feeling a sudden rush of achievement. It was years since someone had asked her to do anything so important.

Mara said, 'I'll see you to the door, Olu,' following him out.

'Is Charleen upstairs?' Jay asked, peering short-sightedly at the door.

'She's in the girls' room,' Desiree said.

As Jay wandered off, Verona asked: 'What'll happen to him?'

Desiree shook her head: 'I not sure. From what Olu say, the police case not strong . . . they was probably hoping to squeeze a confession outa him.'

'Is Olu Mara's boyfriend?' Verona asked tentatively.

'No, he just a friend. He done cases for her centre, when a couple of the youths got arrested for burglary.'

Mara had scarcely got back into the sitting-room when the sound of a key in the front door told them John was home.

Verona frowned. 'He's early. I thought he was doing overtime today.'

Desiree nodded, but made no response as John came into the room.

'What's this about the Babylon arresting Jay?' he asked, moving to his favourite chair and dropping into it.

'How did you find that out?' Mara asked.

'Winston come by on his way to BUF. He was going to bring it up at the meeting, and he ask me to come down.' John paused. Then he added: 'Look, Des, I was going to leave work early anyway. Is my grandmother, yeah . . .'

If he seemed somewhat uneasy and on edge Desiree didn't notice; as far as she was concerned, he appeared laughably self-important.

'I thought you don't have no time for those meetings any more,' she said.

'You know, but this is something that affect all o' we; from them start downpressing the youth, is not the future them attacking?'

She wanted to say that they were oppressing the youth all the time; but she knew so little about it. Until today it had just been something on the edge of her mind, like immigration and bad housing. Somehow it had never seemed real; it didn't happen to the people she knew. She felt ashamed at how little she had really cared.

'I'll just get something to eat and then we can go,' John said to Mara. Since Desiree came out of hospital, he had begun serving his own meals, as if she might not get better if he didn't help out.

'Where exactly "we" supposed to be going?' Mara wanted to know.

'To the meeting. Winston said I should bring you and Jay down. The girls can stay here with Des.'

'I'm not going anywhere, John. I'm fed up of the BUF lot – all you know is talk. When it come to doing something you don't even know it need doing.'

'That ain't fair,' John denied heatedly. 'When that bloke got beaten up last year and everything, ain't we have that march and organise that picket?'

'Look, I not going spend hours talking about what I aready know, and I ain't have no intention of marching around like idiot while they sending my son to prison. So you go do your marching while I do what I can to make sure he don't get convicted for saving to buy a leather jacket.'

'I think I going to come along.' Desiree hadn't meant to say that though she realised she did want to go. She found Mara's attitude puzzling. Surely it wasn't right to judge the whole organisation by one person. When John had been active in the party, he had done a lot of things – selling papers and going on demonstrations, even helping to organise meetings.

'You!' John was surprised. 'Why you want to go down to BUF?'

'Because Jay is my friend son,' she said quietly. 'Anyway you all should try get ordinary people along, 'stead of always putting them off.'

'It ain't that,' he said, 'just that I ain't been down there for a bit, and I don't know what the policy is now.'

'The same as always,' Mara said drily: 'he who has the biggest voice speaks loudest.'

'I wouldn't mind tagging along as well,' Verona put in.

'That all right,' Mara said. 'Lyn and Carol can come round by me and go to school from there tomorrow.'

'You not serious!' John exclaimed.

'Sure thing,' Mara said. 'I think they wasting they time, but if Des and V want to go, I don't see why they shouldn't.'

'Well, I suppose I can't stop them,' John agreed grudgingly.

'Damn right,' Verona muttered under her breath.

# Eleven

The meeting was held in Winston's house in the heart of Balham. When Desiree and Verona arrived with John, there were about a dozen people lolling around on a seven-seater corner unit, new since Mara left. The place reeked of prosperity and ganja smoke and Desiree felt uncomfortable and out of place in the stifling atmosphere. John was soon swallowed up in a little group by the door, Winston at the centre with his two sidekicks, Longers and Beeny, looking ridiculously self-important as they stuck close to him.

Verona and Desiree sat on an African-print floor cushion beside a hostile-looking woman who pointedly turned her back on them while joining eagerly in a discussion about the role of the African woman. Desiree squeezed Verona's hand as she felt her squirm with pique beside her. The atmosphere was bound to be better once the meeting was over. After all, they weren't here to socialise, just to do something about Jay.

After what Winston had said earlier at the Law Centre, she was surprised when he called everyone to attention. He chaired the meeting and, as the evening wore on, it was obvious that he was firmly in charge.

Verona and Desiree shifted restlessly in mounting frustration as the meeting meandered from one discussion to another. Having never been to a radical meeting before, Desiree was a little disappointed, realising why Mara had been so sceptical. But it was when they started talking about a joint Northern Ireland Solidarity March that Verona finally exploded.

'I never came here to listen to no politics about Northern Ireland,' she said. 'You talk all kind of crap 'bout the youth and that, then 'bout marching round like a bunch of idiots – I don't see no Irish doing nothing for no black kids. Come to think of it, I don't see nobody doing nothing, not even you bunch of jokers.'

There was stunned silence in the room and Desiree wanted the floor to swallow her up as all eyes turned to them. Winston's thin face was tight with rage, and she didn't dare look at John, sure he would be equally angry.

Winston leaned back on the dining-chair he had insisted on using, his wiry body reflecting his contempt. 'Ah, Verona,' he drawled pityingly, 'is nice to see you not reading that white trash you like so much.' He paused, and his audience did not disappoint him, though the laughter was a little strained. 'But you must be prepared to be guided by wiser, more conscious people, sister.'

Verona hissed through her teeth. 'Don't be so stupid – you go on like you is some leader or something, but I don't see no ordinary people like me here.' There was a titter of laughter. 'Yeah, go on, laugh,' she snapped angrily, 'see if I care. You ain't nothing, none of you! As for you, Winston, if you is such a big-shot, how come Mara leave you and get more education than you?'

'No stupid woman ain't insulting me and getting away with it!' Winston was all bluster now, jumping to his feet threateningly.

'Yeah, you big with me, ain't it?' Verona sneered. 'But that's through I'm black – you always was ready to attack black people, specially those that really doing something or don't 'fraid of white people. That's why you lot always quarrelling with everybody else and attacking all them black people minding their own business. If you too scared to do nothing about what's happening to the kids out on the street, why don't you just say so?'

Desiree closed her eyes and prayed. Winston's temper was notorious, especially when his bravery was questioned. Like several of BUF's members, he used to belong to the Socialist Workers' Party, leaving to organise and lead black people when the white people wouldn't take them seriously; and in common with many radicals-come-lately, he was very touchy, convinced as he was that his apprenticeship in the white left made him superior to black people and their natural leader.

It was Longers who intervened, talking urgently to Winston, persuading him to sit down and then turning to Verona:

'Sister, you are not a member of the organisation, so you have to follow the procedure for non-members if you want to speak.' He went on to outline the appropriate procedure, while the others nodded in approval and Winston gazed at her with disdain clearly visible on his face.

Verona tapped her foot impatiently, her large bulk swaying gently with the rhythm, and Desiree dared a glance at John. He looked thunderous and she ducked her gaze, knowing she would not hear the end of it that night.

'I not interested in no procedure,' Verona said dismissively as Longers came to the end of his tortuous explanation. 'All I hear is yak, yak, yak. We know what you saying already; what we don't know is what to do. Can't you even organise some solicitors or something? Ain't there no way to complain to your MP or the papers and that?'

They laughed her to scorn.

'Some of us has been in the struggle for years, and for your information I know more about how hopeless the legal situation is than anyone here,' Winston said patronisingly, looking sure of himself again.

'Yeah?' Verona's hands came to rest on her ample hips. 'Then how come is Olu had to get Jay out of prison cause you was too shit-scared of the police, eh?'

'Some of us don't sell out yet,' Winston countered. 'If you want to raise your consciousness, sister, you have to get rid of that know-it-all attitude and those white values of yours.'

Verona shrugged. 'I ain't staying here to listen to no more crap. I might as well go and read my white trash – saves me hearing it secondhand.'

There was an uncomfortable silence as she marched to the door, and for a moment Desiree was too shocked to move.

The slamming of the door shifted her and she ignored John's warning glance as she scrambled after her sister. She agreed with everything Verona had to say, and more. God, people like Winston made her sick. Everyone knew he had never looked at a black woman until Mara, thinking them beneath his intelligence . . . and then look what he had tried to do to her friend.

She caught up with Verona at the end of the street. Her sister was walking fast and breathing hard from the unaccustomed exertion.

'God, Des, I dunno what came over me in there. Me legs ain't half shaking,' Verona confessed as Desiree came alongside.

Desiree hugged her. 'You were right, you know. I don't know much more about them things than you, but I did want to say something like that.'

John had not come with them so they walked along, full of sudden high spirits, giggling at his reaction to Verona's words.

'You should've seen his face,' Desiree said, choking back the laughter. 'I thought he was going to have a fit.'

Verona grinned. 'I ain't half glad I never look. God, I just saw red! I mean, I ain't saying they shouldn't join other people and that . . . but nobody not doing nothing for black people, is just everybody using idiots like Winston to use us, ain't it?'

John was not back until late. Desiree was just finishing tidying the kitchen as he came in. She stiffened as she heard his key in the door, expecting him to be in a foul mood. Instead he came in looking preoccupied and uneasy. She was puzzled, especially when he tried to engage her in conversation, even though his mind was obviously elsewhere. He made no attempt to bring up Verona's outburst, content to indulge in stilted conversation about the children and Jay.

After half an hour, still puzzled by his strange behaviour, she left him with a cup of tea and two slices of the Jamaican hardough bread he was so fond of. Somehow, she got the feeling he was trying to humour her, almost like a small child softening the effect of bad behaviour.

It was after twelve when his heavy tread on the stairs pulled her out of the drifting relaxation of pre-sleep.

The familiar sounds of him preparing for bed were oddly soothing and she moved lazily as the mattress depressed beside her.

'Des, you sleeping?'

'Mmm?'

'I got a letter from Jamaica yesterday.' John was peering anxiously at her through the faint glow from the streetlight outside.

She frowned, the last wisps of sleep clearing away at the premonition that he must have bad news. He often received letters from Jamaica. One of his three brothers still lived there with his grandparents and they kept in regular touch. Also, he had lived there for his first eighteen years and still kept contact with many friends. Desiree often envied him that, wishing she could have maintained some link with Guyana. But it was unusual for him to mention his letters like this and with such strain in his voice.

'Is anything the matter?' she asked, coming closer to him.

'Granny Ruby and Grandpa Clifford coming . . . for a visit.'

'John, that's great!' In her excitement she missed the slight pause in his words. 'I've always wanted to meet them – when are they coming?'

He cleared his throat. 'Well, I thought I'd warn you to get things ready, seen? Yeah, and V could move in with the kids little time, no true?'

Desiree looked at him suspiciously, his evasiveness finally registering. 'When they coming, John?'

'Well, the plane landing about ten-thirty tomorrow morning.'

'What!' She was wide awake now.

'Well . . . I suppose I shoulda mention it from the last letter, but they wasn't sure till three weeks ago that Granny Ruby would be well enough to travel, and it did take nearly three weeks for this letter to reach.'

'Why you don't tell me they thinking of coming over?' she demanded. 'And what you expecting V to do with all her books?'

He bristled at the implied criticism. 'Something wrong with the bin?' From his defensiveness she sensed there was more to it than he had let on.

'Wait a minute,' she said on a sudden thought. 'Granny Ruby and Grandpa Clifford been going to the States to visit your brothers for so long . . . why they want to come here so sudden?'

'Papa spend twenty years of him life in England, why his father can't come?' He sounded cornered and aggressive.

'I don't say they can't come. I just think it's strange, is all.'

'Well, if you must know, Granny Ruby need an operation and it's too expensive in the States,' he volunteered grudgingly.

'So who's paying for it?' Desiree asked, on a note of rising alarm. 'John, is a lot of money for people who don't live here to have operation since the Conservatives come in government, you know.'

'This government racist, you think I can forget that?'

*Not reading that trash you call a newspaper*, she thought, remembering the copy of the *Sun* he had fished out on his return from the meeting. She had made out the word BLACKS in bold print in the headline and it didn't take much imagination to guess the nature of the content. She wondered sadly if he even noticed the contradictions . . . to think he would once have been in the vanguard calling for a boycott of that paper.

'I never suggest you forget the government racist, I just wondered where the money coming from to buy expensive operation for your grandmother.'

'Is aright, we don't have to find all of it.'

'How *much* we have to find?'

'About a hundred pounds. Grandpa Clifford bringing most of the rest . . . Junior and Delroy send it from America; and Carley paying their fare.'

'John, how you expecting me to manage two old people when I don't even know nothing 'bout them?' Her voice was quiet in the silence.

'Noh you just say you wanted them to come?'

'When I say that, I never know they were practically on we doorstep.'

'So what you want me to tell them . . . don't come?'

'I never said that.' She hung on to her temper with an effort.

'I shoulda hope so too. My grandparents them mean a lot to me. Is them raise me, yeah, so I expect you to make sure and show them a good time.'

'You don give your orders? Anything you forget?' she asked sarcastically.

'Yes . . . you can do something 'bout your renking sister for a start. I don't expect her to disrespect me and shame me again like she do tonight.'

Desiree smiled, thankful that the darkness hid her expression. She had known his reasonableness was too good to be true, especially as Verona's outburst earlier must have embarrassed him. He looked up to Winston, and the other man would surely have taken out his humiliation on John.

His annoyed voice interrupted her reflections: 'You listening or what?'

Desiree brought her attention back. 'V didn't mean to upset you.'

'Who's talking about that?' he asked, in a voice that told her it was exactly what he had been referring to. 'It's her whole attitude, know what I mean? She ain't pulling her weight, seen, and you can't expect me to deal with that and everything else as well.'

Desiree sucked air through her teeth. 'Leave V out of this!' she snapped. 'My sister is nothing to you.'

'Oh yeah! So what she doing in my house nyaming out my food?'

'You did have another story to tell when she was cooking it. It's just through she don't let you step on her. When you going realise you can't keep doing that, John?'

'What you mean?' he taunted, now that he heard her anger: 'Women are all the same, they love it.'

'If that's a joke, I not laughing,' she said evenly, turning over and presenting her back to him.

# Twelve

'What time the old people getting here?' Mara asked the following evening as she came down the stairs after she had finished preparing the bedroom for them.

Desiree was opening the front door to her sister and the question was swallowed up as Verona entered, saying penitently: 'Sorry, Des; forgot me keys, didn't I? Oh, hello, Mara,' she added, 'I never expect to see you here.'

Mara smiled. She had lost the drawn look of the day before, which was as well considering the new tensions created by the imminent arrival of John's grandparents. Desiree was relieved that Olu had phoned to say they had managed to contact the witnesses to Jay's arrest who were willing to give evidence. 'Des asked me to come over to help settle John's grandparents in,' Mara explained to Verona, 'not that running a black elderly luncheon club gives me no qualification for the job.'

'Come off it,' Desiree teased, 'you know how well you get on with old people.'

Verona's mouth thinned as she listened to their banter. 'I think it's a real liberty him dumping them on Des like that, especially as she's not long out of hospital.'

'Is months I been out of hospital,' Desiree protested, hoping that Verona wouldn't take one of her dislikes to the old couple.

Mara might have been thinking the same thing: 'Don't go take set on them, V,' she warned, 'you can't blame them because John so thoughtless.'

'Are the kids all right?' Desiree asked Mara, to forestall argument; she really regretted that V had been too young to remember their own grandmother, and she made up her mind that Granny Ruby and Grandpa Clifford would be made welcome in the house.

'Lyn said she's going to read for another fifteen minutes and Carol's finishing her maths homework,' Mara reported. She sat beside Desiree at the kitchen table and repeated her earlier question: 'What time they getting here?'

'About nine-thirty.' Desiree glanced at the hall clock which was showing a quarter past nine. 'The plane delay two times, so they running late.'

'I'll make some tea, shall I?' Verona suggested, filling the kettle. Her stomach growled with appreciation as the smell of the lamb escaped from the pot. 'You eaten?' she asked of no one in particular.

'No. We ought to wait till the old people come,' Desiree said firmly.

Verona sighed. 'They probably won't feel like no food,' she muttered ungraciously, reaching for the breadbin.

'Don't eat too much of that,' Desiree cautioned, 'you don't want to keep filling yourself up with stodge, you know, V.'

The sound of a car pulling to a halt caused instant tension, the slamming of car doors loud in the sudden silence in the kitchen.

Desiree's stomach churned with nerves. 'Is them,' she whispered, rubbing her palms against her thin summer skirt. 'V, you sure you clean everything out your room?'

'Everything,' her sister assured her.

'Do you mind, V?' Mara asked. 'About giving up your room like that?'

'Didn't have much choice, did I?' Bitterness edged Verona's voice.

Mara chose her words carefully: 'Look, V . . . Jay offering to stay round he auntie's for a while if you want to use his room.'

Verona was touched and she felt tempted to accept. She was still upset about being turfed out for these people, and only the knowledge that she had no job had prevented her walking out this morning when she heard the news. She sensed her sister's anxiety now, knew that Des wanted her to stay.

'I'll bear it in mind in case,' she said gratefully to Mara, 'but I think Des might need some help, you know, what with the kids and John's grandparents and all. Tell Jay I say thanks anyway.'

Desiree smiled appreciation. 'Thanks, V . . . but if is what you want, you go, hear. I couldn't blame you after the way we treat you over the room.'

The front door opened, preventing a response.

'Desiree . . . come meet Granny Ruby and Grandpa Clifford,' John's voice came through to the kitchen.

Desiree looked panic-stricken.

'Go on,' Mara encouraged, 'I bet you'll like them.'

'You all don't understand,' Desiree protested. 'I never have nothing to do with old people since Papa mother died when I was eleven.'

Verona was putting a low fire under the pots. 'You'll be okay,' she said bracingly. The kettle whistled and she turned it off. 'If all else fails, you can always offer them a cuppa.'

'Come with me, V, *please*,' Desiree begged, as the activity in the passage told them the arrivals had moved into the living-room.

'Go on, V,' Mara urged, 'at least it will get her out of here.'

'Okay,' Verona said with resignation, 'but we'd better go, or John'll start bringing the roof down.'

The first thing Verona noticed was how the frail old man sat protectively beside the wheelchair . . . *Wheelchair!* She felt her jaw drop, Desiree's tension telling her it was as much of a surprise to her. Granny Ruby couldn't walk.

She saw the shifty look in John's eyes and swallowed bitter words. How the hell did he expect the old lady to get up and down their steep stairs?

The old man looked at her gravely, his face lined with suffering and history yet full of humour and compassion. His eyes moved to Verona, their sharpness suddenly full of mischief, then back to Desiree.

'Come here, man, mek me look on de ooman Jahn manage fe capture. Come in de light,' he urged when she hesitated, 'me eyesight not so good no more.'

Desiree moved forward reluctantly, and Verona hovered behind her, wondering if she shouldn't leave. She would have liked to sit down but the other chair was heaped with bags and John was sprawled across the settee. She didn't want to remonstrate with him in front of the old people.

Grandpa Clifford held out his hands, taking Desiree's in them. 'I is very pleased to mek your acquaintance. I hear a lot 'bout you from de rascal you married to and I hope we visit doan inconvenience you.'

'No, not at all,' she said hastily, and he gave her a shrewd look as she added: 'The children can't wait to meet you.'

'Likewise here,' he said drily. 'Ruby, this is Melba son wife.'

Raising her leathery face, the old woman studied Desiree before turning her attention to Verona. 'So who dat in de background?' she asked directly. 'Come, Miss, come mek me say howdy.'

Verona felt even more awkward, not knowing how to take the abrupt tone. She stood uncertainly a few feet away. 'Hello,' she said lamely.

'Bwoy, what a way England people unfriendly.' The old woman shook her head, a twinkle in her eyes taking the sting out of her words. 'I suppose is true we just meet. I waan something to eat, England Miss – no, not you,' she corrected when Desiree made a move, 'I want dis miss fe get it. De way dat plane food favour horse and dawg I did as good starve dan eat it and get pain a belly.'

She turned to her grandson: 'Jahn, bring de big blue grip, de one I tell you cousin Mavis send gi we from Canada.'

John got up and moved steadily to the door.

'Mind you doan drop it,' Granny Ruby cautioned as he hurried to put it on the floor in front of her. 'Dat bang belly bwoy a Kingston airport make it fall pon Clifford foot, nearly mash off ihm big toe.' She leaned back satisfied, then noticed that Verona was still there, blinking with surprise. 'You no go get de food gi me?'

'I'm sorry,' Verona apologised, recovering. She had been so fascinated by watching John jump to attention, she'd clean forgotten the old woman's request. Now she couldn't wait to get to the kitchen to report back to Mara.

'You should see the way John's granny is ordering him

about,' she burst out as soon as she opened the door, 'and she's in a wheelchair at that!'

Mara looked up from stirring the pot, face lighting with amusement as Verona added: 'The way he was jumping about you wouldn't believe he was the same he-man John.'

'What's she like?' Mara asked.

'She's dead old,' Verona said frankly, fetching two plates from the dresser, 'both of them are – but they seem real nice.' She frowned.

'What's the matter?'

'I was just wondering what she's going to do when John ain't here. Her husband could never take her up and down them stairs and I can't see her stuck upstairs all day somehow.'

'He going to have to work something out,' Mara said.

The door opened and they both looked round guiltily. Verona stiffened with embarrassment when Grandpa Clifford walked in.

'Is all right, man,' he said, noticing her expression, the gleam in his eyes telling he had heard some of the conversation. 'You right, I too old fe lift Ruby. Me bone dem pain bad aready widout me mash dem down more.'

Mara rubbed her palm against her jeans. 'Hello,' she said, holding out her hand, 'I'm Mara, Desiree's friend.'

'So why you a hide? How come you never come say howdy do? We doan bite, you know.'

Mara laughed. 'I didn't think you'd want me to get in the way.'

'What you say you name is again?' he asked, sitting in the chair she pulled out for him. 'Mara . . . I tink me and you gwine get on.'

Verona turned and quietly shared out the food.

'Just dish out little bit gi me,' Grandpa Clifford said, before returning his attention to Mara.

By the time the food was put in front of him, the two of them were laughing and talking as if they had known each other for years and Verona envied Mara her ease. She put the other plate on a tray with a knife and fork, and some of the Grace pepper John was always eating.

'No bother with de pepper,' Grandpa Clifford directed, 'it burn she belly and from she see it, she gwine waan use it.' He cast a critical eye over the tray. 'And just give her one spoon; she doan have time fe de airs and grace oonu like to tek on inna England.'

Verona complied, hesitating before adding a glass and some water;

'You doan have syrup?' the old man asked in surprise.

Verona opened the cupboard with John's Jamaican things and deliberated between the strawberry and the grape. She wanted to ask which one Granny Ruby would prefer but didn't want to interrupt the conversation.

'If you have strawberry, is de one she like best,' the old man directed, between mouthfuls of food and conversation.

As Verona manoeuvred the tray round the door, Granny Ruby said acidly: 'I did tink you did haffe go cook it . . . Jahn, wha wrong with you?' she turned on her grandson. 'You no see de gal deh a struggle – take the tray from her, noh.'

John moved to comply, his eyes resentful as they met the amusement in Verona's.

'Dis England mek ihm rude,' Granny Ruby confided to Desiree, who now occupied the chair vacated by the old man. 'Doan pay ihm no mind, and 'member what I say 'bout no mek ihm step pon you neck back.'

Desiree nodded, bemused, and Verona thought she looked shell-shocked.

'But dis ting fresh,' Granny Ruby said, taking a sip of her drink as John laid the tray across her lap.

Verona was amazed; she had made the drink just as John liked it – far too sweet for any of the rest of them to stomach – and she wondered how much sugar Granny Ruby took in her tea.

'Jahn, put little more syrup inna it gi me, noh.'

John took the drink, glaring at Verona before stomping off.

The old woman looked up at Verona still hovering uncertainly in front of her. 'Bend down open de grip,' she said, tucking into the succulent meat.

Verona knelt and unlatched the case, feeling envy as she heard a wave of laughter from the kitchen.

'I see Clifford find smaddy to gi joke,' Granny Ruby observed placidly. 'Mek her wait till she hear it nuff time . . . she gwine run go hide come time she see ihm a come.'

Verona sat back on her heel in surprise when she saw the case's contents. She had expected food, but instead it was packed with odd-shaped newspaper-wrapped packages.

'Dig under de yam tek out de fever grass,' Granny Ruby instructed.

Verona looked at her blankly. What on earth was fever grass?

'You no know it?'

Verona shook her head, embarrassed.

'You know it?' Granny Ruby asked Desiree.

'I think so,' the latter said unsurely, approaching the case and rummaging around until she came up with a brown-paper bag full of a greenish-yellow grass-like thing.

The old woman nodded satisfaction, waving Desiree back to her chair. 'Is you I did bring it for. I hear say you never well.'

Desiree was lost for words.

'Someting else in dere too fe draw dung de pain. Clifford will bwile it fe you a morning time and you must sure and drink it.'

Desiree nodded, totally off-balance, and Granny Ruby continued:

'I know say we spring pon you. I sorry say Jahn never 'member ihm manner sufficient fe warn you . . . and I hope you gwine bear wid us.'

'I'm glad you're here,' Desiree assured her warmly, pulling herself together. 'I always wanted the children to know their relatives.'

'You come from Guyana, no?'

She nodded. 'But I was only eleven and V was seven . . . our grandmother who was looking after us died.'

'So where your parents dem?'

'Both dead.'

'I sorry fe hear dat,' the old woman sympathised. 'Jahn mother . . . dat's me daughter . . . she dead too, and ihm father inna 'merica now.'

When the plate was still half full, she put down her spoon. 'So what you gwine do bout Jahn?' she asked.

'Do?' Desiree felt embarrassed again. Was the woman trying to test her?

'Eeh-ee, I know ihm spring we pon you, ihm tell me dat in de taxi. Ihm too rude . . . I doan 'gree wid dem tings deh.' She passed the tray to Verona. 'De food did nice,' she complimented. 'Is you cook it?'

'Mara did it,' Verona smiled.

'De gal Clifford a gi joke in de kitchen? You must mek me meet her 'fore she leave; and tell Jahn doan bother wid de syrup.'

'Would you like something else instead?' Verona offered.

'No, man. Just tell ihm fe come tek me up de stairs dem.'

Verona nodded, accepting the tray. 'I could make you some tea or coffee.'

'No, man, me doan business wid dat a night time . . . me bring some chocolate-tea fe me morning but me no drink coffee-tea no more.'

Verona retreated. Desiree felt her heart warming to Granny Ruby. At first she had found her abrupt manner off-putting and, when she had turned to Verona instead of her, had been afraid the old woman had taken a dislike to her. But now she realised that was probably just Granny Ruby's way. Yes, she liked John's grandparents, and she felt in her bones that things in the house were going to get a real shake up.

# Thirteen

'Auntie V!'

Someone was shaking her, rough hands full of eager impatience. She came awake reluctantly, mind still clinging to the last few wisps of dream.

'Auntie V!'

Verona groaned, feeling as though she had only just gone to bed. She, Mara and Des had stayed up talking long after John and the old couple retired.

'Watch his mouth,' Des had whispered as John moved sulkily to the stairs, 'you can see is fight he want tonight. I making sure he well asleep before I going up there.'

They had drifted into the kitchen, Desiree coming to a full stop at the sight of how clean it was.

'Grandpa Clifford and I did it,' Mara volunteered.

'Grandpa Clifford!' Desiree exclaimed.

'Girl, that is a different man – the way he been looking after Granny Ruby for the last ten years.' Mara cocked her head to one side in consideration: 'You know, I don't think he too well. Can't quite put my finger on what it is, but something not right.'

Verona marvelled. She herself hadn't been over-concerned about Grandpa Clifford's frailty, but then she was unfamiliar with old people, who often looked ill to her.

'How's the job-hunting going, V?' Mara had asked as they sat drinking coffee.

'Not too good,' Verona said cautiously. She had been looking on and off, being interviewed once or twice, only to be turned down after they took up references. In desperation, she had contacted Stoneford's, but their answer was the same: they had dismissed her for dishonesty and were not prepared to give a reference saying otherwise. She had found out from one of the permanent staff that there had been a spate of thefts; fifteen women in all had been sacked, but there was no longer talk of redundancies. Verona's suspicions were confirmed.

'How about the voluntary sector?' Mara suggested.

Verona looked at her blankly. 'The what?'

'Never mind,' Mara smiled. 'A couple of community groups looking to hire someone for their accounts; they putting together to hire one person between them. You interested?'

Verona's spirits lifted. Was she interested! 'Yeah, that would be great,' she said eagerly, seeing a job materialising. Any job would do, so long as she could work.

'Right, I'll send you the application forms. The closing date is next Friday so you have to hurry.'

Verona's excitement ebbed, leaving her deflated. She had thought Mara was offering her a job, and the knowledge that she would have to apply was discouraging. No one was likely to let her at their accounts when they found out she was branded a thief.

'Yeah, I'll do that,' she had said, trying to keep the enthusiasm she was no longer feeling in her voice. She would have gone straight to bed after that, depression settling on her shoulders, but she was afraid of arousing the other women's suspicions.

'*Auntie V!*'

'Shut up, Carol, you'll wake Mum,' Lyn hissed as the younger girl's voice rose to the edge of a shout.

'No, I won't . . . she can't hear anyway.'

'What time is it?' Verona's voice was blurred with sleep and muffled by the pillow she was burrowed into.

There were whispers, then Lyn answered: 'It's ten past six.'

Verona groaned, curling further into a ball under the covers.

'Auntie V,' Lyn said, 'Dad says Granny Ruby wants you.'

'Where is she?' Verona asked with an effort.

'She's downstairs,' Carol piped up. 'They don't half get up early.'

Verona silently agreed, wincing as she sat up, closing her eyes against a stab of sunlight. It had been a warm night and she felt clammy and sticky from sweating. She stretched her aching bones, rubbing her eyes in an attempt to get rid of the gritty feeling. When she opened them, Carol was gone and Lyn was sitting at the bottom of her bed, regarding her solemnly.

'You go down and meet them while I get dressed,' Verona suggested hopefully, doubting that she could manage otherwise. Even with the wardrobe moved to the hall, there was only squeezing room with her bed in here.

'I've already met them. Grandpa Clifford makes me laugh,' Lyn wrinkled her nose, 'but Granny Ruby is a bit scary, isn't she? She looks cross, and she's in a wheelchair.'

'That's cause her feet can't support her. She ain't half nice when you get to know her,' Verona coaxed. 'You gotta get used to her, that's all.'

'Well, at least she told Dad to let Mum sleep,' Lyn observed approvingly. 'It's not fair she should get up so early every morning, is it, Auntie V?'

'Sometimes she has to,' Verona said diplomatically, 'and anyhow she don't do so much since she come out of hospital.'

The child looked unconvinced, but her mind had skipped on. 'Is it true Mum's going to leave us to go to college?' she asked now.

Verona could guess where she had heard that. 'Your mum's taken the exam and she's waiting to find out if she got in . . . but she'll only be gone days, like you go to school.'

'But Dad said he was going to have to look after us.'

*I bet he did*, Verona thought sourly. John still opposed Des going on the access course, and only her determination and his belief that she would fail kept him humouring her. She had sat the exam for Vauxhall and Brixton colleges, hoping to get into one of the two.

'I think I'll like Mum going to college, then she won't look so sad.'

Verona digested that. Lyn's perception never failed to surprise her. She seemed so mature in her thinking.

'Shall I go and put the kettle on?' the child asked, happy once more. 'I think Granny Ruby wants you to make a drink with those brown things she's got . . . is that what real chocolate looks like?'

'I don't know,' Verona confessed. 'I can't remember the West Indies too well.'

'You remembered some, 'cause my teacher liked the thing I did on Guyana.'

'That's great,' Verona said absently. 'When you go down, tell Granny Ruby I'm coming in a minute.'

Alone, she edged her feet to the ground, looking ruefully around the girls' room as she got out of bed. They couldn't live like this for too long. Even her books had been relegated to the loft and she wondered if it was too late to take up Jay's offer. She pulled her suitcase from under the bed, rummaging through it for jeans and T-shirt, taking her current novel from under her pillow and putting it in before closing the case.

When she finally came downstairs, Granny Ruby was in the kitchen, one of the chairs moved so her wheelchair was close to the table, where she was slicing some hardough bread.

'We did bring two loaf like oonu did ask,' the old woman explained when she saw Verona's surprise. 'From you never come when I send Lyn fe call you I did tink you was sleeping.'

Verona smiled, wondering where Grandpa and the children were.

'Dem all gone dung de road with Jahn. Ihm not too good right now . . . I tink old age and hard work a kill him.'

Verona remembered Mara's words from the night before. 'But I thought it was you that did need the operation,' she said.

Granny Ruby laughed. 'Ee-eeh? But you is forward, Miss. You is right, is me de operation for.'

There was a bang, followed by a yell and muffled laughter from the sitting-room.

The old woman sat forward, startled. 'Is wha dat?'

'Only the kids,' Verona said.

'But dem gone a de shop with Clifford.'

'I can check if you like,' Verona suggested, seeing her agitation. She looked so frail, Verona felt nervous about being left alone with her in case something happened and she didn't know what to do.

'No, stay here,' Granny Ruby said.

'Ere, what's going on in there, you two?' Verona shouted instead.

There was a series of giggles. 'It's Carol,' Lyn shouted back, 'she just knocked over the lamp.'

'Go up and have your wash,' Verona ordered, 'and don't take too long; breakfast is nearly ready.' She watched at the door as they went obediently. 'I'll tell them not to make so much noise, shall I?' Verona offered, turning back to the old woman.

'Is aright, man . . . I just haffe 'member is England we deh now.' She looked up from her slicing. 'Run go get me de bag a chocolate in de big straw bag . . . de one wid de blue flowers pon de broad side dem.'

The doorbell rang. Verona hurried to answer it, surprised to find Grandpa Clifford there by himself.

'Thank you and good mornin, Miss V.'

'Good morning,' Verona responded politely.

He came in, wiping his feet on the mat. 'I tek a walk wid Jahn, but it too cold for Ruby fe go nowhere.'

'It's always like that in the morning. It might get warmer later.'

He looked unconvinced, his eyes dropping to the brown bag in her hand. 'Is de chocolate dat?'

'Your wife asked me to bring it.'

'You must call her Granny and me Grandpa like all de other smaddy dem.'

Verona nodded, not sure she could do that. He was holding out his hand for the bag.

'I gwine bwile it up . . . you waan some?'

She nodded again, not wanting to hurt his feelings, though she felt decidedly wary about the strange brown balls.

'Ruby in de kitchen?'

'Yes,' Verona acknowledged as he headed towards the door.

She watched him go, deciding she might as well check on the girls, otherwise they were unlikely to be ready on time. Surprisingly they were both dressed, Lyn struggling to comb out Carol's hair ready for plaiting.

'Don't Granny Ruby and Grandpa Clifford talk funny?' Carol said, at the sight of Verona.

'Ca – rol!' Lyn exclaimed, clunking her younger sister in the scalp much as Desiree would have done. 'That's how people talk in Jamaica, is all.'

'Yeah?'

'Yeah!'

'Then how come Dad don't talk like that?'

'Your Dad's been in England a long time,' Verona said. 'You think about it, Carol . . . in other countries they'd think you talk real funny.'

'Naw, they won't,' Carol denied with passionate disbelief. 'I'm English, ain't I?'

'Lots of people speak like Granny Ruby,' Lyn pointed out.

'How come you don't say nothing about them ones down Brixton Market?'

'I still think she talk funny,' Carol insisted stubbornly.

'Well, I like Granny Ruby and Grandpa Clifford, they're really nice, aren't they, Auntie V?'

'Yes,' Verona agreed, 'and I bet she could tell you lots about black people that you can't learn in England.'

'I never said I didn't like her. It's Lyn that was scared of her . . . I sat down with her and she told me about that earthquake in Kingston that happened when she was younger than me. Do you know she's ninety-two!' Carol said, astonished. 'Anyway, I like the way she talks, even if it does sound funny.'

Verona suppressed a smile; trust Carol to try to have the last word.

'Well, I like Grandpa,' Lyn responded to the challenge. 'He knows a lot of jokes and he knows about them Maroon people that beat up the British.'

'What Maroon people?' Carol asked, sounding put out.

'They were black people in Jamaica, ain't it, Auntie V?'

Verona nodded, hoping she wouldn't start questioning her. Apart from the fact that Maroons existed and that they had something to do with runaway slaves, she knew nothing about them.

'Anyway we learn about black people in school,' Carol said sulkily.

'Only bad things,' Lyn contradicted, 'they're always saying that white people gave us everything and we don't have no brains and that's why they have to tolerate us.'

'No, they don't!' Carol was indignant. 'We learn that we must respect everybody and slavery was bad and that's why all them people like Wil . . . something or other – he was a Christian . . .'

'You mean Wilberforce and them other white people?' Lyn was scornful. 'Grandpa says if the slaves didn't fight and make it hard for the white people, and them Maroons never go to war, we'd all be like South Africa now.'

They seemed to be squaring up for a fight and Verona intervened quickly. 'I'm sure you both have a point, but now you better hurry up or you'll be late for school.' She stepped between them as they continued to glare at each other. 'Lyn, go down and give Grandpa Clifford a hand.'

After the child had gone, Verona relaxed, leaving the room with a smile.

As she was passing Desiree's room, her sister called out. She was still in bed, looking as if she had not long opened her eyes, when Verona popped her head around the door.

'Are they up?' Desiree whispered conspiratorily.

'Yes, they got up when John did; seem like they always get up early.'

'How you didn't wake me?' There was panic in Desiree's voice.

'Calm down – me and John already agreed to let you sleep when you don't wake up in the morning.'

'I sure they think I lazy and rude.' Desiree worried at her bottom lip.

'I doubt it. Granny Ruby wouldn't let nobody disturb you, and you know how considerate John's been acting since you came from the hospital.'

There was a yell from the children's room and the sound of a scuffle. Desiree climbed out of bed hastily.

'V, go and see what they're up to,' she said, grabbing her dressing-gown and washbag. 'God, they must think the kids don't have no manners.'

Verona shrugged. 'Okay, but don't get in a twist, you know; they're all right really.'

Her sister smiled, slowing down on her way to the door. 'I know . . . look, you ignore me, hear? I just never had to look after John's relatives before, and with them so old, I don't want them to think I don't have no respect.'

The smell of fresh chocolate and nutmeg greeted Desiree as she came downstairs and she felt a stab of familiarity, reminded forcefully of Guyana, warm images she had thought long gone forming in her mind.

She stood in the kitchen doorway, taken aback to see Grandpa Clifford grilling bacon and frying eggs. It was one thing to know that he looked after Granny Ruby, another entirely to see how competently he moved about the kitchen.

The two of them were absorbed in each other, chattering as if they had lived through a long absence, rather than having been together for over sixty years. Granny Ruby was sitting at the table, a pile of neatly sliced hardough bread buttered in front of her. The old woman noticed her first and a smile warmed her lined face.

'I see you finally wake up,' she said with good humour. 'How you do dis morning?'

'I'm fine, thanks,' Desiree responded, adding solicitously: 'Did you sleep well? Was the bed all right?'

Grandpa Clifford gave his wife a warning look but she ignored it. 'De bed did aright, but dat puffy blanket it never long enough fe tuck in.'

'Ruby, stop complain,' Grandpa Clifford admonished. 'Anyway Jahn say is a quilt, not a blanket, and is fe dem bed . . . de one dem sleep pon is de one dem borrow from smaddy through dem did only have de one.'

Desiree felt ashamed of John; but Granny Ruby seemed unruffled. 'Nutting wrong wid de bed, and de spread did warm . . . but de way Clifford shift, shift a nightime it just tek time creep dung till it fall aff.'

'I could let you have some blankets instead,' Desiree said.

'No, man, de quilt aright,' Grandpa refused.

'Move off, Clifford! Is not you caan sleep cause cold a bite you? Throw two blanket pon de bed, tek dat quilt ting off,' the old lady instructed Desiree, 'no mind ihm.'

'She doan haffe do dat now,' Grandpa Clifford chided. 'Ruby, you no 'member de gal sick?' He pulled a chair out. 'Come, man, tek de weight offa you foot, I bwile up little herb fe gi you.'

Desiree was touched by the gesture, though she eyed the dark, bitter-looking liquid suspiciously when he put it in front of her.

The old people smiled encouragingly.

'Drink it, man, it not gwine bite you,' Granny Ruby urged.

Desiree sipped cautiously, just stopping her face wrinkling up. It tasted strange on her tongue, but she decided she must get it down.

'No bodda hide say it bitter,' Granny Ruby advised. 'It gwine gi you blood.'

Desiree nodded, watching with envy the way they related to each other. She tried to imagine John and herself growing old together, living with each other long after their children's children had children of their own.

'Clifford, mind you doan strain youself,' Granny Ruby cried out in alarm as the old man started to shift the heavy-looking black plastic bag John had taken from the rubbish bin and sealed earlier that morning.

Desiree looked up sharply, to see Grandpa leaning heavily against the work-surface.

'You shouldn't be doing that,' she said, lowering him into a chair, feeling as anxious as Granny Ruby looked.

'Is nutting, man, just old age. I gwine set fe a minute, den move de bag where Jahn say it go.'

Desiree shook her head. 'I'll move it,' she said firmly.

'I doan helpless yet,' the old man protested.

Granny Ruby sucked air through her teeth. 'Clifford, how you so stubborn? You know doctor say you fe tek it easy since de last attack.'

'Attack!' Desiree almost shouted, an awful apprehension growing inside her. 'What attack?'

'Ihm sick, man. Doctor say ihm no fe work so hard. Is why me need de operation, so me can get up look 'bout him.'

'But what's the matter with him?'

'Nutting,' Grandpa insisted, looking sheepish. 'Ruby, why you waan frighten de chile? Look how she tinking I gwine drop dead pon her.'

'But is what doctor say gwine happen if –'

'Doctor no know nutting.'

'No say dat,' Granny Ruby ordered crossly. 'Is ihm tell you 'bout you bad heart when it stop de first time.'

Desiree's mind was buzzing as the implications of this revelation dawned, and her vexation with John increased. No doubt he had known about this as he escaped to work, she thought resentfully. She had a brief vision of being stuck at home with two sick old people come September. She gritted her teeth with determination. *I'm going to college come what may*, she resolved. Then the hopelessness of the situation came back with fresh force.

'You should have told us,' she reproached. 'We never would have let you do so much.' She was going to brain John. This was the last straw, the last time he was going to land her in it like this.

'I is not a invalid,' came Grandpa Clifford's protest. 'I been looking 'bout Ruby since him leg dem gone.'

'You fe tek help when de good Lord sent it, Clifford,' his wife said gently. 'Dis is not like stranger, is you son, son wife, and you did say she aright.'

The children were coming down the stairs, for once not arguing.

'No mek de pickney dem hear none a dis,' Grandpa said hastily. He looked relieved at the interruption and, despite her concern, Desiree smiled, seizing her chance:

'I won't if you agree to come to the doctor with me this afternoon.'

'Doctor gi me one bottle a pill Friday week,' he pointed out. 'I doan need no more fe de time been.'

Desiree refused to budge.

'You better, Clifford, dis gal mean business,' Granny laughed.

He nodded unwillingly. 'But is just waste a time.'

After breakfast, Desiree helped Verona to lay Granny Ruby on the settee, pulling up an easy chair for Grandpa.

'Oonu get on wid oonu work,' Granny Ruby said, after Verona brought her the big straw bag she had carried as hand luggage. 'Clifford and me gwine aright.'

Desiree watched in fascination as she pulled out something large and lacy, settling back against the cushions at her head and moving the crochet needle with speed. She had never seen anything quite so fine, and she envied the skill in the old woman's withered hands.

'Doan mek me keep you,' Granny Ruby said, not bothering to look up.

Desiree told Verona as soon as they were in the kitchen: 'Grandpa sick.'

'I know; Granny Ruby mentioned something yesterday. But he'll be okay, no?'

'Is the heart. V, I think he's real sick; the way he so thin and all . . . and he already have one heart attack.'

Verona looked at her sharply. 'Heart attack!'

Desiree nodded. 'I taking him down to the doctor this afternoon. The trouble is, when I rang they could only fit him in at four o'clock and I have to go up the school when Mara come.'

'Well, I've got a interview this morning, but I'm sure I'll be back in time to take him, if you want me to.'

'Could you?' Desiree was relieved. 'Would you really?'

'Yeah, course. I like him. He's real different from John.' A thought occurred to her: 'Will they see him though?'

Desiree was collecting up the breakfast dishes, frowning at Lyn's untouched plate. 'What? Oh, I didn't tell them he just arrive. I only said he's my granddad.'

'I ain't telling them nothing. Is disgusting the way they refuse people. If you're foreign you could just drop dead, from you're black, ain't it?'

Desiree watched thoughtfully as her sister cleared the sink. If only their father had lived; things would surely have turned out differently. There was so much in Verona that was just going to waste. She straightened from wiping down the table.

'V, everything all right with the job-hunting? This job you after, what's it for?'

Verona's whole concentration was suddenly on the water running into the washing-up bowl. 'It ain't a proper job, just volunteering round that community place near Mara. They pay your fare and give you something to eat. If they like you, they send you to Morley College for one of them twelve weeks' training courses in advice work.'

'It not too late to apply for the college. You'd get the exam no problem.'

'Des, I never have the O-levels. Anyway, I ain't doing no sociology.'

'Is plenty other things at Vauxhall. How about that electronics course, the one you was so keen on? And you have the maths and CSE English.'

'Look, Des, I just change my mind, all right! I don't want to do it no more, and that's that.' Annoyance showed in every line of her posture.

'Well, good luck with the interview anyway,' Desiree said. There was an uneasy silence as she moved about wiping the surfaces unnecessarily.

Verona looked up from her bowl of soapy water. 'Why you don't go into the sitting-room with them?' she suggested impatiently, her sister's constant fussing getting on her nerves.

Desiree agreed.

Granny Ruby was humming softly, the ticking of the clock and the slight rustle of her crocheting keeping company with the tune. Grandpa Clifford had fallen asleep, his newspaper lying discarded on the floor.

Desiree had not realised how cool and restful this room could be. The brightness of the sun outside intensified the peace inside. She cleared her throat, wondering whether the old man was comfortable with his head twisted so awkwardly to one side.

Granny Ruby looked up. 'You finish you work?'

Desiree shifted from foot to foot, feeling like a child. 'Is there anything I can get you?' she asked hesitantly.

Granny Ruby shook her head. 'Clifford sleeping, but when ihm wake I will send come tell you if I have a need.'

# Fourteen

'I tell you, Miss V, England cold, no neck back.'

Verona smiled at the old man's words as she pulled the thin cotton dress away from her neck, trying to stir the warm air. Although it was only April, it was an unseasonably hot still day, but she was used to the vagaries of the English climate, where temperatures could edge into the mid-sixties in spring or drop to the forties in summertime. Today the sky was pale and the sun caused an ache behind her eyes. She wondered how Grandpa Clifford could bear walking about in a cardigan and one of John's heavy railway jackets without collapsing from heatstroke, much less be complaining about being cold.

'We're nearly there now,' she encouraged. They were within yards of the house and she fumbled in her bag for her keys.

'Doan tell Ruby what doctor say,' the old man begged as they reached the gate. 'She have enough tribulation without dis crosses pon her head.'

Verona paused in the action of pulling up the gate catch. 'How long you been sick, Grandpa?' she asked worriedly.

'Is years,' he admitted, 'but don't bodder 'bout de white doctor. I not so sick I can't mind Ruby.'

'But the doctor's right, ain't he? Is not your heart.'

He looked uncomfortable, but Verona made no attempt to open the gate.

'I did go one doctor up a Milk River and ihm send me go a University Hospital,' he muttered.

'Did they say what wrong with you?' Verona persisted, willing him to tell the truth.

'I have a weak heart,' he said, not quite meeting her gaze.

Verona shook her head; the doctor had been very definite: it was not the heart condition alone that was causing the old man to eat away like that. But Grandpa Clifford had stubbornly refused to be referred for more tests.

'No, man, dem do dat up a University Hospital aready,' he said, hardening her suspicion that whatever was wrong, he had known about it a long while. 'I tell you, Miss V, if someting wrong is too late fe haller and bawl now.'

His eyes met hers steadily this time, and she saw determination in them. She pushed the door open with a sigh, but just at that moment Mrs Evans – Nosy Dora – came rushing across the road.

'Hello, love,' she panted to a halt, and Verona's heart sank as Grandpa turned back before she could hustle him inside.

'I saw them arrive last night,' the woman went on, her beady eyes fastened avidly on her reluctant prey.

Verona hid her irritation. 'Hello, Mrs Evans,' she said, making no attempt to introduce Grandpa Clifford. The woman wore a washed-out sundress that had seen better years, and the exposed skin of her arms and shoulders was red and peeling from too much sun.

'Aren't you going to introduce me then, love?' she prompted.

The smile on Verona's mouth did not reach her eyes. 'Grandpa Clifford, this is Mrs Evans from across the road.'

He smiled, holding out his hand. 'Howdy do, Miss Evans.'

'He. . .llo, lo. .ve,' she said, stretching out the words as if he wouldn't understand, her voice rising as if he was also deaf. 'Bit hot for all that, eh?' she grinned at her own joke about the old man's attire.

'He ain't half old.' She turned back to Verona. 'They going to be here long? Only there's already five of you living in them three bedrooms . . . mind you, it's your culture, ain't it?' She leaned closer, confidingly, and Verona noticed that the bleach was growing out of her lank hair, leaving the sparse roots grey. 'I ain't prejudiced, you know, love; live and let live, I always say.' She gave the old man another patronising smile, nodding at him as if he were a small, not very bright boy.

'Grandpa Clifford understand English, Mrs Evans,' Verona said pointedly. 'He ain't stupid neither, so don't push up your face to him like that.'

'Well!' The woman gave her an affronted look. 'No need to be like that, dear, I was only trying to make him welcome.'

'Well, next time perhaps you should tell him – he can hear, you know.'

'No need to be so rude,' the woman said, walking off, muttering under her breath. She didn't go far, just as far as next door, where the Alsatian went into its usual antics at the approach of visitors.

Verona sighed, knowing their conversation would be about her and Grandpa.

Desiree appeared immediately at the door, pulling it open before Verona could insert her key.

'What you doing out here so long? Is things all right?'

Verona gestured to the two women next door who were now openly staring as Grandpa Clifford struggled up the path. 'Nosy Dora caught us.'

Desiree shook her head. 'V, you have to stop insulting her.'

'What for? She insulted Grandpa.' Verona gave the two women a baleful glare, grinning when they turned away. 'Silly old bats.'

Desiree moved aside to allow the old man in. 'Hello, Grandpa . . . here, let me,' she came forward to help him with his coat.

'Who say me a invalid?' he asked, looking put out as he stepped back to shrug out of the garment himself.

'What did the doctor say?'

'Ihm waan me fe go a one next hospital, even gi me letter fe carry.'

'When the appointment for?'

'Me not going.' Grandpa was adamant. 'Me did aready go a University Hospital – why me waan go a one next one again?' He dropped his coat over the banister, rubbing his hands together, his face recovering its humour. 'Bwoy, England cold . . . a no summer yet?'

Desiree shook her head, looking defeated. 'Is quite warm out there . . . it's through you not used to it.'

He looked doubtful. 'Ruby in there?' He pointed to the sitting-room.

'No, she in the garden.'

He looked alarmed. 'What! You mek her go out inna cold breeze.'

'Is not so cold and she has a blanket around her,' Desiree said patiently.

'Is she did ask fe go?'

Desiree nodded. 'The kids and I washing down the patio chairs and she said she'd keep us company. Is warm in the sun,' she added coaxingly.

He looked tempted. 'So de children out dere?'

She nodded again.

'Aright, if you can get one blanket fe gi me.'

Verona watched Desiree through the open kitchen door as she settled Grandpa Clifford beside his wife. The old woman had a wide-brimmed straw hat jammed on her short silver hair and was fanning herself with one of the children's schoolbooks, though she was still firmly wrapped in the fluffy pink blanket Des had picked up in a closing-down sale in Brixton a couple of years before. Verona wondered how they could say it was cold. She always saw herself as someone who hated the cold and today even she was hot. On top of that the south-facing garden was still drenched with sun. The little patch of land was full of colour and interest, reflecting John's keen interest in gardening.

'Okay. What wrong with him?' Desiree could hardly wait until she was back in the kitchen.

'Dunno,' Verona frowned, 'but it ain't just a weak heart. The doctor looked dead worried when he was questioning Grandpa and he even try and send him to hospital straight away. Des, Grandpa insisted on walking to the doctor's and back, and it took us near an hour each way.'

'I thought you did have a big queue or something.'

'Naw, we ain't wait long. Good thing we left here in time, though.'

As the kettle boiled, Desiree moved to turn it off, then dropped some of the herbs the old people had brought into a pot. 'So what the doctor say?'

'Well, I never went in with him at first like, but the doctor calls me in after . . . said he couldn't understand Grandpa.'

'What a cheek! If is me I would tell him something.'

'What's the point? Wouldn't have made no difference anyway . . . all I wanted was to make sure Grandpa got seen proper.'

'Which doctor you see?'

'You know that new one, Dr Lightfoot – the one with the dishy smile.'

'Honestly, V!' Desiree exclaimed. 'Why you don't transfer to him one time, since you think he so good?'

'I might just do that,' Verona teased, sobering as she saw the worry in her sister's face. 'You know, Des, I think he did suspect what it was, but you know how doctors stay . . . saying he need to refer Grandpa for test, and Grandpa keep saying he already had them tests in Jamaica. We was in there twenty minutes, then the doctor just write this letter and ring up for an appointment down Camberwell.'

Desiree was taking two mugs out of the cupboard. 'Did you get no trouble about them seeing him?' she asked over her shoulder.

'No, but this nosy parker on reception kept on about passport.' Verona laughed. 'Oh, you should have been there, Des! Grandpa wasn't half funny – kept asking: "A who fe passport ihm want? A me ihm a talk to?" I had to tell him was to sit down and let me deal with it.'

'What you say to her?'

'Just that he was from up north and was sick. And then Grandpa must've get tired of sitting 'cause he come back and tell her she going on like he have hog tail growing on his bottom and she too faas anyway. I think she was a bit scared of him, 'cause she just shut up from that.'

'Serves her right; them people well out of order. If he was white she wouldn't care, but from he black she want him to drop dead? Come out with me,' Desiree invited, picking up the tray, 'the other chairs must dry by now.'

Verona held the door for her. 'What're the girls doing?'

'They finishing the last chair, then they going to do their homework.'

Verona thought longingly of the book she had begun to read just before the old people came; dismissed the thought. Somehow she couldn't see Granny Ruby or Grandpa Clifford approving of her reading material. From the few chats she had had with them, she knew they were deeply religious, and she wondered if John realised he was going to have to take them to church.

'We doan mind not going to de Church a God,' Grandpa had volunteered helpfully, 'but we haffe worship de Lord in fullness and truth . . . so we will go a de Baptist if it nearer.'

Now he said, equally helpfully, as he took a sip from his mug: 'When you mek Cerosee tea, you must mek it draw little more time.' He drank silently for a few moments, his enjoyment obvious.

'When Jahn gwine done work?' Granny Ruby asked, blowing on her steaming drink to cool it.

'It depends,' Desiree responded, stretching out in the deck-chair beside her and fingering with fascination the delicate lace she was working on. 'Sometimes he stop around now, and other times he go on till ten . . . and every four weeks he does a week of nights.'

'How come dis country come in like slavery so?' the old woman asked, disgruntled.

'Is not that bad,' Desiree defended automatically. 'Is just with me not working, and the kids always needing something, things not easy.'

'It's 'cause you have to pay a lot of money for the house as well, isn't it, Mum?' Lyn said.

'But wait! Hear dis now,' Granny said, looking fondly at the child. Lyn had got over her initial wariness of her greatgrand-mother and was now always hovering around her, badgering her to teach her and tell her things.

'You suppose to be doing your homework,' Desiree said.

'I'm finished my maths, and I have to get my other book for the English,' the child explained.

'Well, who stopping you?'

'I'm going.' She got up from where she had been sprawled beside her sister on the grass and moved reluctantly to the open kitchen door.

'Is not a criticism I was making before,' Granny Ruby said, 'but I never know say oonu work so hard a England; Jahn always a write say it not so bad.'

'It no come like Jamaica whe de people dem a work till dem drop and pickney still have bang belly,' Grandpa contradicted.

His wife bristled, thrusting her empty cup at Desiree and sitting straighter in her chair. 'Is Seaga and de way him a go on with de 'mericans mek Jamaica mash up,' she insisted.

'So what you waan dem fe do, take Manley back? When ihm did in power, de shop dem empty and lockup and people fe dead a hunger and gunshot.'

'No de same ting wid Seaga?' Granny Ruby said spiritedly. 'Food inna shop is fe pure decoration, 'cause people caan buy.

Look how Miss Lorna did haffe go a credit union fe pay ihm light bill . . .'

'Me never say Seaga good –'

'But is you say Manley worser.' She shook her head. 'God gwine punish ihm, y'know. Look how much young gal a sell demself fe go a school and 'member how Sweetie Baby mother nearly go a prison 'cause she borrow money fe maternity and couldn't pay de interest.'

Grandpa shrugged. 'What we need is a next man now – a one dat not gwine go 'merica or Russia but jus fa de people . . . Yes, we need a one dat not gwine fa heself nor inna no backshee nor none a de tribal politics.'

Granny Ruby nodded, picking up her crochet where she had left off to drink her tea. 'Him woulda haffe fa de poor people first though.'

Her husband sucked his teeth in exasperation. 'A no so me say! Cho, Ruby, sometime me tink wax hard inna you earshole de way you no hear good.'

She looked unruffled, her needle flying in and out of the material. 'Jus drink de tea 'fore it cold, Clifford, and tell me what doctor say.'

'Ihm say de same ting like de next doctor a Jamaica, nutting more dan so.'

'Clifford! Tell me de truth noh, man.'

'I is telling you de truth.' He glanced pleadingly at Verona but she looked away. 'Him say de same ting as de next doctor whe Delsey did carry me go.' Then to Desiree: 'Jahn say you fe carry we go a church Sunday.'

Granny Ruby folded her arms. 'No change de subjec . . . no bodda vex me, you hear, Clifford?'

'Guess what we talked about at school today?'

Verona and Desiree turned to Carol with relief, as she scrambled up from the grass and came to sit on the small paved patio.

'Yeah, what'd you discuss?' Verona asked quickly, not wanting Granny Ruby's attention to turn to her.

'We talked about Jamaica,' the child said proudly.

'That's good,' Verona chipped in, watching the old lady out

of the corner of her eye; 'specially with your Granny and Grandpa here.'

'It's only 'cause she told them Granny and Grandpa was here.' Lyn had come back carrying her book and she sat in the vacant chair.

'So what, you never waan we fe come look fe you?' Grandpa asked.

'Yes, I did,' Lyn looked anxious. 'I really like you and Granny Ruby.'

The old woman beamed, and the child turned to her, wheedling: 'Granny, will you tell me another Ananse story? The girls in my class really liked it. Beverley says she's going to ask her mum if she knows none.'

'Oooh, I never heard no story,' Carol complained, laying her head against Verona.

'That's 'cause you were messing about,' Lyn said. 'Granny Ruby's going to tell me lots of things and teach me to crochet like her, aren't you, Granny?'

Granny nodded, content. 'I could teach de both a oonu.' She gave Carol a sharp glance. 'No bother push out you mouth like dat, gal.'

Carol looked even more sulky.

'You better watch smaddy no step pon it pull it off,' Grandpa said drily. 'Oonu pickney must heed de older head dem.'

'Stop it, Carol!' Desiree said sharply, embarrassed at the child's behaviour. 'Go upstairs and straighten your bed, and you can do the rest of your homework while you up there.'

'Aw, Mum!'

'Is cooling down out here anyway,' Desiree relented, as the fresh breeze that had sprung up ruffled the table parasol.

'You're always picking on me,' Carol moaned, not appeased.

'Hush up and tek time do what you mother tell you,' Granny Ruby said sternly. 'You can hear story when you finish you school work. You pickney born a England lucky – me never get de schooling when I did young like you, and plenty pickney born a Jamaica caan go a school still.'

Carol was unimpressed: 'But you're going to tell Lyn a story.'

Lyn got up abruptly. 'Come on, Carol! Stop being so rude. I

have to finish my schoolwork first, isn't it, Granny?' The old woman nodded, and Lyn added: 'Let's finish ours together, Carol.'

Desiree sighed with relief as they left. Sometimes she wondered how she would control Carol without Lyn. A born diplomat, the older girl always seemed to know what to say to get her sister to toe the line.

'Turn de television on mek me listen to de big news,' Granny Ruby said as soon as they were back inside.

Using the remote control, Desiree flicked to Channel 4. Grandpa looked longingly at the slim silver box and she passed it to him. He was fascinated by it and by the video. 'Dem bwoy dey 'merica dem have cable box fe get channel, but dem never like me fe touch it case it mash up and dem haffe pay fe it,' he had said, face lighting up the first time he saw the large square television and video.

'Think I'll go get dinner,' Verona said from the doorway. 'Shall I share yours, Grandpa?'

'Mek me come keep you company,' he offered too eagerly, passing the remote box to his wife and getting to his feet.

Granny Ruby gave him a look that said she had not given up her questioning.

'Come sit by me, Desaree,' she ordered, patting the chair that Grandpa had just vacated. 'You look sad – you and Jahn doan 'gree?' she asked bluntly.

Desiree was straight away on the defensive: 'No, it's nothing like that. I'm just a bit tired is all.' She was wary of the old woman's perception but she didn't want Granny Ruby to misunderstand and feel unwanted.

'You doan haffe cover fe Jahn, Desaree, ihm did always de same from ihm little bit. Curley and de other bwoy dem did haffe mek gang fe beat him up. True, ihm did haffe big inna everyting.' She shrugged. 'Jahn is a man dat mean well, but ihm no know how best fe do it.'

Desiree felt the responsibility of the old people keenly. It was all right for John to bring them here, but she was the one who had to look after them . . . and she was worried sick about Grandpa Clifford.

'You can tell me, you know,' the old woman coaxed, 'if is through we dey ya, I not going to feel grudgeful.'

'Is not that, is just I want to go to work,' Desiree blurted out.

'And ihm a try stop you.'

'Well, yes . . . but is the college, you see.'

'You mean you waan go back a school?' The old woman was puzzled now.

Desiree nodded. 'Yes, is not that he trying to stop me . . . he just make me feel real guilty and selfish.'

'What ihm 'fraid a?'

Desiree hadn't expected that one, and she answered without thinking: 'He think I might end up earning more than him.'

'But ihm have exams,' Granny Ruby puzzled. 'Ihm job a gi ihm trouble?'

Desiree decided that the old woman had too much on her plate already without being burdened with their problems, and John could tell her himself if he wanted her to know. 'He just don't believe women should work,' she said.

'If you waan go back a school, go back, man. No mek nobody stop you, for is you gwine regret it. Tek me, now: when I did young I was with a next man and ihm never waan me fe have de little stall I did build up, t'rough I waan to better myself. All ihm waan me fe do is breed till bwoy pickney come.'

Desiree looked at her in surprise, rapidly revising her opinion. She had not imagined women Granny Ruby's age ever doing anything so radical.

'Yes, man, me was young gal one time,' Granny Ruby smiled, focusing her mind back. 'Dem day me never care 'bout nothing but de pickney dem. It did hard widout a man, but I did use to hard life t'rough me mother did raise nine a we, after Puppa drown a boat accident.'

She paused. 'When Clifford come a Brown's town fram Annatto me never even waan say howdy. Me did feel say me get rid a one disrespectful smaddy and me never waan one nother one . . . but him did aright.'

She sighed, her fingers stilling as she looked steadily at Desiree. 'If you caan 'gree wid de man, is best you fe lef him . . . like dat friend you have, de one Jahn complain 'bout and

Clifford always a gi joke. Is aright inna England, you can find life fe lead when you lef dem.'

# Fifteen

It seemed little time before the two old people became an integral part of life. Granny Ruby's operation was scheduled for the end of August; but as the heat of June pushed into another month, Grandpa Clifford seemed increasingly tired and was obviously in pain.

In the midst of her concern for him, Desiree got her replies from the colleges, both coming together in the Saturday post. It was shortly after Mara had arrived with Charleen and Meeli, who went straight outside to play.

Desiree felt almost sick with the anticipation of failure when she saw the envelopes bearing her name, realising immediately what they were.

'What's the matter?' Mara asked with a shrewd look, noticing the way her hands shook as she tore open the first envelope.

Desiree shook her head mutely, handing her the envelope with unsteady fingers. Mara read it, both women ignoring Verona's curious gaze.

'I'm sorry, Des,' she said sympathetically.

Desiree blinked back tears. 'Should've expected it, I suppose.' She tried to smile: 'Here, you might as well open the other one.'

Mara took it without a word. She scanned the contents without expression, then her face broke into a huge grin.

'You've done it!' she yelled. 'Des, you've done it!' She danced around the room, hugging first Verona then Desiree.

Desiree could hardly take it in so soon after the disappointment, staring in stunned surprise at the flimsy sheet of paper Mara thrust into her hand.

Even John's appearance made no impact. He had been sitting with his grandparents watching football and he looked annoyed.

'What's all this noise? What going on in here?'

Mara waltzed over to him, hugging him too. 'Congratulate Des, John, she on her way to college come September.'

It was as if he had been struck, taken totally off guard: 'College? You mean she get in?'

Desiree watched him with bemusement, some of her euphoria evaporating. John looked sick . . . scared and sick.

'Des, you going?' he asked incredulously.

The jubilation left Mara's face and she sobered at once.

'I'm going.' Desiree said, looking away from the pleading in his eyes.

'Yeah, she's going.' There was triumph in Verona's defiant glare at him.

Only Mara remained quiet. 'It's what she need, John,' she said, 'is what you both need.'

He looked from one to the other in a last desperate appeal, then he turned and stalked out, slamming the door behind him.

'So much for him being happy for you,' Verona said, going over to put a comforting arm around Desiree. 'He ain't nothing but a slob anyway.'

Mara shook her head. 'There's more to John than that, V. Can't you see he scared he going to lose Des, that she going to do what I do to Winston? You have to try be more understanding, you know, V.'

Verona looked annoyed and Desiree stepped in diplomatically: 'You all don't want to celebrate?' she said quickly. 'We can open that bottle of Pomagne I bought last week – is not champagne, but is all right.'

The other two agreed eagerly, and she went to the fridge, still too dazed to take in fully the news from Vauxhall College. An access course in Law . . . she, Desiree, was going on a course – who would believe it, eh? She savoured the thought, rolled it around, sipped it with her Pomagne. She had achieved something, done something, and already she felt better about herself.

It was in the evening, after the children had gone to bed, that the subject of Grandpa Clifford came up again. Charleen and Meeli were staying the night, so Mara was in no hurry to leave. The old people were watching a Channel 4 programme on Jamaica, arguing good-naturedly about it being full of lies. Grandpa Clifford coughed frequently, the sound tortured and painful.

Desiree frowned. 'I going try get he to come see the doctor again,' she announced worriedly as she sat with Verona and Mara on the patio in the fading light of the setting sun.

'That ain't gonna work,' Verona said. 'I been on at him for ages but he don't listen.'

Mara agreed. 'Mmm, I had my go. Remember when we took them down the black elderly luncheon club that Thursday? Girl, I had one go at him in the kitchen when he came to help Mrs Leary with the chicken.'

The club had just been set up by a black woman, Linda Groom, working in the local social action centre. Linda, a trained mental health nurse, was new to voluntary sector work and had the sort of energy and commitment everyone kept saying wouldn't last. Mara had become involved with the advisory group after answering an advertisement for volunteers, and she spent a lot of her spare time helping to develop it with Linda. Desiree wondered where Mara got the energy, and no one could say she ever neglected her children.

Granny Ruby and Grandpa Clifford loved the club, going as often as the volunteer who drove the mini-bus came to fetch them. Desiree valued those afternoons, using them to read up about law from the booklist she had got from Vauxhall College, in case she was accepted on the course.

Verona often went with them, dropping the children off at a nearby play centre now the school holidays had started and leaving Des to study in peace. The old people always came back full of animation. By all accounts, they were usually the centre of attention, swapping memories with other club members or joining in songs from various of the islands. But the last few times, Grandpa Clifford had come back looking ill. After the most recent occasion, Desiree had to force him to go to bed for a while, warning the children not to make any noise.

'John going to have to deal with it,' she said finally. 'The way he keep brushing it off, is like he scared to admit Grandpa sick.'

'Pretending to care more like,' Verona sneered. 'I tell you, Des, when he's trying, like he is with you now, it ain't half awful.'

'At least he's trying,' Mara said. 'Des, Olu said he could lend you that book if you still can't find it.'

It was a particular textbook that the college recommended students became familiar with if they were offered a place on the course, but everyone must have had the same idea, for Des couldn't find it anywhere. 'I did mean to ask him at the court yesterday, but to tell the truth I was a bit scared.'

'I really appreciated you coming, and, V, it was nice of you to granny-sit.'

'That's all right. I'm just sorry I couldn't be there too.'

'Mara, was Olu right to go for Crown Court?' Desiree asked. 'You know, with the magistrate saying it'll be more serious if he's found guilty there.'

'The magistrates seem to hate black people, specially the youth; if they tried Jay, they'd more than likely find him guilty.'

'Even though there ain't no evidence?' Desiree was shocked. She knew black people often went to prison for what they hadn't done; but this time it was obvious that the police had no case.

'I ain't saying it happen all the time, but it happen to three of the youths down by the club, and I didn't like that sour-face woman magistrate at all. If that other man was presiding I would have been a bit happier.'

'Yeah, but the jury bound to be all white, ain't it?' Verona put in.

'That's a problem, but at least there's more chance they won't convict he with no evidence.' Mara shrugged. 'Still, I feel confident, and Jay's dealing with it well.'

The conversation had drifted to Desiree's course when John walked out from the kitchen, taking them by surprise. He had obviously been drinking, and he looked surly.

'I don't know how Des can go to college when Granny Ruby's just going to be out of hospital, and Grandpa Clifford not too well,' he said bitterly.

'John!' Mara and Verona said at once, the latter adding: 'Don't you dare try and make Des feel guilty. I don't see *you* caring for your grandparents.'

'You think it's easy?' Mara added. 'I don't suppose you even think about the times you come in and your grandmother is upstairs. You think she and the wheelchair fly up there?'

John looked taken aback at the force of the attack, especially after Mara's earlier concern. 'Hey, I was only joking,' he retreated, 'can't you lot even take a joke no more? Every little thing and you jump down my throat.'

'I told you before, John,' Desiree said quietly, 'this course is *not* a joke to me.'

'I've said you can do it, didn't I? What more you expect? You know as well as I do that it's a waste of bloody time . . . but I ain't never going get no peace till you see for yourself.'

'Big of you, John,' Mara butted in. 'Is a good thing she don't need you for encouragement, no?'

He clamped his mouth shut, looking as if he regretted ever having opened it. He moved around, muttering to himself, before retreating to the kitchen for his dinner.

Desiree got up abruptly. 'I'm going to talk to him about Grandpa,' she said determinedly. 'You lot stay out here for a bit, will you?'

She must tackle him about his grandfather some time and this was as good an occasion as any. He had been in this defensive mood since his grandparents came, due, Desiree suspected, to the fact that he couldn't keep up his macho image with his grandmother; and he certainly wouldn't get any better now she had been accepted at college.

'John, I want to talk to you about Grandpa Clifford,' she said as soon as she closed the door.

He turned, putting the pot back on the cooker. 'He's really sick, isn't he, Des?' He sounded young and bewildered, adding: 'He won't go to the doctor and I just don't know what to do now.'

Desiree's heart went out to him. At times like this, when he did something so considerate and unexpected, it seemed there was a chance for them yet. 'If only we had an idea what was wrong,' she said, her last hope gone of anyone being able to persuade the old man to see reason.

'I've never seen anything like it before, Des. Carley said Grandpa was losing weight, but I was shocked when I saw him down the airport, and he's been losing more since he come.'

A sudden foreboding hit Desiree. 'I wish you did confide in me before,' she said heavily. 'Honestly, John, I really feel like you landed me in it.'

'I know, Des; I'm real sorry. I just never knew how to tell you.' He sighed. 'Trouble is, I was there trying to tell you they was thinking 'bout coming, then you sick, and I feel so guilty and useless, and I go on so bad about the job, but I was really worried about you . . .' Once he had started, he seemed unable to stop. 'Things just go wrong one after the other, and I just put it off and put it off, till I couldn't do it no more.'

Desiree rested a gentle hand on his arm. 'Maybe we should try talking a bit more,' she said tentatively.

'You no see it,' he agreed readily, but from his embarrassed look she knew he regretted his impulse to confide in her and was talking to submerge his fear. He had opened up in a moment of weakness, and she wished she knew how to get through to the man she had first met, the man she was beginning to believe was still in him somewhere.

'Let we start by planning how to get Grandpa to the hospital, shall we?' she suggested gently. 'We can do that after you eat.'

She got up from the table as he sat down, but he put out a hand, withdrawing it uncertainly when he saw her surprise. 'You can stay if you like,' she said offhandedly, and she sank back into the chair, knowing that his pride prevented a more direct request.

For the first time in years she felt positive. She had got into college, and suddenly John didn't seem all bad. It was going to be all right; somehow, she was going to make it all right.

# Sixteen

Something had happened to Verona. Something so fantastic, she hugged it to herself like a miser, taking it out only in the secrecy of her sagging bed, with the gentle breathing of her nieces to accompany the savouring of it.

She was walking on air, and now it didn't seem so bad that she had no privacy and had to go to the park to read her novels. What did it matter that she had to cancel her romance subscription from lack of money, or that the books in the library were ones she had already read? Even the fact that she had lost five whole pounds in weight seemed small potatoes now.

She had met *him*.

Who would believe it? She, Verona, had met a real man. She was walking on cloud nine. This was love!

There she had been, still just inside the door of the benefit office after shuffling along for half an hour, when he had come from the desk, nearly bouncing into her in his haste to escape. She could see he felt as she did, the shame in his blue eyes matched by a tide of colour at his awkwardness, and suddenly it didn't matter that 'H' always seemed to be the longest queue. He muttered 'Sorry,' and she grinned at him, having a good long look. Well, no one could stop her dreaming.

When she came out, he was waiting outside, smiling at her with even teeth, and her heart had skipped a beat. He asked her if she wanted to have coffee with him . . . he knew a place which was quite cheap. The offer jarred on her a little, but he smiled again and her legs felt weak.

'Yeah, why not?' Verona tried to sound casual, detached,

though with him smiling like that, her words came out breathless and over-eager. It was broad daylight, but she didn't care – who'd be afraid to be seen with such a gorgeous hunk? She raised her head high when some black people paused to stare at her disapprovingly. *Let them think what they like*, she told herself, *I bet it's jealousy anyway*.

'By the way, my name is Steve,' he said, putting a steaming cup of coffee in front of her.

'I'm Verona,' she responded, pulling the cup towards her.

They drank in silence for a while, she sipping like one of the heroines in her books, gazing attentively at him while he leaned back easily in his chair.

'What d'you do, Verona?' he asked with a smile. 'I mean usually, when you're not unemployed.'

He had some kind of Northern accent, probably Liverpool, which he seemed to be consciously trying to suppress. Not that she minded; in fact, she quite liked it. He reminded her of that dishy Terry in *Brookside*. Mind you, Steve was much nicer, with his unruly blond hair and his honey-gold moustache. He had an open, friendly face and a boyish grin that flashed out often. Not even several discoloured and crooked teeth could detract from his attraction.

'Well?' he repeated when she just continued staring at him dreamily. 'You saying you always been unemployed? Don't look like the type somehow.'

Verona blinked, some of the cloud evaporating from her head. 'I'm an accounts clerk,' she said warily, adding shyly: 'What about you?'

He grinned. 'I'm a writer. Technically I ain't really unemployed, but I need some bread while I work on my book.'

Verona's eyes rounded; she was more than impressed. A real writer – someone who wrote books! 'I read a lot,' she volunteered. 'I bet your book's gonna be great. I'm going to buy it as soon as it get finish.'

'You couldn't read stuff like mine,' his voice had a faint edge of contempt; but he was smiling, and somehow nothing else mattered.

'Yeah, I suppose not, but I'll buy it anyway.'

Steve's grin flashed on like a Christmas tree light. 'Well, you have to wait a bit; I ain't rushing it. When I do someting, it got to be good.'

They met regularly after that. At first it was only on signing-on days, Verona getting there earlier than her time in order to queue with him. They would spend the day together, walking in the park and sharing a portion of fish and chips; one portion was all Steve could afford and he was too proud to take money from her. Anyway she always made up for it in the evening, tucking into Desiree's cooking with hungry relish.

After the first few weeks, Steve invited her out on a different afternoon. They didn't do much, just walked around the park talking and holding hands. Verona stifled the niggling disappointment that there was no wine, roses or car. The weather was a cool and uncertain, the sky having been overcast most of the day, and when it started to rain they sheltered under a spreading sycamore tree since neither of them had an umbrella.

They went back to his place, a small cluttered flatlet, littered with the debris of many meals. Every out-of-the-way corner had accumulated inches of dust, and she wondered if the cooker could possibly be white.

It was just like in *Concertina Love*, she recalled, where Alain went into decline and April found him in squalor when his mother urged her to visit him. Verona felt happier thinking of it in that context. Poor Steve, no doubt he was so busy, so sunk in his work, he hadn't been able to find the time to clean up . . . and anyway it really was no job for a man.

Hesitantly, she offered to help and he jumped at the suggestion, sitting cross-legged on his futon, which he told her was a Japanese bed-settee, to be out of her way.

Verona had underestimated the dirt in the place and it took her the better part of the evening to clean up. She felt a little guilty when a glance at her watch showed it was nearly seven. She had promised to get back to stay with Granny Ruby and Grandpa Clifford from six-thirty, so that Des and Mara could go to a meeting. Since that BUF meeting when Verona had challenged Winston, Des had developed such an appetite for politics that even Mara was beginning to flag.

'Here, what's the frown for?' Steve asked.

'I was going to granny-sit for my sister.'

'You do a lot for her, don't it?' his tone was admiring.

Verona nodded, ignoring a twinge of conscience at how affronted Des would be to know about him. But they were hardly likely to meet – not if she could help it. 'It seem the least I can do since I'm living there.' She had confided her home situation to him, bitterness unknowingly creeping into her voice when she explained about moving into her nieces' room.

'You're like a trapped bird,' he murmured, watching as she attempted to fluff up the rug under his feet before straightening to look around.

She liked the image he painted of her, even while the sensible half of her wondered what he could possibly see in her.

'You've really worked wonders on this place,' he said with appreciation, catching her hand and tugging her down beside him on the futon.

She had expected to land on softness, and her body jarred against the hard cushion, taking the wind out of her. Despite that, she felt a shiver of excitement move down her spine, a familiar ache between her thighs. Was he interested in *that* way? God, she hoped so . . . She squeezed her legs tightly together, afraid to allow the feelings rein. It was months since she'd had a man, the humiliation of meeting Mara and Olu when she had been with Guy holding her in check. Now, with Steve, she wouldn't have to fantasise about the heroes in her novels.

Steve started to touch her, clumsily exploring her loose bulk under the pink cotton sundress she had bought specially because of him. It was a long while since Verona had worn anything bright, but to see the surprise on his face as he had caught sight of her alighting from the bus made her feel it well worth all the sweets she'd had to forgo.

She shifted, giving him more access as he pulled down the thin straps of the dress, peeling back the clinging material, before kneading inexpertly at her ample breasts. His mouth was grinding down on hers and he began to breathe hard as he fumbled at her hemline, his hand hot and impatient on her thigh.

Verona wished he would go more slowly, be a little gentle. She wanted to be stroked slowly to life, to have each garment peeled away with little kisses . . . but none of that really mattered. Steve was everything she wanted, and she had to bear with his need. After all, he'd no doubt been saving himself for her since they had met, and four months was a long time for a man to go without.

She ran her fingers through his untidy blond hair, along his narrow back and flat bottom, fantasising that in response he was tenderly caressing her quivering white flesh . . . that the fingers tweaking at her short hair were really tangling in her imagined long golden tresses.

When she was just beginning to get used to his touch, he fumbled for his zipper, rolling on top of her and arranging himself on the cushion of her fat. His fingers tugged urgently at her panties and he sighed with satisfaction when they finally pushed inside her.

For a fleeting moment it crossed her mind that it might be any body he was using, that he was turned on simply by his need for sex and certainly not by her. She squashed the thought. Steve was young and vital, not greedy and selfish like the leathery old bodies she was used to.

Now he was shifting again, squeezing himself between her ample thighs and she shifted automatically, the better to accommodate him, telling herself stubbornly that it was great.

Afterwards, she felt aching and unfulfilled, thinking longingly of the bath she had scrubbed back to whiteness.

'Can I have a quick bath 'fore I leave?' she asked tentatively.

He smiled at her, looking relaxed and satisfied. 'Go? I thought you were gonna stay the night. We can cook something up and . . . just talk.'

Verona agreed readily, eager for anything that would bring back the sense of wellbeing that knowing Steve had brought until now. She needed to distract her mind from the empty aching still inside her.

As guilty thoughts of Desiree threatened, she told herself that there was no point rushing home now. Des would already have missed her meeting anyway.

'Can I just ring my sister to tell her I ain't coming?'

He nodded. 'Don't be too long though.'

Verona felt a sense of unreality as she dialled, an awkwardness that had not been there before, as she watched Steve out of the corner of her eye. He was moving about restively, scuffing his toes as he glanced towards her, speculation in his eyes.

Desiree's anxious voice came on the line, demanding her attention: 'V! Where are you?'

Verona thought fast, remembering she had not told her sister she would be out all afternoon. 'Sorry, Des, I met this friend and clean forgot the time.'

'Is this friend male or female?' Desiree's voice was full of suspicion.

'Female,' Verona responded promptly.

There was a pause. 'One of John's mates say he saw you with a white man the other week,' Desiree said quietly. 'V, you sure your friend is female?'

'Course I'm sure! And you can tell John and his mate to mind their own blooming business.' *Worse than Nosy Dora some of them men!*

'So what time we can expect you?' Desiree sounded annoyed.

Verona bristled. Anyone would think she was still a child the way her sister fussed. 'I ain't coming back tonight.'

There was a disapproving silence. 'Well, I hope you know what you doing. Just be careful, hear, V?'

Verona felt a surge of alarm as she replaced the receiver, her sister's words ringing in her ears. For the first time she felt uneasy about the fact that she was still 'resting' from the pill. Trust Des to spook her with her constant worrying. *Anyway it's my safe period*, she reminded herself resolutely, *and is too late to do nothing now.* This wasn't the first time she had slept with someone without taking precautions, though she only indulged when there was little danger. It was a calculated risk, and she had never yet had an accident.

She dismissed her qualms firmly, concentrating on Steve. Right now she was hungry for him and all the fantasies she had never dreamt could come true.

Rising early the next morning, Verona made breakfast and went to wake Steve. He was snoring peacefully, head thrown back, lips slightly open, with a thin line of saliva at the side of his mouth. He didn't look so pretty now, and she averted her head, determined to keep hold of the fantasy.

Today he seemed impatient to be rid of her. 'I can feel my muse,' he said.

Verona nodded blankly. If truth be told, she herself wanted to get out. She had been cooped up in this tiny space since the previous evening, and she needed to stretch her legs and breathe clean air.

*Might as well walk home*, she thought as she dried the last of the breakfast dishes. She had bathed, using her slip as a makeshift flannel, and she felt fresh and optimistic after a good hard scrub. Suddenly the whole day was full of possibilities and she couldn't wait to go out and sample them.

It was nearly ten o'clock when she eventually left. The sun was hot on her back, soaking through her clothes, making her want to stretch right out. She toyed with the idea of spending the day in the park, imagined lying on the grass under the warm rays, letting her mind drift in and out of sleep. She had a book with her, but it seemed tame compared to the night she had just spent. In the end she decided on the library, glad to find it almost empty. Stopping to choose a couple of books from the romance shelf, she cut through the children's library and went down the stairs to the courtyard.

It was pleasant there. The variegated ivy which had once fanned out in a huge semi-circle covering a quarter of the paving slabs had been cut back, yielding to nettles, thorns and other quick-growing summer weeds. She eased into a chair, positioning herself so that the sun beat on her back, seeping through her in a continuous blast of wellbeing.

She opened the first book avidly, losing herself in the characters and the situation with ease, despite her earlier reservations. The way the sun was shining, she was glad the story of *Harem Queen* was set in the heart of the desert.

Verona stayed in the library until the growling in her belly reminded her she was hungry. Rummaging in her bag, she found twenty pence and she bit on her lip in vexation; that wouldn't even buy her a chocolate bar.

In the end she decided to go home, buying some crisps to fortify herself on the long walk.

'Where you been?'

Verona blinked at her sister's harassed face. 'I went down the library,' she said, feeling sun-dazed and spaced out. The coolness of the hallway was a welcome relief after the hot, airless walk.

'I been phoning all morning – I call everybody I could think of.' Desiree sounded unusually distressed.

Alarm feathered along Verona's spine. 'What for?' Had Des found out she had been sacked? Verona's heart was racing as she searched her sister's face, her insides weak with dread.

'Grandpa collapse this morning . . . the ambulance take him to hospital.'

Verona was stunned. Guilt engulfed her when she thought of the lazy morning she had just spent. 'Christ, Des, I'm sorry, yeah. I could have been back already and all . . .'

Desiree smiled wanly. 'Listen, you can stay here with Granny Ruby while I go down the hospital? John there but I bet he not coping too well.'

'Course,' Verona agreed, eager to make amends. 'Look, Des, I ain't half sorry I wasn't here before.'

'Miss V, you come back?' Granny Ruby's voice floated in from the back garden. 'Come tell me what happening.'

Desiree watched her sister go with relief. Granny Ruby had been on at her since Grandpa Clifford collapsed that morning, badgering her for information she didn't have. The old woman looked lost and frightened without her husband. Desiree dared not think what would happen if the old man died.

She glanced at her watch: quarter past one. She could make the half-past bus if she left now.

Desiree reached the bus-stop just as the bus was pulling away, but fortunately the traffic lights ahead turned red. She ran to the door, banging on it and looking pleadingly up at the driver, and she all but tumbled in when he suddenly opened the door.

'In a hurry, are we, love?' he asked cheerily, issuing the fifty-pence ticket.

'Can you tell me when we reach the hospital, please?' she panted.

The driver nodded, dispensing her change and letting the clutch out almost in the same movement, as the lights changed to red/amber.

At the hospital she had trouble locating the right ward, getting shunted from person to person as they explained that Grandpa Clifford had probably not been 'processed' yet since he had only been admitted that morning. Desiree persisted, and in the end she tracked down the ward, walking in to find Grandpa sleeping, and John sitting at his bedside, face in hands. She touched John's shoulder lightly, feeling him tense.

'Let we go have a coffee,' she said gently.

John looked up at her uncomprehendingly. 'Coffee?'

'Yes,' she said firmly. 'You not doing Grandpa any good, sitting here like this, John.'

'You tell him, dear,' a nurse passing by agreed. 'I've been trying to get him to go get a spot of lunch, but he ain't budged.'

Desiree nodded politely, waiting until the nurse was out of earshot before returning her attention to John. In the end he let her lead him, following obediently as she headed for the hospital café.

She sat him down, fetching him some sandwiches and coffee for them both.

'How come he never tell us how sick he was, Des?' he asked in bewilderment, as she pushed the plastic cup of steaming liquid towards him.

'I think he was trying not to be a burden.'

John didn't seem to hear her. 'Is my fault. If it hadn't been for me, none of this woulda happen.'

'John, blaming youself not helping nothing. Let we just find out how we can help Grandpa.'

He nodded, a spark of hope briefly lighting his eyes before fading again.

Desiree toyed with her coffee, finding it too bitter to drink. She pictured the old man lying so frail and still, nearer dead than alive. Despite what she had said to John, she too blamed herself for not seeing Grandpa Clifford's collapse coming. She closed her eyes in remembered horror, wondering if the children were all right. She had sent them over to Mara's, afraid that the shadow of death might cloud their consciousness. It was a pity school had broken up for the holidays.

'Why it have to happen in front of the children?' she murmured softly.

'What?' John looked dazedly at her.

'Nothing. I just talking to myself.'

She couldn't get the children out of her mind. Before his attack Grandpa had been in their room, sitting on the bed when Desiree looked in. Seeing how enraptured they were by the story he was telling, she had withdrawn quietly. She had gone to sit with Granny Ruby and in fascination was watching her crochet the endless lace when there was a sudden commotion on the stairs.

'Mum! Granny Ruby!' Lyn's voice was panic-stricken, squeaky with fear.

'Wha wrong? Wha a gwaan?' Granny asked, fingers stilling in her lap.

'Let me just go and see.' Desiree hoped she sounded calmer than she felt. Her heart was thudding heavily as she raced out of the door.

Lyn and Carol were at the top of the stairs looking small and frightened. Desiree's heart leapt and her feet were momentarily rooted to the spot. What had happened to Grandpa Clifford?

'We didn't do nothing, honest, Mum,' Carol sobbed as she reached them. 'He just went all bendy and started making this funny sound.'

'I think he's dead, Mum. I tried to wake him up . . .' Despite her tears, Lyn's arms were protectively around her sister. 'He was telling us a story and showing us this dance and he just sort of folded up.'

Clutching each other for support, the children followed her anxiously as she went towards the room.

'Oh, Lord!' Desiree couldn't prevent the exclamation as she saw the bent and twisted body. She took a deep breath to steady herself, forcing herself to sound calm: 'Lyn, you all to go to Mummy's room quick, call a ambulance.'

'Is he dead?' Lyn asked tearfully.

'No, but he well sick, so he need that ambulance quick.'

As the children left reluctantly, Desiree had stared in horror at the old man. What if he was dead? She could hardly breathe from the fear.

*You have to straighten him out*, she told herself, frantically searching her mind for the knowledge gleaned from hours of television. Yes, that was what to do, straighten him out. She hovered over him, fingers recoiling each time she thought she had plucked up the courage to approach him.

Grandpa Clifford was always so dignified, yet here he was, a collapsed heap, and she was standing there, too scared to touch him in case he was cold and clammy . . . like when her grandmother had died and she had been forced to kiss her, before the lid of the coffin was drawn across with that horrible grating sound. Her eleven-year-old self had wanted to scream; and her shaking and crying had been fear, rather than the grief her grandmother's relatives had thought her overcome with.

'This is real foolish,' she said aloud. 'He can't just lie there.'

She approached the still form with caution, wishing Mara was there. She would not be dithering like this, afraid of a man because she thought he might be dead. Mara was far too practical for that.

There was a faint stirring by the bed, and Desiree's stomach squeezed, her feet stumbling backwards automatically. Self-contempt and guilt forced her forward; and she had straightened the buckled limbs with shaky hands.

Downstairs, she had waited restlessly at the front door for the ambulance. She could hear Granny Ruby humming contentedly to herself and wondered how she was going to find the courage to tell her the truth.

*V bound to get here soon*, she consoled herself, glancing at the clock. When her sister stayed out overnight in the week, she always came back by ten, and it was five to that hour now.

The ambulance arrived within five minutes, the two men creating a real commotion. Desiree could hear Granny Ruby muttering to herself; she was bound to guess something, but though Desiree knew she must speak to her, she dragged things out, hovering around until the ambulance sped off down the road, blue light flashing. Closing the front door, she stooped automatically to reposition the mat the men had disturbed.

'Desaree?'

Desiree had hesitated, torn between the anxious old woman calling her and the frightened children huddled together upstairs. She made her decision.

'Is wha wrang?' Granny Ruby had asked as she came into the sitting-room.

'Grandpa Clifford collapsed and they taking him to hospital.'

'You mean de ambulance? Is ihm heart? Ihm ha one other attack?'

'I don't know – I don't think so,' Desiree tried to sound unflustered, wanting to go to the children. 'Anyway I rang John at work and he going down the hospital right away . . .'

John broke into her reflections now: 'Des, let's go see if there's any change.'

She sensed that he was suggesting it for something to do, and she understood the need. The situation reminded her unbearably of her father – of going down to St Thomas's Hospital and wandering in a daze, desperate for something to take her mind off the broken, bandaged form that had only recently been her grave, understanding father.

She slid her arm around John's waist and he hugged her to him, looking as if he needed that contact as a lifeline.

'There's still no change,' a nurse said, stopping them before they could enter the ward. 'Doctor will be finishing his rounds soon and he wants to have a chat with you.' She led them to the small, cluttered ward office, her uniform rustling stiffly with starch.

'Can I get you some tea or coffee?' she offered, but Desiree shook her head automatically, just wanting her to leave them alone.

She watched the woman walking away, resenting her calm. *If only I was like that . . . not this mass of nerves.*

She could see the doctor at the other end of the ward, two

other white-coated figures with him. His head bent towards the ward sister. He was coming back now, pausing as the nurse who had intercepted them stopped him to say something, her shifting eyes and gestures telling Desiree that the conversation was about them.

Now the doctor was coming towards them, looking weary as he pushed into the small, cramped space. The grey hair and wrinkled face should have inspired confidence, but suddenly Desiree wanted to run, terrified of what he had to tell them.

# Seventeen

'Cancer!' Verona couldn't prevent the exclamation. Of all her fears for Grandpa Clifford, that was the furthest from her mind. 'How come?' She realised it was a stupid question even as it was voiced, and she clamped down on her instinctive horror at her sister's words.

'Whe it dey?' Granny Ruby asked in a strained voice. 'Which part a ihm get it?'

Desiree looked pleadingly at John, but he was slumped in his chair, looking stricken. Verona felt a stirring of sympathy for him; it was plain he was taking the news hard. He had come back with Des, saying little to anyone except Granny Ruby, collapsing into his chair and staring vacantly ahead. She willed him to cry, to release some of the pain that was eating away at him. But she knew he wouldn't; he would count that as weakness, would rather retreat into himself where he could scream silently.

'He's got stomach cancer,' Desiree's response was faltering as she hunted for the right words again. 'The doctor says Grandpa been suffering from it a long time.'

Granny Ruby's eyes sharpened with a sudden memory. 'Is one year gone . . . is not de bad heart dem tell ihm 'bout when Delsey carry ihm go a University Hospital.' Her voice dropped and she added almost to herself: 'Dat mussa why ihm did waan me fe have de operation . . . Cho, how much time me tell ihm a no worm mek ihm start mawga down so.'

Desiree felt inadequate in the face of the old woman's distress. 'Well, the doctors doing all they can,' she said finally, spreading her hands in helpless gesture.

'I waan see ihm.' Granny Ruby's withered hands were still, her crochet falling to the floor, forgotten in the horror of the news.

John roused himself. 'I don't know, Granny –'

The old woman cut him off: 'When I can see ihm?'

The despondency in John's face moved Desiree impulsively to drop a hand on his shoulder and she felt rejected when he shrugged it off.

'I've got to get back to work,' he muttered, getting out of his chair.

Watching him go, Desiree wished there was something she could say to console him. She had tried to be supportive after the doctor told them, but John had rounded angrily on her, desperate for someone on whom to vent his frustration. They had been barely clear of the ward when he chided her:

'How come you was with him all these weeks and never did nothing, eh? How come you always whining about something wrong with you and never even notice how sick Grandpa was?'

It didn't help that she already felt guilty; she needed reassurance, not accusations. But she had told herself with grim stoicism that he was in shock, floundering about for an explanation. It was pointless to lay into him. All she could hope to do was try to reason with him.

'John, look how many time we talk about Grandpa Clifford – all four o' we talk and talk and none o' we even suspect this thing.'

'Go on then, blame me too!' he had virtually shouted, attracting curious stares. 'It's always the bloke's fault, yeah?' he had prodded as she walked beside him, head averted, embarrassed and near to tears. 'Women! You lot never to blame for nothing.'

'That's not fair, John.' Desiree had kept her voice level with an effort. 'Look, I know right now you upset about your grandfather, but –'

'What you mean you know? You don't know nothing.'

She did know that nothing was to be gained from trying to talk with him in this mood, so she had followed silently, nursing her wronged feelings. What was the use of saying she knew something of what he was going through? As far as John was concerned no woman, with the possible exception of Mara, could possibly understand.

Now the front door slammed behind him and Desiree relaxed, sliding into the chair he had been using. The room was shrouded in an air of depression; what was normally pleasantly cool and shadowy now seemed cold and gloomy.

'Would you like to go into the garden, Granny Ruby?' Desiree asked.

The old woman nodded, eyes haunted with worry. 'Is a shame Clifford no here fe feel de sun hot,' she commented as they manoeuvred her chair down the kitchen stairs. 'Ihm always say when sunshine hot, tings never so bad. I tink ihm read it inna one a dem book dat 'merican preacher call ihmself missionary did gi we.'

Desiree wished she possessed Verona's ability to sit so naturally beside the old woman. By contrast, she felt awkward in the face of sorrow, not knowing what to say, how to act, wanting to withdraw from it. Not that she felt any less concerned about Grandpa Clifford. She had come to like the old man a great deal in the few weeks she had known him. It was just that all the bland words of comfort seemed false somehow. How could she even pretend to understand Granny Ruby's emotions? Her husband had been with her for sixty-five years. They had lived and grown old together, and for ten years he had been her legs.

Verona was the sensitive one, always seeming to know the right thing to say on every occasion – the sort of person who broke news of tragedy best. It was a blessing that the old lady could turn to her. Desiree had not been surprised on returning from the hospital to find that Verona had calmed Granny Ruby and was listening attentively while she attempted to teach her the rudiments of crochet. In other circumstances it might have been comical: V was hopeless at any type of needlework and could barely knit three rows without dropping a stitch.

Desiree frowned as her sister's face came into focus now. Come to think of it, there was something different about Verona, something she couldn't quite put her finger on. She seemed younger somehow . . . less tense, and Desiree wondered what could be responsible for that look of contentment that came to her sister's face when she was still.

'V, you found a job yet?'

Verona stiffened at the question, the wellbeing engendered by thoughts of Steve shattering. 'No,' she said cautiously.

'Mara said you didn't apply for that job she told you about.'

'Course I did! What she mean?' Verona forced herself to sound affronted, praying her sister would believe her. 'I sent me application first-class at that. It must have got lost in the post or something.'

Desiree looked sceptical but didn't pursue the matter, asking instead: 'Where you get to last night?'

Verona felt a surge of remembered pleasure, but caution guided her tongue. 'I met up with this friend I ain't seen since school and we got talking.' She was thinking on her feet, looking for a plausible answer. 'We just clean forgot the time and she never had a phone neither . . . and with me not having no bus fare so I thought I might as well stay the night.'

She was determined not to let her sister find out about Steve, recalling the first and last time she had ever taken a white boyfriend home. She had been twelve, just beginning to notice the opposite sex, and Brian was one of the nicest boys in her class. He would talk to her at break and she often helped him with his maths. Inviting him home that time had been purely innocent. She had been horrified to find that because he had lost his key he had to wander the streets until his mother returned from work at six o'clock.

Desiree had been off work that day, and her warm greeting

had choked off as her eyes fell on the awkward, greasy-haired youngster.

'What you bring this . . . boy here for?' she had asked in tones that were cold, unfriendly.

'Des, this is Brian – remember I told you 'bout him?'

'You never said he was no white boy.' Desiree's eyes had been hostile. 'He only using you 'cause he no good at maths.'

Verona had been furious. 'How come you never thought that before?'

Desiree shrugged, totally ignoring Brian. 'If he was black, he might have really liked you.'

It was the first time Verona had come face to face with the ugliness of race. She was shocked, wanted to ignore her sister. What did Des know anyway? Just because she was sixteen and working didn't mean she was right. It had nagged at Verona, things falling into place in her young mind. She had refused to speak to Desiree for a whole week, not accepting her apology or her explanation that she had been taken by surprise. The doubts had already been planted; and somehow she and Brian had drifted apart.

'I know you have a boyfriend.' Desiree's voice pulled her back to the present with quiet vehemence.

Verona was caught off-guard. 'Yeah? What if I have?'

Desiree looked relieved, to Verona's irritation. Her sister could be so transparent sometimes, the way Des watched with anxious eyes when she thought she wasn't looking. Verona knew her well enough to guess she was dubious about her sexual practices.

'But that's great, V!' Desiree said with genuine pleasure. 'I don't know why you hiding him. What's his name? When you going bring him round?'

This time Verona was prepared: 'He's a bit funny about strangers, and what with Grandpa Clifford sick . . .' She let her voice tail off, feeling a little guilty at the disappointment on Desiree's face. Well, the way Des felt about black women associating with white men she'd be a lot more upset if she ever met him, Verona thought wryly.

Grandpa Clifford's condition worsened steadily, and John was at his bedside at every opportunity. Desiree couldn't help noting the contrast with his behaviour towards her after her operation. She didn't begrudge Grandpa the attention; indeed, she went to see him every day too. At first both children came with her, but Carol found the visits depressing and quietly dropped out.

It was Verona who impressed her, dividing her time between her hidden man and visiting the hospital, never forgetting Granny Ruby. When V was home, she often begged Desiree for money to take Granny by taxi to see her husband. Verona also accompanied her to the black elderly luncheon club to help to take the old lady's mind off things. The distinctive van from the Social Action Centre, driven by an improbably small woman who always seemed to be chomping on something, took them to the club which went on until three o'clock, and from there they would go straight to the hospital.

Three weeks after being admitted to hospital Grandpa Clifford died.

The phone had rung in the middle of the night, the sound slicing Desiree out of a restless sleep. She jerked upright, fear squeezing at her heart, as John rolled over and snatched up the receiver. He hadn't been sleeping too well since the old man went into hospital, his temper becoming more frayed as the days slid into weeks.

She snapped on the bedside lamp, watching his face anxiously as panic started to creep into his eyes.

'Wh-when?' Stunned disbelief made him stumble over the word. 'No, no, I'll come down . . . Yes, that's all right.'

Desiree didn't dare to say anything when he put down the phone. Watching his frantic haste, she guessed that Grandpa Clifford was dead.

A deep sadness descended on her, making her want to slide back into the soft warmth of the bed and pretend the last few weeks had been all a bad dream. She didn't want to believe the humour and sparkle that had emanated from the old man's wasted body had finally gone out.

She looked helplessly at John. If only there was some way she could reach him, show him that she shared his grief. She was depressed at how hard they found it to communicate these days. She wished she could go with him to the hospital. *If only Verona was here instead of spending the night with her mysterious boyfriend again . . .*

John was cursing and swearing, looking for his shoes, and Desiree rolled across the bed silently, fishing them out from where he always left them when he came in too tired even to have a wash.

It was still early morning when he returned from the hospital, looking stony-eyed and bitter. Without waiting for him to slump wearily into his chair, Granny Ruby asked:

'Jahn, is true Clifford dead?'

He nodded dazedly, getting up again. 'I have to go to work.'

Desiree felt exasperation mixed with panic. What was he trying to do, kill himself too? 'I rang your work and told them, John,' she said, bracing herself for his rebuke.

John hated white people to know his business, feeling that they would use it against him. Normally Desiree sympathised; but he was beginning to look ill, and his trousers sagged where his belly had once kept them up.

'Why don't you go lie down?' she suggested gently. 'I'll bring you up something.'

To her surprise he nodded, making no comment about her pre-emptive action, and with relief she watched him leave.

'When Miss V gwine come back?' Granny Ruby asked wistfully as Desiree got up and stretched.

'I not sure. She said something about fetching the girls from Mara later.'

'She stay wid her man last night?'

Desiree nodded, awkward now. Verona often accompanied Granny Ruby to church and she knew the old woman was keen to convert her.

'When she come, send her fe see me.'

As Desiree moved about the kitchen preparing a meal for John, she shook her head. 'What a mess,' she muttered. She felt an urge to get away from the whole tangle, just to leave, move out with the children – do a Mara.

The harsh sound of the kettle banished the idea. She could never do it, she realised. She wasn't Mara. But nor she was any doormat. Her mouth tightened at the thought of how John had walked all over her when she had been sick. *That's the trouble with men; anyhow you lay down they good to walk right on top of you.*

She balanced the tray carefully, heading for the stairs. Granny Ruby was humming a slow, mournful tune, and Desiree felt tears stinging her eyes. The old woman was on her own now; she just prayed that her operation went all right next week.

'Verona back yet?' John asked sleepily as she pushed the door open.

'Not yet. She going pick up the kids on the way back.'

He hesitated before saying: 'Des, I been thinking. You know I kinda never treat the two of you like I should, seen . . .'

'Eat this before you go to sleep,' she said tactfully, putting the tray on his lap.

'No, really,' he insisted, 'I been thinking a lot since Grandpa get sick. Did I tell you is him and Granny Ruby that raise me and me brothers them?'

Desiree nodded, humouring him, concerned at the way he rambled on.

He picked over the fish without interest. 'You know that day Grandpa fall sick? Well, I meet this woman from V's work and she tell me V get the sack for stealing.'

Desiree's whole attention was on him now. 'Stealing!'

'Yeah, they say she take ten pounds or something stupid like that from a coat in the cloakroom. Anyway this woman say she sign some paper admitting she did take it.' He sighed. 'I was going to confront her in the evening – shame her so bad she'd treat me with a bit more respect.'

Desiree could hardly take in what he was saying. Her mind flashed back to the two men with the dusty red Cortina. So that's what the bastards were up to! *Why the hell didn't I keep them inside?* There was no doubt in her mind that Verona was innocent, that she must have been framed.

John was speaking again and she pulled her mind back with an effort.

'I know I keep on at you when I don't get the promotion, and I didn't nice about the college – but, Des, is through I don't want to lose you . . .' His voice wavered and cracked.

Her heart went out to him. 'John, let we talk about it another time. You tired now.'

He shook his head. 'No, is important. I been thinking about it, yeah. Look how Mara leave Winston when she get her education, and he not even like me – he's got brains and he had education as well.'

Desiree was appalled. Winston prided himself on being more intelligent than the other men he associated with, but she never imagined that John took his friend's boasting so seriously.

'You have your Ordinary National Diploma and the City and Guilds, John. That's education too. Is only racism stopping you get that promotion.'

'Seen, but supposing it isn't, Des? Winston always saying black people have to be ten times better than white people to get as far as he got . . . supposing I ain't even as good? And when you go to college and get through, you going to leave me too.'

She knew it was his shock and grief at his grandfather's death that was making him bare his soul like this. 'John, I not leaving you just because I going to college, and Mara leave Winston long before she go.'

'But what happen when you earning more money than me? I can't have my woman keeping me.'

Desiree hid a smile. He looked such a child in his big man's body, and somehow now she had the confidence to say what she really believed.

'John, we supposed to be in partnership. I don't think you keeping me – you out there earning the money, but I doing my share in here.' She paused. 'If we both sharing, things would easier and we could even spend more time together, 'stead of drifting away from each other.'

'If I could get a promotion I wouldn't need do so much overtime.'

'Why don't you look for another job?'

He looked at her as though the thought had never occurred to him before; but she could see by the tentative excitement growing in his eyes that he did not find the idea unpleasant. 'Des, you think I could?'

She nodded firmly. 'When you go to the railway there wasn't much jobs, but I been looking round and now there's a lot more for people with your skills.'

He seemed intrigued. 'But what if I ain't good enough? I don't have no O-levels, you know.'

'You don't know OND is the same thing?'

'But Winston say –'

'I don't want to hear what Winston say. *Mara* say is the same and she have more education than him.' She hadn't meant to belittle the other man, but she felt angry at Winston's way of always trying to put others down.

'Suppose no one want me?'

'Just think about it and let we talk another time.'

He nodded, putting the tray on the bedside table. 'Des, stay with me, noh?' he asked.

She hesitated, thinking of all the things she needed to do.

'I just want to talk to you,' he pleaded.

Desiree relented. This was the closest she had felt to him since her illness. What he had confided to her made so many things clearer, fitted in with the man who had done so much to help when they had met fifteen years before.

As his even breathing told her that he was drifting into sleep, Desiree vowed to hold on to that. After all, she and John still had a lot going for them if only they could keep talking, and she was determined not to let their marriage slip back into the morass of resentment and misunderstandings it had become of late.

# Eighteen

Verona lay on the bed-settee, still only partly dressed. Steve was writing as if his life depended on it, wedging his typewriter into a space on the desk by the simple method of ramming it into the mass of paper and wriggling it about. She watched him for a few minutes, awed by the speed at which his fingers flew across the keys; but soon the novelty wore off.

*I might as well go*, she told herself, realising that he was unlikely to surface for several hours. She debated about breakfast, deciding against it. He hated the smell of frying first thing in the morning, especially when he was in a writing phase. She had some chocolate in her bag; that would just have to hold her until she got round to Mara's to collect the children.

There was something brooding and desolate about the house since Grandpa Clifford went into hospital, she thought as she walked back with the girls. Something waiting, that dragged at her spirit each time she approached it.

'Will Grandpa be out of hospital yet?' Carol asked wistfully.

'Don't be silly, Carol,' Lyn said, 'he's dying, ain't it, Auntie V?'

'He's very sick right now,' Verona evaded.

She was glad when Carol suddenly sped off down the road. 'Bet you can't catch me,' she shouted back to Lyn.

The door was open when they reached the house, Desiree standing there grim-faced as she watched their progress.

Mrs Evans from across the road came out of her house, moving to the gate to shout across: 'How's the old man, love? I saw the ambulance and been meaning to ask one of you but you're never around these days.' She leaned against her gate confidingly. 'Must be all the to-ing and fro-ing to the hospital . . . quite a shock, was it?'

Verona's lips tightened; trust Nosy Dora to be trying to ferret out the facts. Before she could reply, however, Desiree said from the door:

'Why you don't keep your nose in your own business, 'stead of always in things that don't concern you?' She was deliberately rude, ignoring the woman as she stepped aside for the now giggling children to enter.

'Lyn, go into the garden with your sister,' she said as soon as they came into the hall, 'and if you all got any homework left, make sure it's done. Don't forget school start next week.'

'Not till Wednesday, Mum,' the child protested.

'Do what I tell you.' Desiree gave her an impatient look.

'Is he dead?' Verona asked in an undertone when Lyn was out of earshot.

Desiree nodded. 'Granny Ruby asking for you,' she said.

'How's she taking it?' Verona gave her sister a shrewd look. Des was acting strangely and she sensed it wasn't all to do with Grandpa Clifford's death. Something else was wrong. 'Look, Des, everything all right? Does John know? He been bothering you, is that it?'

'Is John did go to the hospital. He in bed sleeping now.' She stopped as the children's voices rose in an argument. 'Listen, V, I'll talk to you later.' Her eyes slid away from direct contact.

Verona frowned, heading for the sitting-room. If Des had something to say, she'd find out what it was soon enough.

It was as they were preparing dinner that it came out.

'V, why you leave Stoneford's?'

Verona halted abruptly in the act of washing lettuce leaves under the running tap. 'What do you mean?'

'I mean, why didn't you insist on your holidays or something?'

'I told you. I tried but they never listen, so in the end I just gave in my notice.'

Desiree was observing her closely. 'Remember that woman from Trinidad you introduce us to at the last dinner dance?'

Verona felt the breath leave her lungs as if she had just been kicked in the stomach. 'What about her?' she asked faintly.

'John met her down Brixton couple of weeks ago. She told him you got the sack for thieving.'

'So?' Verona didn't know how else to respond, hiding behind defiance as a cloak for the sickness inside her.

Desiree's temper flared. 'V! Look, is true or not?'

'What if it is?'

'That's what those men wanted, wasn't it?'

Verona shrugged; what was the point hiding now? Des already knew anyway. 'Yeah, it's true.' She wondered why John had kept it to himself. That certainly wasn't his style. He was more likely to confront her with relish, taking pleasure in watching her try to squirm out of it.

'You could have trusted me, you know, V.' Desiree sounded hurt.

Verona felt uncomfortable under her sister's steady gaze. 'Ain't you gonna ask if it's true?' she challenged.

'Of course you didn't do no fool thing like that. But why you sign that paper, V?'

Tears prickled in Verona's eyes. Desiree believed her! She felt happiness mingled with shame. She should have trusted that her sister would always take her side. 'You were real sick, and they was saying about the newspapers. And I know how bad things are up at the school already.'

'But what you going to do now?'

'What about John,' Verona countered, 'I bet he thought I took the money?'

'Course not . . . I know you don't like John no more, but you got to realise what he's going through. Remember when Dad died, how it was?'

Verona nodded. Of course she remembered. Their father had been all the parent she really knew. She had been nine when her mother died, but she had only been with her in England two years, and in truth her grandmother was the one she really thought of as mother.

'I'm sorry, Des,' she sighed, 'I guess John must be really suffering.'

'He'll survive.' Desiree brushed the comment aside, bringing over the rest of the salad vegetables to her. 'What I worrying about is getting you a job.'

The bell rang, preventing an answer.

'That must be Mara. I ask her to come over after work,' Desiree said, moving towards the door. 'Jay's in court soon and I'm going with them.'

At the door, Mara said concernedly: 'Des, they told me down at the hospital. How's John taking it?'

'He's sleeping,' Desiree responded, closing the door and hesitating before asking: 'Mara, could you go see Granny Ruby for a bit? The truth is . . . well, I just don't know what to say to her.'

'Is she taking it bad?'

'Not really.' Desiree sounded as if she had just made the discovery herself. 'She just talking, talking about when they were young. V can talk to her, but since this new man of hers she's out most nights now.'

'What's he like?'

'Wish I knew. Every time I try to invite him round, she telling me how he shy. Mara, you think she hiding him?'

'I think I'll go and see Granny first.' Mara ducked the question, heading for the sitting-room before Desiree could make any protest.

Grandpa Clifford wasn't to be buried in England. John was furious at the suggestion.

'Not bloody likely! Grandpa ain't staying in no racist country, even if I have to sell the house to do it.'

Desiree made no comment, making allowance for the pain he must be feeling.

'Dem bwoy dem deh 'merica can find some a de money, and Clifford and me did have one little bit put by,' Granny Ruby said.

'I'll ring your brothers, John,' Desiree offered, 'and what about your uncles in Canada?'

It was Granny Ruby who answered: 'Me know say Delsey no have no money, but Delroy and Samson good fe help out. Doan worry youself say you a go lost you house.'

Desiree was determined that wouldn't happen. She felt a little mean, but no way was she going to sell the house to send the old man back. It was all right for John; he didn't really have to worry. As he saw it, children were the woman's problem. She shook her head; maybe that was a bit unfair. John had always been a good provider, and if they didn't see eye to eye much of the time, the conversation they had had on the day of Grandpa Clifford's death proved John was still capable of opening up, and she had begun to feel more optimistic about their learning to communicate better with one other.

She wondered if the mess would ever sort itself out. College started in less than a month and even though John could be made to pull his weight, almost letting her direct him, emotionally he was practically sitting on her. Sometimes she had to grit her teeth to stop from lashing out at him, wishing he would snap out of it. All he ever did was work and mope around. She couldn't wait for college to start, so she could get away from the oppressive presence of death that had seeped into every corner of the house.

'Yes, Desaree, you telephone Canada and 'merica. You can mek de call colleck if you ringing Delroy and Samson – dem no go vex 'bout it.'

Desiree nodded, satisfied. It was far better actually to be doing something, rather than living with the uncertainty of the past few days. She knew Granny Ruby wanted things settled before she went into hospital the following day and she was glad this at least was decided. She could see the old woman was pleased that her husband would be laid to rest in the family burial ground she often spoke about. Granny Ruby had spent many years tending the little patch reserved for them; she needed to know he would be there waiting for her.

# Nineteen

'It's positive.'

Verona felt stunned, looking at the gentle-eyed woman as if she had just delivered a death blow. 'But it can't be, I'm on the . . .'

She tailed off, remembering. That first time, when she hadn't long met Steve, she'd been 'resting' from the pill. It was a common enough practice for her; if there was a long gap between times she would come off until she met a likely somebody. So many alarmist television programmes and vague warnings had made her nervous of the pill; rumours and half-snatched bits of conversation had convinced her that without 'contraceptive holidays' she would get cancer and die before anyone found out.

Pregnant! The thought provoked a host of conflicting feelings. Did Mara suspect . . . was that why Mara had insisted she come down to the Women's Centre to have the test? It hadn't occurred to Verona before, but people didn't take pregnancy tests just in case.

'What can I do about it?' she asked in a small voice.

The woman looked at her through warm grey eyes, her face reassuring as she picked her words carefully: 'For a start, you must make up your mind whether you want to have it or not . . .'

Verona was hardly taking in any part of it, her mind wrestling with the implications of pregnancy. *What's Des going to say?* she wondered unhappily. She could imagine her sister's initial reaction – Des would be full of joy but anxious, searching her face to make sure that she really wanted it. All that would be gone when the truth came out about Steve being white. *She ain't never gonna forgive me when she finds out.*

Verona pulled up sharp. She was thinking as if she had already decided to have the child. Nothing was decided yet, she told herself firmly, half-aware of the voice still droning away on the edge of her conscious mind.

Somehow she was through the heavy wooden door, glad of the warmth of the late sun after the coolness of the place. She walked along the side of the fenced-off green where children from a nearby nursery played, skirting the rubbish that choked up the path to the extent that people using the crèche could no longer get past. She stepped gingerly through a veritable field of broken glass, wondering how a place that advertised workshops for children with such bold posters could leave so glaring a hazard in their path.

Far below, where Thurlow Arms faced Woolworth's and the outer edges of the cemetery marked the boundary where the number 2 bus turned, the traffic lights changed. Three lanes of traffic rushed towards her, and she hurried across the road, heading for the modern starkness of the library.

It was only three-twenty. Hers had been the first appointment at the pregnancy-testing service. She was to meet Desiree and Mara in Peckham later, after they had been to the court for Jay's case; John for once had agreed to take half a day off so that when Granny Ruby came back from the luncheon club someone would be there for her.

Verona hesitated at the library door, tempted to go down the road and see how the old woman was doing. Granny Ruby was using the club regularly again since coming out of hospital after the hip replacement. It had not been successful but Granny Ruby had remained philosophical, returning to her crocheting and surprising them all with her resilience. Every Thursday night she would start looking forward to her outing to the club again, her conversations full of the happenings and doings down there. She still grieved for her husband but she seemed to cope by holding on to the memory of the good years they had shared together.

Verona sighed. If only the hip operation hadn't failed . . .

thank goodness Granny Ruby was so accepting. It was John who had been floored by it. He seemed broken and defeated, watching over his grandmother like a hen with chick. They had all pinned so much hope on the old woman walking again, and the thought of what was to happen to her was never far from their minds.

Verona picked a couple of books at random and headed for the courtyard. It was hot and silent, the brown tiling a restful contrast against the glare of afternoon sun. She sat down, feeling a certain disappointment that someone had been fighting back a new tide of variegated ivy, cutting the root strands and rolling back a part of it like a carpet.

The sun was warm on her, but she felt too queasy to read. The atmosphere was airless, but she enjoyed the warmth and peace. She often imagined this was what holidays abroad must be like, judging from the glossy pictures she saw in travel agents' brochures. Even the intricate brick pattern of the courtyard looked as if it would have been at home trailing bougainvillea and edged by hibiscus in some sun-drenched Mediterranean villa.

Verona had the sudden urge to eat a Caramac bar, but her stomach lurched as the thought registered. It seemed weeks since she had first started feeling sick and she was constantly sucking mints to keep the sensation at bay. It was so hard to keep on her feet. All she wanted to do was lie on her bed letting her misery wash over her, never having to get up again.

When she finally walked up Peckham High Street, Desiree and Mara were waiting outside the bookshop, the brown bag Mara was clutching evidence that she had been unable to resist nipping inside. Mara's big interest at the moment was children's books; she insisted on buying ones written from a black perspective for Charleen and Meeli, who devoured them as fast as she could find them.

'How did it go?' Verona asked as she came up to them.

They had been deep in conversation and they looked up together.

'Hello, V,' Mara said, while Desiree nodded, scanning her sister's face.

'What happened?' Verona asked, impatient to find out.

Mara smiled. 'Case dismissed.' There was quiet triumph in her voice. 'I could have kissed Olu.'

'I'm sure he would have understood,' Desiree teased, 'you kissed just most everybody else in reach.' She sobered: 'V, are you all right?

Verona forced a grin. 'Why shouldn't I be?' She wished the sick feeling streaming inside her would subside. Her head was aching from the bus ride, and it was an effort to keep her body from slumping on itself.

'You've lost weight,' Mara said, looking at her critically.

Desiree nodded in agreement, a frown on her face, and Verona hid her surprise. She certainly hadn't herself noticed any change in her size. If anything, she felt heavier and more sluggish with this nausea inside her. She couldn't even lose herself in romance any more, feeling too unwell and worried to concentrate on the dancing words in the pages.

Mara's expression was thoughtful and she edged closer to Verona as Desiree was distracted by a commotion across the street. 'You do what I tell you?' she asked quietly.

Verona pretended she hadn't heard; the last thing she wanted was to confirm the suspicions of Des's best friend.

Mara shrugged good-naturedly, and said, pitching her voice so Desiree could hear: 'Let's go eat. I thought we could go to that Caribbean restaurant in Streatham, the one I told you about up Greyhound Lane. They say it have some sweet, sweet food.'

Verona wondered with annoyance why they hadn't just told her to meet them up there. It certainly would have been easier on her stomach. She could have walked down to Leigham Court Road, from where it was only a short bus ride to the High Street. She hated the route she'd had to take, the one-way system making it a particular nightmare with the driver's tendency to brake sharply and jerk the bus whenever they were slowing down or speeding up.

Mara had parked in a dead-end street, flanked by a pub and a fenced-off construction site bordering the main road. Verona climbed into the back of the small car with trepidation, doubtful that she would survive the lurch and swing of the car in motion. She leaned her head against the door, willing herself to relax, lest the others guessed her secret.

Mara drove through Brixton, coming up from Camberwell along Coldharbour Lane. Verona just wanted to die as they snarled up by the half-closed market in the start of the rush-hour traffic. There were prickles of sweat under her arms, a clamminess on her palms, and she wondered if her legs would support her. She had developed an increased need to go to the toilet and the urge came on strongly by the time they were bearing off towards Streatham Vale. She was thankful when they finally arrived, excusing herself and heading straight for the ladies' the minute they entered the restaurant.

Desiree gazed after her with troubled eyes, while unenthusiastically following the waiter to the table he indicated.

'Mara, tell me something: V strike you like she acting strange?' she asked, as soon as the man had presented them with menus and retreated.

Her friend looked up, seemed about to say something then changed her mind. 'She don't look well, does she?' she admitted instead.

'She's gone off her food, and she's been sick a couple of times.'

'I thought she was dieting for the new man . . .' Mara started half banteringly, tailing off as she saw the concern in Desiree's eyes. 'You think she might be pregnant?' she suggested, watching the other carefully.

'I could be wrong,' Desiree was almost apologetic. Putting her fears in words made the possibility far too real.

'She ain't mentioned anything to you?'

'No. I probably being too suspicious. V's nearly twenty-eight, she much too sensible to do something so fool.'

'Girl, ain't that always the way?' Mara responded sceptically.

The meal was an uncomfortable affair and Verona was glad when it was over. She had toyed with her fish, finding it physically impossible to raise the fork to her mouth after the first bite lodged somewhere in her throat and threatened to bring the contents of her stomach up. She was aware of Desiree watching her, and only willpower kept her sitting there. The smell of the food was too rich. Willing tears not to come, she drank the iced water greedily, trying to numb the queasiness that was growing steadily worse. It seemed for ever before they had finished and were ready to go, and she stumbled out of the restaurant feeling as if her insides had been thoroughly battered.

She huddled wretchedly in the back of the car all the way home.

What was wrong with her? Surely pregnancy should not make her feel this ill. She couldn't recall Desiree going through this. Forebodings of a disabled child, loss of her womb, pregnancy in one of her tubes, now terrified Verona beyond the point where she dared approach a doctor. All she wanted to do was ignore the changes happening to her body.

Afraid that Desiree had guessed her predicament, Verona avoided her all evening, helping the girls with their homework and then talking to Granny Ruby. When John eventually took the old woman up to bed, Verona ducked into the kitchen, running hot water into the washing-up basin.

'V, I want to talk to you.' Desiree sounded ominously serious.

'Can't it wait?' Verona made her voice as discouraging as possible. 'I ain't half got a headache.'

Her sister came across to lay a cool palm across her forehead, reminding Verona of the countless times Des had looked after her when she was ill. 'Well, you don't have a temperature,' Desiree confirmed.

'That don't mean it ain't hurting.'

'V, you pregnant?'

'No!' She could have bitten her tongue off, the denial heavy in the air. Desiree looked unbelieving, and Verona wished she could have called it back. 'What gave you that idea?' she asked casually.

'All that morning sickness and the way you been off your food this long time now.'

'I thought you supposed to get cravings when you're pregnant,' Verona challenged.

'Not everybody does. Why you don't talk to Mara about it? She did some course down at South London Women's Centre.'

'I don't need to,' Verona denied.

She had burned her bridges now, the half-formed decision she had tried desperately not to make forced on her by circumstances. She was going to keep this child. Why not, anyway? Okay, Des and Mara were always talking about mixing the races and how bad it was, and Verona agreed that black people shouldn't be forced to take sole responsibility for the children just because white people rejected them.

But she and Steve had a good relationship, and he wasn't one of those ignorant racist white people. They'd make a good life. She was sure they could get rehoused from his flat when the council found out they were expecting a baby . . . and they might even get married.

Once the decision was made, telling Desiree was next. Verona couldn't imagine her wanting to have anything to do with her once it came out that Steve was white. *But I've got to lead my own life*, she told herself. She supposed she should talk it over with Steve first. He had given her a key to his flat, complaining that she always interrupted him when she came. She would keep herself busy cleaning the place, often taking his dirty clothes to the launderette, then getting in something to cook on the way back.

Fortunately, Desiree refused to take any of her benefit money and Verona spent most of it on Steve. When she wasn't doing for him, she would sit and read a romance, slipping easily into the role of the latest heroine, Steve's features superimposed on the description of the wonderful hero.

# Twenty

It was Friday before the subject of Verona's pregnancy came up again. College was starting the following Monday and Desiree was preoccupied and tense throughout the week, checking and rechecking with John the arrangements they had made for Granny Ruby. The children had been back at school for a few weeks and they were doing a lot more for themselves, still wrapped in the novelty of their new freedom to help out around the house.

Desiree and John agreed to ask Verona to take care of the old woman in the daytime, knowing how well the two of them got on. Desiree was to speak to her sister, but when the weekend loomed without a chance presenting itself she resolved to make the space that day to broach the subject.

It started to rain in the afternoon, fat droplets splashing on the tiled sill, through the open kitchen window. Desiree covered the rapidly boiling pot of rice, pulling the window shut as the rain sheeted down. The air had freshened and she opened the back door slightly, welcoming the breeze after the oppressive, unrelenting heat of the past two weeks. After such midsummery weather it was hard to believe they were now three weeks into September. She hoped it wasn't going to turn into an unsettled month. The laurel at the bottom of the garden was beginning to look somewhat downtrodden, with the dead brown blossoms drooping like dirty spots against the deep green of the leaves. It was a late-flowering tree, planted in the wrong season when they had first moved in and making no attempt to change its lifestyle.

A flash of lightning jagged across the premature darkness,

followed by the deep belly-roll of thunder. She hoped Lyn and Carol were all right. They had gone down to the swimming-baths straight from school and didn't have coats. They were to meet Charleen there and go back home with her for the night; then she was to come over for Saturday night.

Charleen had really hit it off with Granny Ruby and often brought her little presents, things made at school or freesias from their garden. Granny was teaching her to crochet, and she would come with a little basket Mara had brought back from a trip to Trinidad a couple of years earlier. Charleen would sit with the old lady, take out her carefully wrapped handiwork from the bag, and they would be singing songs and working in no time. Usually Lyn joined them, listening attentively to Granny Ruby's guidance when the tablemats she was making went wrong. Carol, by contrast, would mope around complaining until her mother humoured her by allowing her to make a cake.

*I suppose I'd better speak to V*, Desiree thought, turning down the fire under the pot as the sizzling of water told her it was boiling over.

Verona was lying down in the children's room, staring through the window at the rain-sodden sky.

'V, you all right?'

Verona turned with a start as the bed depressed. 'Oh, Des . . . I didn't hear you come in. I was just thinking.' She sat up cautiously, reminding Desiree painfully of when she herself had been ill.

'When you going to see the doctor?'

'I'm all right, honest, Des. Anyway I'm feeling a lot better.'

Desiree let that pass for now. 'Actually I wanted to speak to you.'

'Funny, I was thinking of having a word,' Verona sounded wary: 'Des, what would you say about me moving out?'

'Moving out! Verona, why?'

'Well, sleeping in here ain't ideal, for starters.'

'I know, V, and I'm real sorry; but you know Granny going back to Jamaica October twelve, so you can have your old room back in just a month.' She smiled hopefully. 'That not too long. You in here three and a half months now and you never complained before.'

'Maybe I never saw no point. There was only Mara's where I could stay and I didn't want to turf Jay out.'

Desiree's eyes sharpened as she discounted her sister's excuses, focusing on the only other possible explanation: 'Is this new man friend of yours.' She tried to keep the accusation out of her voice, knew from the way her sister bristled that she had failed. 'V, don't you think is a bit hasty?'

'Steve and I love each other,' Verona said with dignity.

Desiree felt the burden of failure. How could V be so naïve? At twenty-seven, she sounded like something out of a bad romance novel. Somehow she had gone wrong with her sister. Something had happened in V's life, and she didn't even know what it was.

'But you seeing him only a few weeks, V.'

'We been together nearly three months, but we know each other longer.'

'Well, four months then. That's still hardly enough time to know a man.'

'Yeah, and nine months was, eh? So how come you ended up with that deadbeat John?'

Desiree flinched. 'Whatever John's faults, at least he's responsible.'

'Well, so is Steve,' Verona responded defiantly.

'At least let me meet him,' Desiree pleaded, worry threading her voice.

'Why? You think I don't have sense to know when a bloke's all right?'

'I didn't mean that. Honestly, V, why do you always hide your boyfriends from me? I never used to keep mine from you.'

'No, you never, did you?' Verona said with hostility, springing to her feet. 'At least I never expose Lyn and Carol to any of mine.'

'What's that supposed to mean?'

'You don't know, do you? You always on about promising Mum you'd look after me – well, you never did a good job when I needed it, so don't bother start now.'

'V, I tried my best. What I do wrong?' Guilt and pain made her shaky.'

'You ever wonder why your precious Ronnie used to come by even when he knew you weren't gonna be there, did you?'

Ronnie? Desiree stared at her blankly. 'You mean Ronnie Gilmour from the youth club?'

'Yeah, Ronnie Gilmour from the youth club,' Verona mimicked her, 'the same bastard you brought home.'

'V, you can't blame me through you go get sweet on him.'

'Oh, get out, Des,' Verona sniffed, her large frame shaking with misery. How could she ever make Des understand that she had long ago ceased to be an innocent child? Her tears fell unheedingly now, tracing furrows along her sun-darkened skin. 'You keep talking about understanding, and black this and black that, but when something really goes wrong none of you ain't around.'

Desiree stumbled backwards, righting herself as she nearly fell over the end of Lyn's bed. She looked devastated, and Verona regretted taking out her fear on her like that. It wasn't really her sister's fault that Ronnie had assaulted her.

She was appalled at herself for the way she had lashed out at Desiree. She had not truly meant those things. Her temper frayed so easily lately. She supposed she would have to apologise again, she thought with resignation. That was all she ever seemed to do these days – snap at people and then apologise.

'Des, sorry about yesterday,' Verona said contritely as soon as her sister appeared at the kitchen door the next morning. She had got up early, finding it difficult to sleep or even to concentrate on a book, and on impulse decided to make Desiree's favourite breakfast.

'That all right,' Desiree acknowledged, eyes sliding away from direct contact. She had passed a restless night, worrying about Verona's words, and she had risen today with every intention of tackling her before the kids came back. John had gone off to work early, and Granny Ruby wasn't feeling too well so was staying in bed until the children returned.

'V, you still mean to leave?' she asked quietly, touching the kettle to test if it was hot, then taking a mug from its hook under the wall unit.

'I never said I was leaving for good . . . but, yeah, I'm going to move in with Steve next week.'

'I wish you'd think about it a bit more first,' Desiree said carefully, fishing a piece of liver from the pan and chewing on it thoughtfully.

'There ain't nothing to think about. Des, I'm twenty-seven, for God's sake, not twelve. Don't you think is time I start standing on me own feet?'

Desiree wondered how she could make her understand. 'Look, you can tell me to mind my own business if you like –'

'Mind your own business.' Verona was smiling, but there was a serious look in her eyes that said she was not joking.

'All right, I can see there ain't no stopping you. But you promise me something, V?'

'What?'

'Just if anything go wrong you going come to me.'

'Yeah.'

It was said too glibly to be convincing, and Desiree might have pursued it had she not been so disturbed about their confrontation in the children's room.

'V, what you mean last night about Ronnie?' she probed.

Verona stiffened, suddenly absorbed in stirring the already finished liver. 'I was a bit browned-off. Don't take no notice of me, y'hear, Des. You know I don't mean nothing by it.'

'V, you were really upset . . . and when I was thinking about it last night – you did start acting odd round that time.'

'Of course I never acted odd,' Verona denied indignantly.

'Let's leave it, shall we?' Desiree conceded, seeing little point in pressing. In a stubborn mood like this there was no shifting her sister. They finished breakfast in an atmosphere of truce and soon afterwards Verona said she was going to see Steve.

John came home around eleven o'clock, and Desiree was surprised to see that Mara and the children were with him.

'John came round to get the kids and I gave him a lift,' Mara supplied to her friend's unspoken enquiry. 'Jay's taken Meeli to her godmother for the afternoon.'

'You hardly ever bring her round these days,' Desiree complained. 'You know how much I like her.'

Mara shrugged. 'She's into six-year-olds right now, my dear, and you know she and Melissa is best friends again.'

'You eat already or you want some liver?'

'Any pork inna it?' Mara asked.

Desiree nodded. 'I forgot. But I have some chicken from yesterday.'

'Girl, now you're talking my kind of language.'

The children were moving about upstairs and Desiree cursed under her breath when she heard them go into Granny Ruby's room.

'It's all right, Des, I'll go see to them,' John said almost immediately, his steps heavy and loud as he climbed the stairs.

'He's changed,' Mara said, jerking her head in John's direction.

'Yes and no,' Desiree said slowly, trying to bring what she meant into focus. 'He really taking Grandpa's death hard. I think he blame himself.'

'Why? The old man had terminal cancer. How could John have done anything, even supposing he knew?'

'I don't know, I just feel he needs help – someone to talk to. I not handling it well, Mara. I wish he would stop being so manly and do some good old-fashioned bawling.'

Mara chewed her chicken thoughtfully. 'You might have something there,' she said, sitting up with a grin. 'Remember I was telling you about Black People in Bereavement, the new counselling service that was setting up? Well, I'll get one of the guys to come and have a chat with John. I suspect he'd find that easier than talking to a woman.'

'Could you really? The truth is, I don't know how he'll manage when Granny Ruby leave next month.'

'I'll ring Mike tonight and see how he's set,' Mara promised.

'Wish you could solve V's problems while you're at it,' Desiree said.

'Is she over at her man's?'

'Yes, she went around ten.'

'Did she say what she going to do about the baby?'

'She said she not pregnant.'

Mara hissed air through her teeth. 'Des, you can't miss it! Even supposing she wasn't having such a bad time, just take a good look at her breasts.'

'I know,' Desiree sighed, 'but I can't do nothing about it.'

'True. She's a big girl now, Des; you can't keep stifling her in protection.

If Desiree felt a little hurt by that she made no comment.

'She'll be all right,' her friend coaxed. 'V isn't as soft as you think. Whatever make her behave so fool sometimes doesn't mean she don't have sense – she probably better at surviving than you.'

'I suppose you're right.'

'So,' Mara said, picking up her plate and heading for the sink, 'looking forward to Monday?'

Desiree felt the fluttering of nerves that thoughts of her course invariably brought. 'Yes . . . I suppose so. V's agreed to keep an eye on Granny Ruby till John get home, and the kids are really being helpful – Lyn gets their tea in the week now,' she said, not hiding her pride.

'You see what I mean?' Mara said obliquely.

Desiree looked blankly at her. 'I suppose so,' she said doubtfully again.

# Twenty-One

Desiree cradled her books in her arms as though they were fragile, feeling a sense of awe and unreality as she mounted the wide entrance stairs to the college. She had seen students in American films carrying their books like this and she had always wanted to try. As she reached the top, she glanced upwards at the VAUXHALL COLLEGE sign, feeling a swell of pride as she fumbled for her identification card for security.

It was the end of November and the air had that cold promise she always associated with the run-up weeks to Christmas. Although she had already been at the college for nearly a term, she still got a thrill just from walking through the door. It had been like that on the first day. She had come early for registration as directed, awed by the enormity of what she was doing in this milling, buzzing crowd of students. When she had come before to sit the entrance exam, things had been quiet and it hadn't seemed such a big step to be taking. Yet although the noise had been somewhat offputting, it felt good to be a part of all that bustle and activity. It gave her a new determination and she was certain she was going to enjoy the course.

Not that it had been plain sailing so far. It had been over twelve years since she had done any studying and she was rusty and out of practice. At first it had been hard to concentrate, the volume of work overwhelming her. She had spent long hours in the college library, and had even attended a course in how to study down at the Strand Centre.

Everyone, apart from John, had been encouraging, particularly Mara's friend Olu, who had dug up several of his old law textbooks for Desiree to use. She smiled, looking back. Those first few weeks had been touch and go even with the benefit of the six-week Strand course.

In her new preoccupation she had forgotten Lyn's birthday. Thank God for Verona! Her sister had made a cake and even prodded John into buying the present Desiree would normally have remembered.

The thought of her sister brought a frown of consternation to her face. Verona had in the end gone to live with Steve at the beginning of October, and no one in the family had even met him. In the early days V still came round regularly, but after a couple of weeks she would only phone. Granny Ruby's departure had been postponed because of complications resulting from the operation, and Desiree wondered whether her sister's staying away could have anything to do with not being able to move back into her old room. Now news had just come that Verona was at Mara's and, from what her friend had to say, pretty much the worse for wear.

Desiree glanced at her watch, quickening her step on the wide stairs. She was going round to Mara's that afternoon, so she had to see her tutor before the morning session began.

Today she had lost all her hard-won concentration. Her mind was on Verona, and she felt uncomfortable and out of sorts after the lecturer had to call her attention several times. It was a relief when the classes were over for the day, and she didn't bother to exchange the usual pleasantries with her fellow students. It was already three o'clock and she had told Mara she would be there by four-thirty. She intended to walk up Lansdowne Road and take the bus at Stockwell, but she would have to hurry if she hoped to get the next one.

Verona curled up on the mattress, not reading, not sleeping, just staring at the tiled ceiling, wondering how Jay had managed to get the picture of the footballer to stay up there. She was determined not to think about Steve. That only made her angry, and then she became short of breath and panicky.

Thank God for Mara. If not for Mara, she might still be traipsing from Social Services to Housing and back again, hoping someone from the council could help her. Verona had seen in the news about how bad the housing problem was; but that was inner London. You couldn't get much more outer than Croydon; and they'd said you had to be housed if you were pregnant. Well, that was a myth. The toad-faced man who talked to her after she had waited over an hour had been really nasty.

It was when she started feeling faint that she had thought of Mara. Her head ached where she had banged it against the wall, and her palms were sore and numb from dragging around the heavy suitcases. Added to that, she felt queasy from lack of food. The draining sick feeling from the early months had come back with a vengeance.

She sighed. None of it would have happened if she had never

met Steve. She wondered why she wasn't heartbroken, decided she had too much bother on her head to think about that now. All she could think of was how stupid she'd been. He had not really wanted her there in the first place, dismissing her proposal out of hand by saying she would never want to live with him. She hadn't realised what he was telling her then, feeling touched that he seemed always to be thinking about what was best for her.

She had gone ahead and moved out of her sister's house on the Wednesday after Desiree started college, accepting gratefully when Des insisted on giving her money for a taxi.

Steve had been out when she arrived and she had busied herself putting the place in order and tidying up his clothes. By the time he got back, she had a pot boiling merrily on the cooker. She had brought some flowers from her sister's garden, arranging them in a couple of milk bottles, and they added a splash of colour to the otherwise drab room.

'What's all this in aid of?' Steve had asked, puzzled. Then his eyes had come to rest on the two suitcases. 'Those yours?'

Verona had tensed, detecting a slightly unfriendly note in his voice. 'I've moved in,' she had said, going to hug him. 'Isn't that great? Now I'll be able to look after you all the time and you can just write, ain't it?'

He had pulled her arms from round his neck. 'How long you staying?'

It was obvious that he was put out, but she had quashed her unease, telling herself he just needed time to get used to the idea.

Time! That was a laugh; he was no different from those white people who were in the National Front. He'd only wanted her because he was trying something exotic. Well, nobody was going to slap her around and call her names. She should have known he was tacky. All his talk about being a writer was simply that – talk. He'd probably nicked that typewriter as well.

Verona didn't know now what she'd ever seen in his greasy straw-like hair, and his face was full of pimples most of the time anyway. It crossed her mind that the only difference between him and Ronnie was that Steve was white and she was older. It hadn't taken long for him to show his true colours.

The way Steve had kicked her in her stomach was the height of nastiness. She was convinced he had been trying to get rid of the child.

'I don't want no black bastard calling me Dad,' he had told her with cruel frankness, digging his fingers into her scalp through her short hair.

She had lashed out at him, kicking and scratching, to protect her child and affronted that her illusion of safety was crashing around her ears.

To think she had thought because he was white he was safe! Boy, had she paid for that. She sucked air through her teeth. *At least this time I really mean it when I say never again*, she told herself wryly.

The door opened and she turned her head listlessly, steeling herself for the cross-examination Mara had had the good sense to put off.

'Des is here,' Mara informed her, 'why you don't come have some tea?'

Verona forced a smile, nodding reluctantly. She had to face her sister some time. She just wished it could be later, when the confused echoes of disappointment would be less fresh in her mind. She could understand now why Des stayed with John; it was all very well for Mara to say that physical violence wasn't the only way of being cruel, but when people started slapping you about . . . Her mind shied away from images of Ronnie suddenly lined up with Steve.

Mara and Desiree were in the lounge listening to a new Sparrow record, both keeping time to the calypso music in their own way while tactfully waiting for Verona to join them in her own time.

Desiree looked up, shock registering on her face, when her sister came in. 'V! My God! Is what happen to you?'

Verona's hand self-consciously covered the bruised side of her face. 'It look worse than it feel,' she said, shaken by her sister's reaction.

'How the man dare do that to you! You not letting him get away with it.'

Was it really that bad? Verona had hoped the stinging

rawness in her face was only an immediate effect of the blows she had received. Fresh anger tautened her lips. *If I see him again . . .* she thought bitterly. *I should have flattened him there and then.* Ridiculous really, she supposed, but she had been too frightened at the time.

'Not much point doing nothing, is it?' she said aloud, as much in answer to her own thoughts as her sister's question. What would they say if they knew that he was white? 'Is best to just leave it.'

'You not going back to him, are you?' Desiree demanded.

'Not likely. I ain't that daft, you know,' Verona said with a spurt of irritation at her sister's concern – as if she couldn't look after herself. Des saw her as her baby sister even now.

'Why you don't come round to the house?' There was pain in Desiree's voice. 'I know we only asked you to keep your eye on Granny Ruby till October, but that was before we realised she had to go back into hospital.'

'Yeah, well, I never want her to know, did I?' Verona said truthfully.

Desiree shook her head. 'V, Granny Ruby probably knew you pregnant way long time 'fore I did.'

'But she couldn't see nothing – I only started showing not too long . . .' She tailed off as she remembered how unsurprised Mara had been at her news, the way Des spoke about it as if she'd known all along.

Mara and Desiree exchanged knowing glances.

'Girl, is weeks you was showing before you drop from sight,' Mara said, amused. 'What you mean is you not long notice it yourself. That's the thing about being pregnant: you the same size in your mind, till the day you catch sight of yourself by accident.'

Desiree sat up, comprehension dawning. 'So that's why you just up and disappear like that? We all been worried sick when you stop coming round.'

'Look, I'm sorry,' Verona said guiltily. 'I've really messed up this time, ain't I?' She wondered what her sister would say when she found out the real extent of the mess.

'I want to meet this Steve,' Desiree announced. 'No way he treating you like this and getting away with it.'

Mara looked from one to the other, noting the determined jut of Desiree's chin and the horror in Verona's face.

'Right now what V needs is to rest herself,' she interposed.

Verona gave her a grateful look, panic subsiding. Trust Mara to come to the rescue. 'Yeah, I still feeling a bit weak,' she agreed readily. 'I think I'll go back to bed if you don't mind.'

As soon as the door had closed behind Verona, Desiree asked anxiously: 'Is she all right, do you think?'

Mara nodded. 'I took her straight down to Casualty when she showed up.'

Desiree was distracted. 'It must have been embarrassing for you, her turning up at the centre like that?'

'I didn't mind. Tell the truth, I was so shocked, I never even have time to feel nothing. That cut on her head was still bleeding so, it look like he bust it open.'

Desiree felt her stomach clench. 'Mara, how V could make a man do that to her?'

Mara stretched, checking her watch before bending to pick up the tea tray. 'It happen,' she said musingly. 'The blessing is that she never stay for it to happen again . . . and she might well have done,' she added almost to herself.

Desiree followed her into the kitchen, picking biscuit crumbs from the table absently as she asked: 'What kind of woman would stay with a man who violent?'

Mara turned from filling the washing-up bowl. Her gaze was steady and direct and she made no attempt to give an answer to Desiree's question. 'You and V have to talk to one another,' she said, 'really talk. Des, you better stop seeing her as your baby sister, 'cause right now is a friend she need and you're the nearest thing to one she have.'

'But she have plenty friends. Look how she was always going pictures and out dancing with them.'

'Girl, you fool or what – you don't see she making them up?'

'What you telling me?' Despite Desiree's expressed shock, in her heart Mara's words came as no surprise. If she was honest with herself, she would remember the many times Verona's explanations hadn't rung true.

Mara sat at the table, gesturing to Desiree to join her. 'I suppose I should have told you before, but I figured V had to work it out for herself.'

'Told me what?' Desiree perched on the edge of her chair.

'Remember when me and Olu went to see *Woza Albert?*'

Desiree nodded impatiently.

'We saw V up Streatham with a fat old white man.'

'V? You sure?' Desiree couldn't take it in. 'Mara, I know V act a bit odd sometimes, what with the romance novels and the secretiveness, but she not that screwed up.'

Mara shook her head. 'Des, I always admire the way you two close, specially with me not having no brother or sister myself; but I have to tell you, there's a lot about V you don't know.'

Desiree wanted to deny it, to say that it was all a huge misunderstanding; but the words wouldn't come. There were too many things that fitted – that strange man who used to call Verona up, and the big car without lights bringing her home, not to mention the way V was so sneaky about going out yet so open about everything else.

Mara had tactfully returned to stacking dishes noisily in the sink and now she changed the subject. 'By the way, was that book Olu lent you on tort any good?'

'What? Oh, Olu's book . . . yeah, my tutor said the essay was good.'

'Mmm, Olu had a look at it and he thought it would get a good mark.'

'You really like him, don't you?'

Mara looked steadily at her. 'You know, Des, there was a time when I used to think a woman couldn't have a man just as a friend, but now I have quite a few of them. If you must know, Olu been married eight years, he has three children and a great relationship with his wife.'

'Is she from Nigeria as well?'

'She's from St Lucia. You must meet her one day, I think the two of you would get on. She really have a sense of humour.'

Desiree glanced at the Africa map clock above the fridge and suddenly it seemed to symbolise all the change Mara had achieved in her life. 'Wish I could find one of those,' she said wistfully, getting to her feet.

'You want one seriously?'

'Of course,' Desiree said eagerly. 'Is years I envying you that clock.'

'Well, I know a guy makes them; I'll ask him to keep one for you.'

'I'd like that . . . Listen, I going now, you hear. I got this essay for tomorrow and I haven't finished writing it up yet.'

Verona heard Desiree leave as she lay in bed watching the gradual fading of daylight through the open curtains. She was sad, as though the last link in the chain that held her to her sister had broken with the quiet closing of Mara's front door.

It had been a shock to realise how much she was showing, but it was hardly surprising. She was six months pregnant after all. So much for thinking she showed late. She might have found her own misjudgment amusing if she hadn't been so pre-occupied, for her baby was due in three months and she was nowhere in her life. It was hard trying to work out what to do next.

'Too late for an abortion now,' she muttered, feeling suddenly desperate. She had been like this since that first visit to the Women's Centre, veering between wanting the baby and certainty that she could not have it, then right back the other way again.

Her major worry was that the baby would be born with major disabilities. *I'm a fool*, she told herself. Here she was terrified that the baby would not be able-bodied, yet she could not face another physical examination. They must think she was being awkward down at the clinic, but no way was she letting them examine her again, however much they promised it would not be internal. It had been awful, bringing back all the memories she had tried so hard to suppress. She supposed it was her own weakness and indecision that caused most of her problems. When the doctor had told her to strip and lie on the couch she hadn't even protested; though she had wanted to say no, the conditioning of years told her she had no right. She had closed her eyes tightly as he examined her internally, her whole body rigid with rejection, getting tenser the more he told her to relax. It had been painful and humiliating, and she fancied he was looking at her with contempt. She had been shaken and angry by the time she finally got up, struggling into her clothes and getting out of there as fast as she could.

At the back of her mind was the dread of labour. She had seen enough pictures in the books in the library, heard enough horror stories to know that she was going to die of shame.

She was depressed and lonely, isolated in the rapidly darkening room. *Funny*, she mused, *is near fourteen years since Ronnie.*

Her eyes were sore, the lining of her nose burning as tears brimmed over. She should have known there was no romance in reality.

# Twenty-Two

'Are you sure V said she'd be in?' Desiree frowned at Mara.

'Sure,' the other responded calmly. 'She asked if she could come round since I was off, and I said I'd fetch her.'

Desiree hid her emotions. Each time she had asked Verona over, offered to pay for a taxi or to pass by after college one day, her sister always refused – not in an obvious way, but she would always have some excuse such as that she was just on her way somewhere. It had been the same for several weeks now but Desiree knew there was no way she could force the issue and she had accepted Mara's advice just to give it time. Always in the background when Desiree phoned Verona she could hear the fretful sounds of a young baby, and she ached for her sister.

From the start, Desiree had been opposed to her going to the unmarried mothers' hostel, arguing that there was more than enough space for a cot in her room at home. They'd have been a little overcrowded with Granny Ruby there, but somehow they'd have managed. But Verona had stubbornly refused all persuasion. So Desiree had insisted on at least going with her to see the place.

It had not looked too bad on the outside – much the same as it did now, in fact, except that it had been a little more denuded. The lush red-leaved trees guarding the entrance had been winter skeletons, and the late flowers looked blackened and blighted from the first days of frost. It had been just after the Christmas holidays and Verona's baby was due in less than a month.

Desiree had been upset by her sister's steadfast refusal to return home, and her equal determination to be alone for the birth. Verona had not even been prepared to say which hospital she would be in, making it clear that visitors would not be welcome.

Now Desiree looked at the house again, relieved that it was so much more pleasant than she remembered. It still looked the worse for wear, the neglected garden bearing the universal stamp of rented property, overgrown with weeds after a month of drenching rain. May was shaping into another dismal summer.

While they waited on the doorstep, Desiree tried to remember the inside of the building as Mara pressed the bell again. It had been as shabby as the exterior. The faded carpets were worn through in places, and the room Verona had been assigned was smaller than the one at home and extremely basic.

'It's due to be refurbished,' the woman who showed them around had offered helpfully, seeing the horror in Desiree's face. 'It would have been done before, but it's the cuts, you know.'

However, it was the size of it that had bothered Desiree most, convinced that Verona would go mad in this place.

'Where you going to put all your books?' she asked.

Verona had rubbed the small of her back as if it ached, standing with her legs apart to balance her bulky body. 'It'll be okay, Des.' Her tone had been reassuring, saying clearly that she understood her sister's concern.

But Desiree couldn't understand why Verona wasn't dismayed, looked positively relieved in fact.

'V, even John saying you should come home,' she had made a last attempt. 'He don't like it, but he wouldn't want you in a place like this either.'

That hadn't impressed Verona. 'Actually it ain't too bad here, and at least I'll be standing on me own two feet.'

The door opened abruptly now, revealing a thin, washed-out-looking woman with lank, bleached hair. 'Yeah?' she quizzed, becoming a little more friendly when she recognised Mara: 'I think she's in,' she volunteered, before sauntering back into the large hallway.

'You go on up,' Mara directed, stepping aside for Desiree. 'I'll stay here while you talk to V.'

Desiree hesitated. 'Won't she mind? I mean, she obviously don't want to see me.'

'Do you want to see her or not?' Mara demanded. 'Is cold out here, and I don't want to stand here arguing and freezing.'

'I'll go.'

'Good,' Mara beamed, huddling further into her duffel coat as the rain started up again. 'I'll go bail out the car. With that leaking roof I liable to drown one day.'

The unlit corridor was gloomy and dismal and Desiree felt an almost tangible depression as she approached Verona's room. She couldn't understand why her sister had withdrawn from her so much. Desiree had been offended when Verona had asked for Mara instead of her during her difficult labour; V must have known she would have come, that she wanted to be there. But what had been even more hurtful was Verona's insistence that her sister mustn't visit her in hospital. Desiree had been tempted to ignore that, but in the end she had respected V's wishes, persuaded by Mara and Granny Ruby. The two of them had pointed out that Verona was probably at her lowest and that it was best not to antagonise her by interfering against her wishes.

It had therefore come as something of a shock that, three long months later, Mara seemed to have changed her view. Mara had phoned her just after she got in from college yesterday, telling her that V was coming to see her the next day. Desiree had been eager to agree with Mara's suggestion that she came along, sure that whatever Verona had against her could be cleared up.

Now Desiree knocked tentatively, almost afraid to make too much noise.

'The door's open.'

Verona's voice nearly made her jump. Somehow she had expected that her sister would be full of melancholy, not sounding so strong and capable.

The door swung open slowly and Verona said brightly, too busy changing the baby's nappy to look up: 'I'll only be a mo. Jason would have to choose now to mess himself, wouldn't he?'

As she finished fastening the pin Verona swung round, puzzled by the answering silence. 'Des!' She couldn't believe her eyes, moving hastily to shield the child on the bed. 'What *you* doing here?'

'Hello, V,' Desiree said nervously, hovering by the door. 'Mara said you were coming over to her, and I ask to come with her to carry you.'

Verona swallowed, moving awkwardly from one foot to the other. 'How are you?' she asked.

'Fine.'

'How's college?'

'All right. I'm really enjoying it.'

An embarrassed silence fell between them and Verona hunted around for something to say, wishing she had not asked to visit Mara.

'Can I see him?' Desiree stepped forward hesitantly. She came to a halt as Verona shifted, and shock and understanding dawned in her eyes.

Verona picked up the child with a defiant look and Desiree stifled the sharp dismay she felt. Jumbled thoughts chased around in her head: anger, disappointment, hurt . . . The knock on the door was heaven-sent.

'V, you ready?' Mara asked, poking her head round the door. The two sisters turned to her in relief.

'I just have to put his coat on,' Verona said.

'Here, I'll do that,' Mara said, coming into the room and taking the baby from her. 'You just get his stuff. I bought some baby food when I was down at Boots, so don't bother with that.'

Desiree retreated to the door, feeling in the way. As Verona and Mara talked, she felt shut out, her mind struggling to understand her sister's choice. No wonder V had hidden her man! So many thing were beginning to make sense now.

'Are we all set?' Mara asked, heading for the door.

Mara talked cheerfully all the way to Norwood, ignoring the quiet tension between the two sisters. Verona was thankful for that, unable to forget the frozen shock on Desiree's face at her first sight of Jason.

She held the baby tightly to her, glad to see that he was drifting off to sleep. He was big for his age, and the arm against which he rested was numb by the time Mara reversed the car into a space outside her flat.

'Put him to lie down for a bit,' Mara suggested, indicating that Verona should take Jason to her room. 'If you leave the door open, we'll hear him when he wake up.'

No sooner was Verona out of earshot than Desiree chided her friend: 'How come you never say one word to me?'

'Des, it ain't for me to faas in, is for you and V to work it out. Listen, I going down the road, hear. Tell her I soon come.' She was gone before there was time for any protest.

Desiree sighed. *Might as well put the kettle on.*

'Where's Mara?'

Verona's return took her by surprise and Desiree unconsciously braced herself. 'She say she soon come.'

'How's John?' Verona enquired stiltedly, following her into the kitchen.

Desiree wondered where the ease between them had gone. 'He not so bad now he join Black People in Bereavement. He takes the kids and Granny Ruby to the meetings with him and Granny have a counsellor now.' She chewed at her bottom lip.

'He's still worried about Granny Ruby leaving but I think he finally accepting that she don't want to stay.'

'Mara was saying she had complications,' Verona said, dropping her eyes.

'She fine now,' Desiree reassured. 'Is a shame she still can't walk, but at least John's cousin Delsey is going back to Jamaica and want her to live with him.'

'When she going?'

'Friday,' Desiree said. 'V, she really want to see you before she go.' She hesitated. 'You always welcome to come round, you know.'

Silence fell between them again, full of awkwardness and secret meanings.

'Why you didn't tell me?' Desiree's voice was reproachful as she pushed a cup of tea across the breakfast bar to Verona.

'How could I?' Verona countered unhappily, following her to the table.

'V, what went wrong with us?' Desiree's voice was sad. 'When Mara tell me about you and the old white man in Streatham, I never want to believe it. Why, V? Why a white one? At least if he was black –'

'I'd think of him like Dad, ain't it?' Verona interrupted.

'But why a white man?' Desiree persisted. 'I mean, I hear women say is 'cause a black man mistreat them, but that never happen to you. The only time you done get beat was your white man did it.'

'And Ronnie,' Verona said quietly, staring into her cup.

'Ronnie!'

Verona smiled bitterly. 'Yeah, just before I was fourteeen . . . remember that day I told you I came on sudden.' She could sense her sister's mounting rage and guilt.

'Couldn't you have told me?'

'I never told nobody,' Verona confessed. 'I did feel real dirty and shame, but I thought it would pass, except it never did.'

'So that's why . . .' Desiree sounded relieved, almost as if she had found a convenient answer.

Verona was tempted to leave it at that. What would be the harm? There was no point now in raking up the past. It was true what she said about the old white men. She had spent a lot of time thinking about it during the weeks just after the birth.

Old black men never came into it somehow. Some of them might well be as bad as their white counterparts; but her experience of them had been men like her father, and Grandpa Clifford. No, it had been the Ronnies of the world who frightened her, the fear that she could end up with one of them. She gave a half-smile; the mistake she made was thinking they only came in black skins.

'Steve wasn't old,' she said.

'But Mara said –'

'That was Guy; Steve came afterwards.' A wry, self-reproaching humour lit her eyes briefly. 'Yeah, he was young and he talk to me like I was somebody.'

Watching her sister struggling to assimilate that, Verona felt sorry for her. 'Things were never easy but they were always tidy for you, Des,' she said quietly. 'You had one bunch of problems: there was John and the children, then you lost your womb, plus you was always looking out for me, and to top everything, John lumber you with Granny Ruby and Grandpa Clifford.'

Admiration crept into her voice as it struck her how far Des had come. 'You know, Des, you just like Mara – look at the way you have John doing whatever now, and Mara says you getting on real well at college. Me now, I don't have nothing to liberate from . . . I mean, I don't have a man nor nothing.'

Desiree shook her head. 'You wrong, you know, V.'

'All right, what I have to get out of? Even this hostel is my choice.'

'That's not what I mean. V, remember when you used to tell me how you thought Mara was a real weed?'

Verona nodded, puzzled.

'Well, I suppose it was the way Mara pull herself together that make me think. You know, when I had the hysterectomy, I really did feel I ain't have no use leave in me – for if I can't have children, what leave? I know I did have two, but all *me* was about was having children and looking after them and my husband.'

'Do you feel all right now?'

'I still feel the loss sometimes – funny, 'cause I don't want no more children – but least now I don't think my whole life was wrapped in that womb. I suppose what I trying to say is that I spent a long time bothering about what everybody was doing to me. It was always how John treat me, what white people was doing, why the children don't listen . . .'

'Yeah, but it was true.'

'Don't you see, V?' Desiree leaned across the table to stare earnestly at her sister. 'The only person that never counted was me. What everybody else did was what my life revolve round.' She sighed, settling back and almost talking to herself: 'The old people coming over did something to me. Till then I never realise there was any other way. I just thought I'd either leave John or buckle under. Something Granny Ruby keep saying, every time John and Winston get together and talk about struggle . . .'

Verona's attention never left her sister's face. This was the first time they had sat down and talked – really talked. Des had never treated her like an adult before and she felt proud and pleased at the same time.

'She say there's nobody to liberate yourself from but yourself,' Desiree finished with conviction. Verona was straining to make sense of it. 'Don't you see, V? When me and Mara spend all our time on the way we get treat, we never have time to think about our own self.'

Verona's nod was slow with comprehension now. 'Yeah, I suppose you can't do everything because of what somebody else do or don't do.'

'Anyone hungry? I got us some take-away,' came Mara's voice.

The sisters looked round, surprised to see her at the door.

At that moment Jason began to cry and Verona got up. 'I'll just go get him,' she said apologetically.

'Chow mein or fried rice?' Mara asked brightly.

'Chow mein,' Verona responded before she left the room.

Desiree looked after her sister with an involuntary frown. 'You think she'll be all right?'

'Des, V's been all right for years, you just never give her a chance to prove it.'

'Why you keep at me like I do V something?'

'You have,' Mara said bluntly, fishing out cutlery from a drawer unit beside the sink. 'Hold on,' she said when Desiree looked as though she was about to explode. 'Des, you keep saying how your mother tell you to look after V . . . but, Christ, girl, that was when she was nine.'

'V has had a lot of difficulties,' Desiree said stiffly.

'Hey, don't vex yourself with me,' Mara urged, a thread of amusement in her voice. 'Des, you probably the best friend I have, and I really value you, and that's why I not going to tell no lie. You were the one stifling Verona. Girl, when did you ever accept how much she did for you?'

'All the time!' Desiree protested.

'Well, you could try show a little more of it to V. I've never known you *not* underestimate your sister.'

Desiree digested her words.

'V spent her whole life trying to please you,' Mara pressed on; 'your approval mean so much to her, if she think you won't like something she does it in secret.'

Desiree couldn't help thinking about Verona's behaviour over the baby, her secretiveness over her men before. Even the way she used to hide her romance novels under the settee cushions when she brought them downstairs. One after another, illustrations of the truth of Mara's words paraded across her mind.

When Verona returned, Desiree watched her carefully, seeing the way her eyes shied away, then the wistful way she looked from her sister to the child.

Desiree moved almost before the decision was made. 'Let me hold him for a moment, noh?'

Verona looked up eagerly. 'Yeah, sure.' She passed the child over quickly, as if afraid Desiree would change her mind.

'He have a look of you,' Desiree commented as she stared down at the light, round face. Whatever happened, she was not going to show her disappointment. Mara was right, V had made her choice and she alone would have to live with it. Desiree couldn't condemn her or the child, and, in time, maybe she might even learn to accept it, conquer the sharp sense of disillusion so strong in her just now.

Verona felt happiness warm her belly just seeing Desiree with Jason. She had been pained by the anticipated rejection she had not dared to face. Her sister was so much to her, and the loneliness in her had been because of the loss of that support and understanding.

She could see the faint reserve in Des' manner, the slight awkwardness she never showed with other children. But even that didn't matter. Desiree had not rejected her or her child, and, in time, would grow used to the idea of the child's heritage.

'V,' Desiree looked at her sister over the baby's head, making no attempt to eat the fried rice she had requested from Mara, 'you going to come see Granny Ruby before she go back to Jamaica?'

Verona became wary again. 'I'd like to . . . but, well, you don't think she might mind – about Jason, I mean?'

'She don't mind at all,' Desiree said firmly, 'she just keep saying she want to see you before she leave.'

Verona wavered, tempted by the thought of seeing the old woman again. 'Look, I'll let you know,' she compromised finally.

Desiree nodded. 'How about if you come back home?' she asked hopefully, ignoring the warning furrows on Mara's brow.

Verona didn't hesitate. 'No, Des; I'm fine, honest. The truth is, I quite like having somewhere for myself. I don't say it's great, mind; but the council say they going to rehouse me soon.'

She wasn't sure how soon was soon, but at least it was a chance of a place for herself, and she was certainly not passing that over. It would be the first time she had somewhere that really belonged to her.

Mara changed the subject with determination, refusing to let Desiree pressure her sister, and the rest of the day passed relatively peacefully.

When eventually Desiree looked at her watch and said she had to go, Verona rose with real reluctance, for once not looking forward to her solitary room.

'I suppose I'd better go as well,' she said, shifting the sleeping Jason in her arms so that she could pull on his hat before swathing him in his sleeping-bag. It had become progressively colder and Mara had been forced to switch on the central heating, muttering the familiar litany about what a Godforsaken climate England had.

'I'll just get a jacket,' Mara said now. 'No, don't turn off the heat, Des. Charleen and Meeli coming back from their auntie anytime now. You want a lift somewhere while I taking V back?'

Desiree declined, but waited for them before leaving. As Verona made to get into the car, she gave her sister an impulsive hug.

'Don't let we drift apart again, eh, V?'

Verona hugged her in return. 'Yeah, and I'll ring you Wednesday about Granny Ruby.'

As the car moved away, Verona waved through the window to her sister's still form.

'Is everything okay?' Mara asked quietly, changing gear as they turned on to Gypsy Hill.

Verona smiled. 'Yeah, everything fine now,' she assured her.

Mara pulled up outside the hostel, letting Verona out of the child-proofed door.

'Granny Ruby would love to meet Jason,' Mara said gently before settling back behind the steering-wheel and pulling away.

Verona was thoughtful as she climbed the hostel stairs. Des was lucky to have Mara, she thought; then she realised how much Mara had been to her. *I suppose we are both lucky.*

The baby was still asleep when she reached her room and she laid him in the cot Mara had passed on from Meeli. The room was neat and cheerless but Verona hardly noticed that. Bouncing on the bed with a sudden surge of energy, she pulled out the two books that force of habit had led her to put under her pillow. The romance novel was almost finished; the other book, a present from Mara, was still unopened, a children's book by a black writer.

Verona looked at the pensive face of the black child on the cover, tracing the large vulnerable eyes with her fingers. 'I suppose some of me's in you,' she told the picture, before replacing the book and bending open her other choice. There was a certain comfort in the familiar ritual, though somehow she was glad she was on the last chapter. Tonight she'd read romance, she decided. *But tomorrow, who knows . . .?*

She had an interview for a job, and Mara was giving her a reference; Jason's name was down for a nursery place, using Mara's address to be near the area.

Verona felt a sense of satisfaction. Tonight she would continue with her *Castle of Desire*. Tomorrow was the beginning of the rest of her life.

Desiree watched as Mara's tail lights disappeared in the premature twilight. She had expected to feel depressed by the meeting with Verona, but suddenly things seemed better. She was reflective as she crossed Knights Hill to the stop outside Norwood Bus Garage, boarding the bus which swung out of the station almost immediately.

'Who would ever think it?' she said under her breath as she alighted at West Croydon. 'V managing on her own.' She felt pleased, hardly noticing the freezing wind that had blown up since she boarded the bus.

Darkness had fallen by the time she reached home. There was a cheerful light burning in the window and she could just make out Granny Ruby through the net curtains. Something looked different about the old lady. The children were sitting beside her, absorbed in whatever they were telling her.

Desiree lingered by the window as John come in sight, looking absurdly awkward with Granny Ruby's dinner on a tray. A half-smile flitted across Desiree's face. She had been worried that he would revert to his former self once he started coming to terms with Grandpa Clifford's death; and now and again character did find him.

She knew he was bound to get worse when his grandmother was gone. But what the heck? John wasn't all that bad. They could have some good years together yet. If it came to it and he started being difficult, she would just have to handle him, that was all.

She was glad he had finally told her of his fears. In fact he had been a lot better since he started looking for another job. True, leaving the railway might not be the whole answer, but if he stayed he was likely to be convinced that promotion eluded him because he was inadequate. So much for Equal Opportunity.

She shrugged, pushing her key in the lock, letting the front door swing open.

'Mum's here,' she heard Lyn say.

'Yeah, let's tell her about the tablecloth.'

*So that's it!* Desiree thought. *She isn't crocheting any more.* She realised it was the first time she had seen Granny Ruby without her crochet, apart from when Grandpa Clifford died.

'Ca-rol!' Lyn was her usual self. 'It's Granny's surprise – we're not supposed to say nothing till Mum goes to the kitchen.'

'Lef you sister,' Granny Ruby admonished, amusement in her voice. 'De way oonu favour mouth a massi, you mother good fe hear aready.'

Desiree grinned, feeling a wave of love for the old woman. Things were going to be much duller after she left, and Desiree found herself missing her already. Granny Ruby had changed their lives so much, and the year she had spent with them had woven her into the fabric of their lives for ever – woven both the old people, she amended silently.

She knew the fragile beauty of the crocheted tablecloth would be spread across the table, a tangible reminder which she would fold away for special occasions. But Granny Ruby's gift was more than that. She would leave them all with new ways of seeing life.

Desiree shrugged off the thought of the old lady leaving them in four days' time, keeping her mind in the present.

This was home, and the truth was it wasn't too bad. Granny Ruby was right: there never *had* been anything to liberate herself from but herself. You couldn't fight when you were already defeated, only mark time.

But now things would be different. The old Desiree was long gone, and all those other battles could come now.